A KILLER'S HEART

THOMAS FINCHAM

A Killer's Heart
Thomas Fincham

AUTHOR'S NOTE

Visit the author's website:
www.finchambooks.com

Contact:
finchambooks@gmail.com

Join my Facebook page:
https://www.facebook.com/finchambooks/

JO PULLINGER SERIES

Ford said, "You two were the ones who responded to the call?"

Laury nodded. "Yes, sir."

"What happened?"

"We received a call to respond to a possible break and enter. A neighbor reported hearing screams and shots being fired." Laury gestured to the sprawling, Victorian-style house twenty yards away. "We arrived, cleared the house, and discovered three bodies on the upper floor."

Ford crossed his arms. "You said there was a suspect on the scene?"

"Yeah," Laury said. "A kid. He was holding the body of the youngest victim in his arms. When we told him to raise his hands where we could see them, a Beretta fell out of his hands."

"Where is he?"

Laury and Schorr split apart to reveal a pale kid in the back seat of their cruiser. He was in a daze. Eyes wide. Unblinking.

Ford said, "You got a name?"

Laury handed Ford a wallet; Ford peeled it open and glanced at the Washington State ID with the name "Tim Morris" underneath the photo.

"He's eighteen," Laury said. "We pulled his record while we were waiting for backup. He's got a bit of a record."

The detective appraised Tim Morris. The young man looked lost. Terrified. Completely taxed as tears welled in his eyes.

Schorr asked, "You know whose house this is?"

Ford handed back the wallet. "Yeah. Rene Stansfield's. He's the CEO of Stansfield-Kellerman Pharmaceuticals."

Schorr's brow furrowed. "Oh, man. He's a big deal, right?"

"A little bit," Ford said. "So, where were the bodies discovered?"

"Well, Rene's body was in the study down the hallway from the young girl's room. His wife was in the master bedroom."

Ford pointed to Morris. "Did he say anything?"

Laury said, "Yeah. He said he didn't do it. But the 9mm shell casings all over the place say otherwise. We checked the weapon he had on him. Half the clip was empty."

Schorr said, "When I asked him who he was when we hauled him down to the car, he said he was the youngest victim's boyfriend. He said he was coming to scare her. I guess she called things off the day before."

"What's her name?"

"Lindsey."

Ford asked, "There was no one else on the scene when you guys rolled up?"

Laury replied, "No."

Ford looked at the street. "How did Morris get to the scene initially? Did he drive?"

Schorr shook his head. "No, on foot. He lives only six blocks from here."

"Did you read him his rights?"

Nodding, Schorr said, "We did."

Ford opened the back door and sat next to Morris, scrutinizing the young man from head to toe as he waited a moment before speaking. "Tim," he finally said.

The young man said nothing.

Kowalski left the study, turned left, and arrived at the master bedroom. Much like the youngest victim, the body of the older woman lay on her back. Eyes wide. Mouth open. Ford spotted multiple shots.

"Panic fire," Kowalski said. "Suspect probably heard the woman screaming, ran in, and shot her as she was running out of the room. First shot hit her in the leg, the second in her belly, and the final shots were drilled into her sternum, the ones that killed her."

The suspect enters through the window, Ford thought. *He shoots the daughter, kills the father, and then shoots the mother to tie off any loose ends.* "Who else is on the scene?" he asked.

"Detective Weintraub."

Ford located Weintraub out in front of the house. The thickset man with the caterpillar for a mustache on his upper lip glared at Tim Morris in the back seat of the cruiser. Weintraub looked at Ford with disdain as he approached.

"Ford," he said.

Ford flexed his brow. "Weintraub."

"How's your night?"

Ford shrugged. "It's a night," he said. "How about you?"

"Not too shabby." Weintraub chuckled. "You?"

"Same old, same old."

Weintraub smirked. "Didn't think they'd throw you a case this big again."

Ford's brow furrowed. "What's that supposed to mean?"

"Nothing."

"Good," Ford said. "Then keep your comments to yourself."

Weintraub shrugged. "I'm just saying, after the last guy they let go, I'm surprised you're still puttering around the station."

Ford ignored the comment and pointed to the house. "Word is that the alarm wasn't triggered?"

Weintraub shook his head. "No, the system was shut off. I checked it myself."

"Strange?"

"It happens."

Taking a scan of the neighborhood, Ford asked, "Who called it in?"

Motioning with two fingers, Weintraub pointed to the house next door. Standing on the lawn, hands clasped in front of her, was an old woman wearing a nightgown and coke-bottle glasses. She was dabbing the tears from the corners of her eyes.

He's holding back, Ford thought. "Then why do you have gunshot residue on your hands, Tim?"

Morris's eyes widened. "The gun range," he said, sounding like he had just solved a math equation. "I was there earlier today. You can go there and see me on their tapes or whatever. I was just taking practice shots. I know the guy who owns the range. He'll tell you!"

Ford moved toward Morris. He sat on the edge of the table; his six-foot-one frame, toned by years of playing as a Wide Receiver for UCLA, followed by a stint in the Marines, towered over the kid.

"Here's how it looks," Ford said. "The neighbor heard screaming: Lindsey's. Then she heard gunshots. She called the police, they arrived on the scene, and they found you inside with three dead bodies, one of which was your ex-girlfriend."

"No," Morris said, shaking his head. "That's not how it happened. I heard the screams when I walked toward the house. I almost ran away."

"Why didn't you?"

"Because I heard the shots go off. I was worried about Lindsey. I scaled the trellis and went through her window. It was already open. I climbed in, and that's…" He looked away. "That's when I found Lindsey. She was already dead."

He shivered and hugged himself.

"And you didn't see anyone else in the house?" Ford asked, curious.

"No. But after I ran down the hallway to check on her parents, I heard shuffling in Lindsey's room."

Ford made a mental note. "Is that so?"

"Yeah. But when I went back to see what the noise was. There was no one in Lindsey's room except for her body." He shivered once more.

Ford crossed his arms. "Tim... I'm trying to see things from your side, but it's still not lining up."

Morris clenched his jaw. "I didn't do this."

"You can say that over and over again, but the fact remains that all of the elements of this thing point to you being the one responsible."

"I didn't fire my gun."

"Half of your clip was empty, Tim."

"Because I was at the range! I told you that. I didn't change out the magazine after I left."

Ford shook his head. "You need to get a lawyer."

Morris said, "It makes me look guilty."

Ford replied, "You're not thinking clearly."

Sitting back in his chair, Morris clenched his jaw. "I didn't do this. Someone killed Lindsey and her family, but it wasn't me."

Ford wasn't convinced. All signs pointed to Morris being the shooter. No two ways about it. Sure, the kid sounded convincing, but guilty people had a penchant for saying anything. "You're in trouble," he said to Morris. "*Big trouble.*"

Morris held his face in his hands. "My mom and dad," he said defeatedly. "Where are they?"

Taking a deep breath, Ford set about informing the parents of Tim Morris that their only child was about to be charged with a triple homicide.

FIVE

Ford checked his watch as he approached the Morris residence's front door: 1:07 a.m. It was going to be a long night. He resigned himself to the fact that sleep would evade him. He knocked twice on the front door of the two-story home and heard nothing but a congregation of crickets chirping in the bushes nearby.

The door opened briskly. Standing in the foyer was a couple in their fifties. Tousled hair. Wrinkled clothes thrown on in a hurry. A look of panic and confusion about them as they looked at Ford like he was a surgeon about to reveal a terrible diagnosis.

"Mr. and Mrs. Morris?" Ford said.

The man on the right, bulky and nodding repeatedly, said, "I'm Jonathan." He pulled his demure wife with sandy-blonde hair in close. "This is Deborah."

Ford shook the man's hand. "I'm sorry you had to be awakened so—"

"*Where is he?*" a wide-eyed Deborah asked. "Where's Tim?"

"Is everything all right?" Jonathan asked. "Is Tim okay? Is he hurt?"

Stay calm, Ford's mind urged. *Stay cool. Stay collected.* "We currently have your son—"

"What for?" Deborah threw up her hands. "What in God's name is going on?"

"Please," Jonathan said, "tell us what's happened."

Ford held up his hand. "Can we speak inside?"

Jonathan stood aside. Deborah trembled as she whispered something into her husband's ear. The couple led the way into the kitchen. Ford spotted a few photos tacked to the fridge with magnets. One was of Tim and his parents. Another was of him when he looked all of six or seven years of age. Smiling while standing on a lawn, clutching a toy truck in his tiny hands. Innocence at its absolute purist. As Ford slipped down into a dining chair, he could feel the tension that had accumulated in the home; it was thick enough that it could be sold by the pound.

Jonathan flattened his palms on the table. He breathed deeply. "Where's our son?"

"Mr. and Mrs. Morris," Ford said calmly, "Tim has been arrested."

Deborah shut her eyes but said nothing.

Jonathan asked, "For what? What happened?"

"Your son," Ford said, "was taken into custody earlier tonight at the Stansfield residence. It appears that the Stansfield's were—"

Say it calmly.

"—murdered."

Deborah collapsed into Jonathan's arms. Ford allowed them a moment to soak in the information before resuming the conversation. "Mr. and Mrs. Morris," he said. "I don't relish telling you this, but the neighbor living next door to the Stansfields called nine-one-one earlier tonight saying that she heard screaming and gunshots. When officers arrived at the scene, they found your son in the house. He had a gun on him, and the gun had been discharged previously. He is currently being booked at the station." Ford drew a breath. "We're charging him for the murders of the Stansfields."

Deborah broke down in tears. Jonathan attempted to console his wife. After settling her in a chair in the living room, Jonathan stepped into the hallway leading to the bedrooms. He stuffed his hands in his pockets. He shifted his weight repeatedly and lowered his voice to a whisper.

"I can't believe this," Jonathan said as he closed his eyes.

"I'm very sorry, Mr. Morris," Ford said. "There's no easy way to break the news like this."

"You're certain that he did it? You're *positive* Tim is at fault?"

"He had a gun with him. Half of the magazine was empty. The shell casings we found and the injuries to the bodies all point to him being the prime suspect."

Jonathan Morris rested his back against the wall. His jaw muscles tensed, and, shaking his head, he said, "This is my fault. I was never tough enough on that kid. I should have done better."

"Don't blame yourself," Ford said, trying to speak as a father. "There's only so much a parent can do."

Jonathan sighed. "My wife went through multiple miscarriages before we had Tim. That made us extra protective of him. It also made us spoil him in every way possible. Instead of reprimanding him for doing something wrong as a child, we looked the other way. We didn't have it in us to see him upset or sad. By being too lenient on him, we may have encouraged his bad behavior."

Ford knew Jonathan Morris was trying to make sense of what had happened, but he wasn't here to discuss parenting mistakes. "When was the last time you saw Tim tonight?" he asked.

"I didn't. I saw him in the morning. My shift doesn't end until eight."

"What do you do?"

"I work for a telecom company as a lineman."

"What about your wife? Did she see Tim at all tonight?"

Jonathan shook his head. "No, she was at a book club meeting a few miles from here. She taught third grade up until a year ago. That was when the cancer hit her. She's in remission now. I insisted that she take some time off work so she could recover, so she's always home."

"When was the last time she saw Tim?"

"This morning."

Ford said, "Did she say anything about that?"

Jonathan huffed. "She said he was copping an attitude. He left early this morning and didn't say where he was going."

Ford crossed his arms. "How aware were you of Tim's relationship with Lindsey Stansfield?"

"Very," Jonathan said with a frown. "They were on and off for a while. Tim can never really control his temper. Lindsey broke up with him the day after he threatened to punch one of her friends. She was in the right for doing so."

Glancing down the hallway, Ford saw a bedroom door decorated with bumper stickers for different rock bands. "Would it be all right if I take a look in Tim's room?"

Jonathan gave Ford his blessing.

The room was unkempt. Clothes were scattered on the floor. The bed was unmade. Everything inside the room was riddled with teenage angst.

Ford walked over to a desk near the window. Next to a closed laptop was a video game controller, along with half-drunk soda bottles and candy wrappers.

Something caught Ford's eye: a series of letters was underneath the game controller. Putting on a latex glove, Ford pulled out the letters. All were addressed to Lindsey. Sifting through each one, the tone went from loving to aggressive:

We're meant to be together. I love you.

Why are you doing this? I'll kill myself before I let anyone else be with you.

Ford replaced the letters. He took a scan of the room. His sights homed in on the nightstand. Approaching, he made out a crumpled receipt resting on top. Picking the receipt up, he noted that it pertained to the purchase of a 9mm Beretta from a vendor called "Saul's Gun Emporium."

The time stamped on the receipt was just six hours before the deaths of the Stansfields.

SIX

Golden rays of sun broke through the clouds and painted the streets in warm hues. Ford, getting out of his Seattle P.D.-issued sedan, peeled off his Aviators. His estranged wife had gifted them to him on his last birthday. He took in the building on his right, which was nestled in the area known as Beacon Hill.

Saul's Gun Emporium. One-story. Made of brick. Wedged between a liquor store and an adult novelty shop. A seedy part of the city, one that Ford had become all-too accustomed to frequenting thanks to his job.

Ford shut the sedan's door and approached the shop. He parted his coat to show the badge clipped to his hip as the doorbell overhead *pinged* to announce his presence. Behind the counter, a heavyset man with a sleeveless flannel shirt and a ponytail took a furtive glance at Ford before turning back to the trashy magazine he was reading. On the walls behind the man were racks of guns ranging from double-barreled shotguns to AR-15s. In the glass display case the man's magazine rested upon were the small arms. A cornucopia of ammunition was stacked on a shelf near a hallway with a sign above it that read: GUN RANGE.

"Help you?" the man at the counter said flatly.

Ford replied by removing his badge and placing it next to the dirty magazine.

The man huffed.

Ford said, "Need to ask you a few questions."

The man scoffed. "Figured as much."

Ford, vexed by his first impression of the gun shop's owner, slowly closed the magazine and pushed it aside. The man responded by sighing, standing up straight, and bracing the sides of the counter.

"What's your name?" Ford asked.

"Lenny," the man replied with a slow blink.

"Well, Lenny, a kid came in here last night."

Lenny shrugged. "A lot of kids come in here. I'm chasing them out more often than not."

"Lenny," Ford said with a long sigh, "I'd appreciate it if you curbed your attitude and helped me out."

"Well," Lenny said, "tell me what you want. I'll try my best."

Ford leaned in close. Eyes squinted. A hiss tracing his words. "Well, you sold a gun here to a murder suspect. Eighteen." Ford pulled out his phone and showed the owner a picture of Tim Morris's driver's license.

Lenny examined the license.

Ford said, "Have you seen him before?"

Examining the photo, Lenny nodded. "Yeah. He came in later in the afternoon." He stuck his tongue in his cheek. "Think I sold him a Beretta."

"How'd he pay?"

"Cash."

Ford reached into his pocket and produced the receipt he'd found at the Morris house. "According to this, he also rented an hour's worth of time at your range."

"Yeah," Lenny said. "Kid's a terrible shot. Only put three in the center of the target."

Huh? Ford thought. "What was his attitude like?" he then asked.

Lenny scoffed. "Like most teenagers."

"Meaning what?"

"You know: brooding, pissed-off, thinks the world owes him a favor. So was the kid that he was hanging with."

Ford's eyes narrowed. "Someone came in with him?"

"Yeah. Same age he was, I figured. High school age."

"You get a name?"

Lenny shook his head. "Didn't bother to ask."

Spotting the security cameras nestled in all four corners of the store, Ford asked, "Mind if I see the tapes from yesterday?"

Puffing his chest, Lenny asked, "You got a warrant?"

Ford lowered his voice to a whisper. "You really want me to get a warrant to search this place, Lenny?"

Lenny's lips tightened into a fine line. He swallowed the lump in his throat and said, "Follow me."

Ford tailed the portly man to a back room of the hall that led to the shooting range. A pungent aroma of burnt tobacco clung to the walls. In the center of the room was a desk. Papers were scattered about. A pair of dented filing cabinets were in the back. To the right of them was a flatscreen monitor showcasing a 4k feed of the security cameras.

Ford said, "Pull up the footage from when that kid came in yesterday."

Lenny obliged. His puffy hand took hold of the mouse sitting next to a keyboard and monitor. Lenny scrolled and clicked away for a brief moment. The feed on the screen started to play back at high speed. Ford watched the timestamp in the corner of the screen roll in reverse before arriving at precisely the time Tim Morris walked into Sal's Gun Emporium the day before.

Ford said, "Play it."

Lenny hit the spacebar. Ford inched closer to the screen, his eyes focused on Tim Morris. He was dressed in black. His face was partially hidden under a hoodie. He looked around until Lenny—on the screen wearing the same attire he was now—told him to take down his hoodie. Morris snickered but obliged. He approached the counter with a kid beside him. The kid's face was turned away from the camera. All Ford could make out was the back of a head, watching as Lenny conversed with Morris before Lenny reached into the cabinet beneath him and pulled out a 9mm Beretta. They talked some more. Morris showed his ID.

"Speed it up a little," Ford said.

Lenny complied. The kid that was with Morris never once showed his face. Ford crossed his arms as he witnessed Morris pull out his wallet and count out bills on the counter as Lenny ran Morris's ID and came back to the counter with a smile.

Ford continued watching the footage. He instructed Lenny to speed it up. Play it back. Slow it down. Speed it up again. Ford tried to make out the face of Morris's friend, attempting to find something, anything that he could run with to get a positive ID. Upon watching the images showing Morris and his friend sauntering off toward the shooting range, he found it. The kid with Morris had his hand pointing to a long-range rifle on one of the shelves. Ford paused the footage. He zoomed in and spotted something on the kid's wrist: an infinity tattoo.

Ford said, "Bingo."

SEVEN

Special Agent Johanna "Jo" Pullinger awoke and clutched her chest. She opened her eyes and took a long breath, realizing she had just endured a nightmare. She wasn't in the hospital. Her chest was not open and not in the throes of receiving a new heart. She was on a 737 inbound to SeaTac. The rest of the passengers were either passed out or staring at the small entertainment console before them. The pilot announced they were thirty minutes out from landing.

Jo glanced out the window at the night sky ripe with clouds. The nightmares she was having were a recent occurrence. She had been forewarned of the physical strains she would have to deal with after the surgery. She just never prepared herself for the mental ones that accompanied them.

"You have the heart of a killer," Jo recalled a fellow FBI agent once telling her. "Maybe that'll give you an edge."

The lines in her mouth melted into a frown. Jo fixated on the fact that she had been gifted the heart of a man she once loved. The dust had long since settled since that day, but the memories still remained. Jo, her mind wandering, began to reflect on the memory of her mother's recent passing.

The sun was shining. The skies were as clear as glass. Jo was holding her mother's hand as she laid back in the hospice bed moments after Elaine Pullinger's nurse, Jackie, informed her that "It was time." Elaine never said much the entire time. She rarely ever did. It was just the way that she was.

Jo watched as the woman who once proudly toted the title of Miss Wyoming was slowly withering away like flames licking at a piece of parchment. Her mother smiled. Jo smiled back. Few words were said in the days leading up to the ordeal. Jo held her mother's hand as the machines around Elaine began beeping. The one monitoring her heart rate began to chirp. Jackie stepped in and gave Jo a look, signaling that the inevitable was about to play out. Moments later, Elaine closed her eyes. She was gone. And Jo was certain she felt her mother's presence drift away from the room. After the funeral, her mother's house was put on the market, and Jo put in for a transfer. Her brother, Sam, had informed her that a bedroom was waiting for her the moment she arrived. The time had come to start anew, Jo knew. She needed to begin the next chapter of her life.

Bridgeton was now nothing more than a word to Jo. That was her past, and Seattle was her future. Jo had already been toying with the idea of making a move to the FBI's field office in Washington for some time, but the moment her brother Sam had found work in the same state, it felt like fate. It took only a couple of weeks to uproot everything, and now that Jo was twenty minutes out from touching down, she inhaled deeply, released it, and whispered to herself, "*Breathe.*"

EIGHT

The sun cast a warm glow across the tarmac the moment Jo's plane touched down in SeaTac. After sitting through the excruciating task of waiting for the other passengers to depart the plane, Jo made her way to baggage claim, fetched her bag, flagged down a cab, and stared out the window as it pulled away from the curb.

The driver, short in stature but overabundant in smiles, turned in his seat. "Where you headed?"

Jo gave him the address to her brother's house.

The driver, adjusting the Sea Hawks cap on his head, put the car into gear. "You got it."

Jo went back to staring out the window. The weather was picturesque: blue skies with billowing clouds sat against the bright and shining sun. A thin layer of moisture coated the pavement, and Jo couldn't help but note how cleaner the air felt as the cab linked up with the freeway.

The driver said, "You in town visiting?"

Jo shook her head. "No, I just moved here."

"Work? Family?"

"A bit of both." Jo smiled.

The driver merged into the left lane. "Seattle's a great place. Yes, ma'am. The entire state of Washington, as a matter of fact."

Jo said, "Are you from the area?"

The driver pressed his thumb proudly into his chest. "I'm a native, myself. From Tacoma, originally. If you ever need a guide"—he grinned—"I'm your man."

Jo said, "What's your name?"

Smiling and looking into the rearview mirror, the driver said, "Joe."

Jo snickered. "That's my name, too, minus the *E*."

"No kidding. Ha! Two Joe's in the same car. What a treat. Who named you Jo?"

"My mother."

"Same here," the driver said. "Sweetest woman I ever met in my life."

The driver's infectious nature was rubbing off on Jo. He was jovial, happy-go-lucky, down to the cheerful way he flicked his turn indicators. "So," he said, "what made you move down here"—he flexed his brow— "*Jo*?"

"I work for the FBI."

The driver flashed the whites of his eyes. "Get out of town."

Jo pulled out her identification folder and let the driver take a quick look at her shield and ID card.

"*Wow*!" he remarked. "Well, isn't that something? I've met a few cops before. Never met an FBI agent, though."

"It's not as glamorous as it is in the movies, Joe."

He waved her off. "Oh, I bet it has its moments." His eyes flickered in the rearview mirror. "You chase down a lot of bad guys?"

Jo laughed. "More than my fair share."

"Crazy gunfights? Anything like that?"

Her mind-wandering to cases from the past, Jo said, "More than a few." She turned and looked out the window, appraising the homes looking down at the city of Seattle on her right. They were nestled in the rolling viridian hillsides with a clear view of downtown, Lumen Field, and the waters of Elliot Bay.

"Tell me," Jo said, "any hot spots I should visit first now that I'm here?"

The driver nodded. "Yes, indeed." He counted with his fingers. "Pike Place Market, Chihuly Garden and Glass, Woodland Park Zoo. You name it. We got 'em!"

"I'll have to check those out."

"Seattle's a wonderful place, ma'am. You picked a great spot to live." The driver held up a finger. "I guarantee it. Don't listen to what the news says. It's a wonderful place to work and raise a family. In fact"—he glanced in the rearview mirror— "your first cab ride here is free of charge."

Jo held up her hand. "Oh, no. I couldn't possibly—"

Waving her off, the driver said, "No ifs, and, or buts, miss! Consider this your warm welcome to our great city. We're happy to have you!"

Resolved to tipping the man generously upon arriving at her destination, Jo thanked him and rested back comfortably in her seat.

"You like Johnnie Taylor?" the driver asked. "Oldies music?"

Jo nodded, recalling the few times her mother would put on a record. "I certainly do."

Thumbing his smartphone tethered to the Bluetooth, "Just the One I've Been Looking For" started trickling through the car speakers as the driver said, "Just sit back and relax, miss. We'll have you to your stop in no time."

Tapping her foot to the beat, Jo smiled as Johnnie Taylor served as the background music while she took in the sights around her and thought, *Not a bad way to start the day.*

NINE

The Medical Examiner was hunched over a folder as Ford entered his office and knocked twice on the doorframe. The ME, a rangy man who looked like his daily caloric intake was just under twelve hundred, smiled, stood, and stuffed his hands into the pockets of his lab coat. He and Ford had had the pleasure of working on several occasions—even on cases that had not gone the way they'd wanted them to.

"Morning, Curtis," Ford said.

The ME nodded. "Detective Ford." He stuck out his hand. "It's been a minute."

After shaking David Curtis' hand, Ford noted the pot of coffee on a bar tray in the corner of the room. "Is it hot?"

Curtis gestured like a bellhop to the pot. "Dive on in."

Snagging a Styrofoam cup from the tray, Ford poured himself a generous cup, skipped out on the cream and sugar, and took a pull. His skin flushed. His body temperature rose to offset the cold, meat locker quality of the ME's office that filled the air.

Ford asked, "How's business?"

Curtis said, "Busy as ever." He held up a finger. "Hey, when are you going to start throwing those July barbecues again?"

The summer shindigs that Ford threw with his wife had to be put on the backburner because of their situation. "Not for a while," he said.

"Sorry to hear that," Curtis said. "You guys okay?"

Ford wasn't in the mood to divulge the tale. "Long story." He waved his hand through the air. "Anyway, what can you tell me about this case?"

Curtis slipped down into the chair on his desk. He tapped a finger on the file he was perusing. "Just finishing up the reports from last night."

Ford said, "That was fast."

Curtis shrugged. "The DA's office already called three times."

"You're surprised?"

Shaking his head, Curtis said, "Not in the slightest." He examined the television in the corner of the room. "Twenty-four-hour news cycle is already in full swing over the whole thing." He huffed. "My thoroughness is a point of pride, but you'd think I was an amateur based on the number of calls that have come in making sure that I cross every T with this thing."

"A wealthy family in a suburb was shot to death. Everyone, down to the people cleaning up the crime scene, is going to have a spotlight cast on them."

Curtis snickered. "Never gets any easier, does it?"

Ford said, "No, it does not." He leaned against the wall and crossed his legs. "What do you have?"

"You want the medical jargon or the gumshoe version?"

Ford smiled. "Pretend I'm a fool."

"Give yourself more credit, detective. You're as smart as they come."

"Likewise, Curtis. So, what's the rundown?"

The ME peeled open the file. "Rene Stansfield," he read, sounding like he was reciting a grocery list. "Fifty-eight. Male. Caucasian. Five-foot-ten. A hundred and eighty pounds. Shot at close range by a 9mm round. Bullet entered the front of his skull and exited through the back. He died instantly."

Ford brought the cup to his lips. "Next."

Curtis turned the page. "Lindsey Stansfield. Sixteen. Female. Caucasian. Five-foot-four. A hundred and five pounds. Shot at close range. Three 9mm rounds shot into her torso at close range. One round pierced her left lung, the other two her heart. Those were the rounds that killed her. She died within a minute."

"And the mother?"

Curtis flipped another page. "Justine Stansfield. Forty-one. Female. Caucasian. A hundred and forty pounds. Shot once in the leg from ten to fifteen feet away by a 9mm round. The second bullet entered her upper intestines. Third and fourth rounds entered her right lung." He closed the file. "Putting it crudely, she drowned in her own blood."

Ford sighed. "Understood."

Hands up, Curtis said, "Pretty straightforward, Detective."

Resolved that the right man was in custody and charged for the crime, Ford said, "Indeed, it is."

The ME shrugged. "Save for one thing."

The lines in Ford's brow wrinkled. "What's that?"

Curtis turned back to his files. "I just got the blood results back. Again, everything's being put on a rush order because of the high-profile nature of the thing."

"I'm assuming something stood out."

"Not at first. When I did the autopsy on Rene's body, I discovered that he had a vasectomy."

Ford pursed his lips. "Nothing unusual about that. His wife was younger than he was. One kid was enough for him."

"*Zero* children are my preferred number." The ME's eyes flickered. "But I found it interesting to note that Justine Stansfield's bloodwork showed that she was on birth control."

It took Ford a quick moment to process the information. "Really?"

The ME nodded. "Yes, sir."

"You're sure it wasn't Lindsey's bloodwork? She was sixteen. Kids her age tend to take birth control."

Sighing, Curtis said, "You sound like the DA's office."

"I'm just making sure. This is high-profile. I can't take the risk of screwing something up."

"I'm telling you." Curtis flexed his brow. "I'm sure."

There are a few different reasons Justine could have been taking birth control, Ford thought. *Don't use the evidence to frame a narrative.* "How soon can you forward your findings?" he asked.

"Couple hours," the ME replied. "Just need to run a few more tests."

"Anything else of note?

"Nothing out of the ordinary. Rene's BAL was just under .08. Same with Justine. They probably had a drink or two before the murders happened. Nothing stood out on Lindsey's panel, save for the anti-depressants that were in her system, but that's nothing to raise an eyebrow at. She was in high school. Prescriptions are doled out to kids nowadays like flowers on Mother's Day."

High School, Ford pondered as something in the recesses of his brain told him to check out Lindsey's educational stomping grounds.

TEN

The thirty-five-minute drive brought Jo to the suburb of Queen Anne. The cab pulled up to a one-story painted blue off of 2nd Avenue, and upon spotting the VW Jetta in the driveway, Jo knew that she had arrived at her brother's home. She paid the cab driver, retrieved her bags from the trunk, and approached the front door. Thumbing the doorbell, Jo immediately made out the clamor of little feet padding their way to the front door. The door swiftly opened to reveal her six-year-old niece, Chrissy, looking up at Jo with a wide smile stretching from ear to ear.

"Aunty Jo!" Chrissy screamed.

Jo laughed and picked her up. "Hello, little lady. How are you?"

The little girl would not break her grip around Jo's neck. "I'm good," she said. "I missed you."

"I missed you, too. Can I put you down now?"

"Nope!"

Jo chuckled. "Why not?"

"Because I'm never going to let you go."

"Never?"

"Never ever!"

"Well," Jo slowly uncoiled Chrissy's arms from around her neck, "we'll have to ask your dad how he feels about that."

As if on cue, Jo's older brother, Sam, moved into the doorway. He was tall, his shaved head catching the light in the foyer above as he pushed back the frames of his wire-rim glasses. He smiled warmly at Jo. Chrissy scurried away and hollered out to her mother that her Aunty Jo had arrived.

"Well, well," Jo said, appraising Sam from head to toe. "Look who it is."

Sam moved in to wrap his arms around his sister. "Hey, you."

The two siblings embraced. Jo, closing her eyes, felt back at home. She held onto her brother and made the time last for as long as humanly possible.

***

Jo dabbed at the corners of her mouth after taking her final bite of the grilled chicken sandwich Sam's wife had prepared. She looked across the table at Kim Davis-Pullinger and said, "Your cooking just gets better and better, Kim."

Kim, her immaculate and charming smile on full display, waved Jo off. "I'm still trying to master this marinade my sister-in-law told me about." She nudged Chrissy, who was seated beside her, gently. "Finish your greens, baby."

Chrissy rolled her eyes before proceeding to finish the vegetables on her plate.

Sam winked at his wife and brushed his fingers across her carob-colored skin. "Kim's been obsessing about this marinade since she tried it last Thanksgiving. The Davis' seem to have some kind of ongoing debate about who can do it better."

"It's not a debate," Kim said with a serious glint in her eye. "It's a no-holds-barred competition."

Jo laughed. "How is your family, by the way?"

"They're good. They came into town a few weeks ago."

"I'm sorry I missed them."

Kim placed down her fork. "Well, the guest bedroom is made up. You're welcome to stay as long as you like."

Chrissy perked up in her chair. "How long *are* you staying with us, Aunty Jo?"

"Just until I get settled, Chrissy Bear," Jo said. "I just need to find my own place." She looked at her brother. "Honestly, I'm not quite sure where to look."

Sam said, "I'll put a call into our realtor, the one who helped us find the house. She'll find you something."

"You're a gem."

Sam raised his eyebrows. "That's what big brothers are for."

The family proceeded to catch up for another hour. By the time the plates were cleared and the kitchen table had been wiped down, Jo proceeded to sit with Sam on the back porch as they shared a cup of decaf coffee.

Sam said, "How are you holding up?"

Jo asked, "As in?"

"In general. You were running around like a madman that past few months getting everything settled."

Jo sighed. "It's all taken care of now. Mom's house is on the market. The realtor said she might have a buyer. As soon as it sells, we can figure out how to split everything up."

"You should take a bigger chunk of the money."

Jo shook her head. "It's a fifty-fifty split."

"Yeah, but you did all the work."

"You had a lot on your plate."

"You did too."

Jo patted her brother's hand. "You did your part with Mom. Don't shortchange yourself."

Her brother shrugged. "I just appreciate the effort you had to put in. Honestly." He looked away. "I felt like I didn't do enough."

Jo squinted. "What do you mean?"

Sam said, "I've just been thinking about Mom a lot lately. I felt like maybe I didn't pull my weight as much as you did during the last few months she was around."

"That's not true at all. You're just misplacing your grief."

Sam laughed. "I forgot you had a psych degree."

"Don't be a smart mouth," Jo said. "You know it's true."

Sam sighed and said, "Maybe you're right. I've been moving so quickly since we came out here that I haven't had a chance to breathe."

"How is the new job, by the way?"

"It's good. The private sector is a nice change of pace. I'm home at six every night. Kim and Chrissy enjoy the consistency."

Her brother was always a brainiac. It came as no surprise to anyone when he landed a job as a forensic accountant for the government straight out of college.

"What about you?" Sam asked. "When do you go into the field office?"

"Tomorrow," Jo replied.

"You know, Dad worked out of the same office for a few months before I was born."

Jo nodded and said with a flat tone, "I know."

"Is that why you chose Seattle?"

"No. I just needed a change of scenery. The fact that you guys were already out here gave me the push."

"It'll be nice to have you around. Chrissy could barely sleep the past couple of nights because she was so excited."

The prospect of spending more time with her little niece elated Jo. "It'll be nice to be close to you guys." She then huffed. "I could barely sleep on the flight over."

"You were that excited, huh?"

Jo recalled the nightmares that she was experiencing. Unsure of what to say, she smiled and looked away.

Sam said, "You're thinking about something."

Jo was not in the mood to speak on the subject. "I'm just tired," she said dismissively. "That's all."

"You're sure?"

"I'm good, Sam." She stared out at the horizon, where the sun was in the final stages of setting. "I just need to distance myself from everything that's happened in Bridgeton, you know."

Raising his coffee mug in a toast, Sam said, "It's good to have you home."

Clinking her mug against Sam's, Jo said, "It's good to be home."

ELEVEN

Kensington Preparatory School evoked feelings of an Ivy League college in Ford as he pulled into the parking lot. The Georgian-style buildings seemed to sprawl on for acres. The lawns and bushes were well-manicured. The students that filtered in and out of the main building were dressed in blue skirts or ties. And the flawless, fresh-faced complexion of each pupil that was in attendance sported the kind of half-smirks that only children who came from immense wealth had.

After checking in with a security guard, Ford moved to the main office and found the headmaster's chambers nestled in the back just past the administration desks. The name, stenciled in the fogged glass above the door handle, read "Dr. Martin Van Hauser: Headmaster."

Knocking twice, Ford heard a booming and authoritative voice call out, "Come in."

Seated behind a rich mahogany desk flanked on all sides by polished bookcases was a thin man with balding hair and falcon-like features wearing a sweater vest over a tie. Behind him on the wall were framed credentials and diplomas from various different schools. Van Hauser smiled pleasantly as Ford entered the room.

"Doctor Van Hauser," Ford said.

Van Hauser squinted. "Detective Ford, I presume?"

"Yes, we spoke on the phone." Ford shook Van Hauser's hand. "Pleasure to meet you."

"Please," Van Hauser said as he motioned to the chair across from him.

Ford sat in the chair. "Thank you for taking the time to see me."

"Can I offer you anything?" Van Hauser inquired as he sat across from Ford.

"No, thank you. I don't want to impose."

Van Hauser held up his hand. "It's no imposition in the slightest. I want to help you however I can."

"Thank you," Ford said. "Quite a prestigious campus you've got here."

"It is," Van Hauser said. "We house some of the brightest the state has to offer. Tell me"—he folded his hands in his lap—"how can I assist you?"

"I just came here to ask a few questions in relation to, well, what transpired with the Stansfield's the other night."

A look of dismay spread across Van Hauser's face. "A terrible tragedy. The Stansfields were a reputable family. Their deaths have cast a dark cloud over Kensington." He gestured to the window that overlooked the grounds behind him. "We're leaving the flag at half-mast for the remainder of the week. A candlelit vigil is going to be held in their honor this Friday. I know that such gestures only offer the slightest bit of comfort to the family, but I'd be remiss if I didn't attempt to honor their legacy."

Ford nodded. "I'm sure that the Stansfield's would be thankful."

Van Hauser shrugged and then said, "I was surprised by your call. To be frank, I'm not quite sure what today's visit can offer you in regard to your investigation."

"I'm simply being thorough, doctor."

"Please"—Van Hauser held up his hand—"you can call me Martin."

"Very well, Martin." Ford shifted his weight. "Well, as I said, my visit is nothing more than a formality. We're certain that the individual responsible is currently in our custody. I'm simply trying to tie off any loose ends."

"All right."

Ford squinted. "Does the name *Tim Morris* ring a bell?"

Van Hauser frowned. "Yes, unfortunately, it does," he said with a sigh. "He was Lindsey's boyfriend. He was caught on the grounds on several occasions: visiting her at lunch"—he winced—"*frolicking* near the athletic grounds, *making out*, as the kids would say."

"I see."

"Yes, and I had to have Mr. Morris escorted from the school many times. The last was two weeks ago. He was stopping by to pay a visit to Lindsey and one of her friends, another student of ours."

Furrowing his brow, Ford asked, "Which student?"

"Kyle Paulsen," Van Hauser said. "I suppose you could say he's part of the friend circle that Lindsey and Mr. Morris were in. Anyway, Mr. Morris attempted to take Lindsey and Kyle to lunch off-campus. I had to call security to drive him away. I then informed Mr. Morris that I would call the proper authorities if he trespassed again."

"Did he ever come back?"

"No, he did not."

"He never started any fights with other students? Vandalism? Anything along those lines?"

Van Hauser shook his head. "No, nothing like that. He simply overstepped his boundaries on a few occasions. Quite frankly, I was shocked to hear that he was responsible for—well, the tragedy that occurred."

"Why is that?"

Van Hauser said, "I've been in this profession for a long time, detective. You meet a lot of young men like Mr. Morris who are, succinctly putting it, full of hot air."

Ford squinted. "How so?"

"You were a younger man once, as was I. I'm sure we both thought we were tougher and smarter than we played ourselves to be."

Thoughts of Ford's youth came to mind. He nodded. "I wholeheartedly agree."

"Well," Van Hauser said, "that's Tim Morris, in my opinion: all flash, no substance."

Ford said, "Can I ask you a little bit about Lindsey?"

Van Hauser shrugged. "What would you like to know?"

"What kind of student was she?"

Van Hauser sighed. "Lindsey Stansfield was…" He sighed again. "Well, she was a popular student. Very bright. Unfortunately, her GPA was on a downward slope these past few months."

"Why is that?"

"She was easily distracted. I fear Mr. Morris played a part in this."

"Did she ever get into trouble? Drugs? Fights?"

"No, no problems like that," Van Hauser said, "at least not in a serious sense." He held up a finger. "But there was one issue that required a meeting with her parents about six months ago."

"What issue was that?" Ford asked.

"Online bullying," Van Hauser replied, shaking his head. "Lindsey was caught—well, shaming several of the female students online through her social media accounts. It prompted me to bring in Lindsey's parents for a discussion. Lindsey was given six weeks of detention as a result. I fear this didn't do much in terms of Lindsey's attitude. As you know, this school houses a ripe supply of some of the wealthiest children in the state. Many of the tropes— arrogance, entitlement, laziness—tend to play out more often than not. Lindsey was no exception. It was a problem with her, quite frankly."

Taking note of Van Hauser's story, Ford proceeded to ask the headmaster several more questions in relation to Lindsey's friends, work ethic, relationship with the teachers, and overall reputation at the school. Satisfied, he shook the headmaster's hand, thanked him for his time, and headed out of the office.

Ford headed back to the parking lot as the school bell rang, signaling the end of the day. Halfway to his car, Ford stopped in his tracks and glanced to his left. Something caught his eye, specifically the two students making their way to a 2021 model Mustang parked in the student lot. Squinting, Ford noticed something on one of the student's arms as he rolled up his sleeves: an infinity gauntlet tattoo inked into his right wrist.

"Well, I'll be damned," Ford whispered as he turned and proceeded to follow the students. Raising his hand, he called out, "Hey! Hang on a minute!" The two students turned and squinted in his direction. Upon seeing the badge on Ford's hip, they ran to their car, piled inside, and the student with the infinity gauntlet on his wrist started the engine before driving it out of the lot.

TWELVE

The kid behind the wheel of the Mustang threw the car into drive and stamped the pedal into the floormat. The tires whisked smoke, screeching like a banshee as it gunned toward the exit that bled out onto the street. Students cleared out of the way. Some of them cursed and waved their hands at the Mustang.

Ford raced to his Crown Vic. He piled behind the wheel, spotting the Mustang turning hard right out of the parking lot. He twisted the key, revving the engine and tearing out of the lot with a white-knuckled grip on the steering wheel.

Ford cranked the wheel to the right. The Crown Vic leaped out of the parking lot, linking up with the street as the Mustang turned left into a residential neighborhood. "Idiot," he grumbled. "He's going to run someone over."

The Mustang was fifty yards ahead of him. Ford closed the gap. His eyes went wide as he spotted a trio of children stepping off the curb and crossing the street in front of the Mustang.

Ford blared the horn. The Mustang screeched to a stop. The children hopped back. The Mustang stopped two inches shy of clipping them.

Ford jumped out of the Crown Vic, pulled his sidearm, ran up to the driver's side of the Mustang, and yelled: "Show me your hands! Now!"

The kids in the car were trembling, with hands held high. They stared at Ford in horror.

Ford, index finger caressing the trigger guard, ordered the kid with the tattoo behind the wheel to step out of the car. He ordered the passenger to stay put. He spun the tattooed kid around and slammed him against the door.

"Take it easy!" the kid shouted.

Ford patted him down. "What's your name?"

"Kyle! Kyle Paulsen!"

Ford slowly turned the kid around and holstered his weapon. "Kyle Paulsen," he said like it was a revelation. "You were friends with Lindsey Stansfield."

The pale-faced kid nodded repeatedly. "Yeah, yeah, I was."

Pointing to the inside of the Mustang, Ford said, "Get in your car. Follow me. If you run, I'll have you arrested."

"Okay, okay," Paulsen said as he slowly got behind the wheel and proceeded to follow Ford's orders.

***

After Ford ordered the kid that was in the Mustang's passenger seat to run home, he drove to a coffee shop two blocks from the school. Five minutes later, Paulsen was hunched over across the table from him with a bewildered look on his face.

Ford placed the cup of coffee down in front of Paulsen and said, "Drink. It'll wake you up."

Paulsen said nothing.

Ford said, "That Mustang is a cherry ride. Your parents buy it for you?"

Nodding, Paulsen said, "Yeah."

"Well, they're going to have to pick it up at the impound after they post your bail for speeding. You're lucky you didn't kill someone."

Paulsen turned visibly sick. "*Please*, man! Don't arrest me. I'm sorry I ran."

"I'm sure that you are."

"You freaked me out, is all. I saw a cop with a badge shouting at me. I didn't know what else to do!"

"What you *don't* do is run away."

Paulsen looked down at the cup and said, "I just don't want to be in any trouble, officer."

Ford pointed a finger. "If you answer all my questions honestly, I'll cut you loose. If you don't, well, let's just say it'll be the second dumbest thing you'd have done today. The first is how you recklessly drove out of the parking lot and nearly hit a group of kids."

Paulsen held up his hands. "I'll tell you everything I know. I swear."

"Good." Ford sat back. "Now, according to your headmaster, you were friends with Lindsey Stansfield."

Paulsen breathed a little easier. "Yeah. Well, kind of."

"What does 'kind of' mean?"

Paulsen shrugged. "We dated for a while. But that was a long time ago."

"You dated Lindsey before Tim Morris did?"

The mention of Morris's name caused a terror-stricken expression to wash over Paulsen's face. "Yeah," he said. "But that was, like, a year ago."

"How'd you meet Tim?"

"At a house party back when I was dating Lindsey. We hung out every once in a while."

"So, then tell me," Ford said as he leaned forward. "Why were you with Tim at the gun range the day he killed Lindsey and her family?"

Paulsen swallowed the lump in his throat. "I didn't have anything to do with—"

"*Answer the question.*"

Closing his eyes, Paulsen said, "Tim said he wanted to buy a gun, and I agreed to accompany him."

"Did he say why?"

"No." Paulsen shook his head. "But most guys our age want a gun. Tim wasn't any different. He thought he was a tough guy. He just wanted to look the part."

"What do you mean *thought* he was a tough guy?"

A smirk formed on Paulsen's lips. "Tim was, well, kind of a wimp."

Ford asked, "In what way?"

"He's always talking smack. Like he wasn't scared of anyone. But when Lindsey broke up with him, he started crying all the time. He was a major drag to be around. He started writing letters, poems, all of that crap. He listened to emo music all day."

Ford recalled the letters he'd found in Morris' bedroom. "I heard something about that, yeah."

Paulsen huffed. "It was stupid, man. Lindsey was a tease. Tim was better off without her. Trust me, I know. That chick was always treating guys like they were clothes: she stuck with one for a while, then moved on to a different one the second the season changed." He shook his head. "Tim was like her 'bad boy' phase or something. She loved how mad her parents got that she was dating a dude from a public school."

"Were you surprised that Tim was arrested after Lindsey was killed?"

Paulsen said, "Kind of, I guess. I mean, he was always getting into trouble."

Ford said, "And did it occur to you that coming to the cops to tell them you were with him the day of the murders might have been a good idea?"

Eyes wide, Paulsen held out his hands. "Officer, I'm sorry. I was scared. I didn't want to get in trouble—"

"Well," Ford cut in, "you were with Morris when he bought the gun that was allegedly used to commit the murders. That's a big deal. That makes you a witness to a crime." He tapped the table. "Consider this a head's up that you're going to be spoken to by my people a few more times."

Paulsen cursed and held his head in his hands.

"Hey," Ford said, "look at me."

Paulsen did.

"You want to make this easy"—Ford shrugged—"then all you have to do is cooperate." Paulsen sat up straight. "Now, the day that you were with Tim at the range, did he say anything? Did he mention going to Lindsey's? Anything like that?"

Paulsen nodded. "Yeah. He did."

"What did he say?"

"Well, it's like I told you: he was pissed off that Lindsey broke up with him. It was actually one of the reasons we started hanging out again. We used to hate each other back when I was dating Lindsey. But after she called it off with Tim, he came to me. I tried to tell him he was better off without her. After that, we started hanging out more. All he would talk about was Lindsey. He'd go from being sad to pissed off every few minutes. Finally, last Friday"—Paulsen drew a breath—"well, he said he was going to do something about it."

Ford, literally on the edge of his seat, waited for the rest.

"Tim told me he was planning on scaring Lindsey into being with him again. He just didn't say what it was he was going to do. He just kept saying, 'I'll get her back. She'll see things my way,' stuff like that," Paulsen said.

"He didn't say anything about shooting her?" Ford asked. "Nothing like that?"

Paulsen shook his head. "No, no way. He was being really vague about it. I thought he was just, you know, talking a lot. I didn't actually think he'd do anything."

"The day of the murder, you were with him at the range. What happened after that?"

"I had to go home," Paulsen said. "My mom was super pissed at me because the school called and told her I signed out the day before. Technically, I'm grounded right now. She had called me about it when we were at the range, so I split as soon as Tim and I were done."

"Did you talk to Tim after that?"

Paulsen shook his head. "No. I heard about what happened the next day when my parents called his parents. The last time I saw him was at the range. That's the honest to God truth!"

The phone in Ford's pocket buzzed. He answered it and heard his Lieutenant's voice on the other end: "I need you to get back to the station."

Ford's brow furrowed. "What's up?"

"The Governor just called," Griffin said. "The FBI is stepping in to take a look at the investigation."

Ford raised an eyebrow. "The Stansfield's case?"

"Yes."

"Outstanding," Ford said with a sigh.

THIRTEEN

The call with Kyle Paulsen's parents lasted close to ten minutes before Ford hung up the phone. Seated at his desk, he played back the colorful language Paulsen's father had put on display after finding out his son was in the wrong place at the wrong time.

Ford checked his watch: 4:08 p.m. He rubbed his neck, curious at how long the day would go on before he would find a sliver of time for himself. The phone on his desk rang. He answered and heard Griffin summoning him to her office.

"Lieutenant," Ford said as he entered the room.

Griffin, a tall woman with dark skin and a pair of eyes that instilled fear in anyone that crossed her, gestured to her cellphone. "Just got off with the Feds."

"What did they want?"

"They'll be sending someone down in a couple of hours. I didn't get a name, though."

Ford said, "I'm sure we'll know who it is when they walk through the door. Feds tend to have an air of arrogance about them."

Shuffling papers on her desk, Griffin's eyes narrowed to slits. "How'd it go at the prep school?"

Ford snickered. "Fine, up until it led to a brief car chase, that is."

Griffin's brow furrowed. "Come again?"

"I crossed paths with the kid who was with Morris at the gun range the day of the murders."

Eyes wide, Griffin said, "You're kidding me."

"No," Ford said. "Hit a lucky streak on that end."

"What happened?"

"I tried to talk to the kid, and he ran."

Griffin shook her head. "Rich kids think they can get away with anything."

"Well," Ford said, "I caught up to him and pulled him over. We then talked for a bit. His name's Kyle Paulsen. Turns out he was romantically linked with Lindsey Stansfield before she was with Morris. Lindsey's break-up with Morris prompted Morris and Paulsen to rekindle an on-and-off friendship."

Griffin sat back in her chair. "Did he shed any light on the situation?"

Ford shrugged. "Nothing we didn't already know. He told me that Morris was stewing after Lindsey broke up with him. He also told me that Morris bought the gun so he could scare Lindsey with it." Ford forked a thumb over his shoulder. "I just got off the phone with Paulsen's parents. They weren't happy to hear that their son was hanging around at a gun range. Apparently, the dad is a big proponent of gun control laws. Let's just say he'd like to amend the Second Amendment if you will. Anyway, Kyle Paulsen will have to testify as a witness if and when the case against Tim Morris goes to trial. I forwarded everything I have so far to your inbox."

"Very good." Griffin checked her watch and sighed. "On a related note, Morris just got transferred to King County Jail. His arraignment is in three days. Judge Hallenbeck is out of town for a funeral, so Morris is going to have to sit in a cell for a few days."

"So," Ford said, "for all intents and purposes, that's it."

"Morris will be charged; every form and piece of evidence has been approved." She shrugged. "So, yes, that's it. Excellent work, Detective."

Furrowing his brow, Ford offered a dry smile.

"Something's wrong," she said.

"No, not really," Ford replied. "I'm just running on fumes."

Griffin wagged her finger. "I know you well enough by now that something is tugging at that brain of yours."

"It's nothing."

"Don't do that. Something is on your mind. What is it?"

Ford thought back to Morris's letters, to the narrative that Paulsen gave him in regard to Morris being a wimp. "Everyone I've talked to," Ford said, "everything that I've seen in relation to Morris all point to him being a blowhard."

"Meaning what?"

"Just that certain people appear shocked that Morris actually pulled the trigger. Everyone who knows him maintains the same rhetoric of him being a punk. They're just having a hard time wrapping their head around the fact that he's a killer."

Griffin interlaced her fingers and leaned forward. "Ford," she said with a bit of concern, "I feel the need to mention Randall Watney at this moment."

Ford swallowed the lump in his throat. The name Randall Watney was one that he was certain would follow him to his grave. "What about him?" he asked.

"Well," Griffin said, "the last time you played on a hunch and tried to follow a different angle, it resulted in a convicted murderer walking free. I just need to make sure that you're not entertaining something that will derail a case that is as open-and-shut as this one."

Ford said, "It's not a problem."

"Good." Griffin stood. "So, once we get this little visit from our friends at the Bureau, I can assume that you'll walk them through what's happened without going off the beaten path into territory comprised of conjecture and wild theories."

"I won't."

"Outstanding," Griffin said with a nod.

Ford turned and left the room. Memories of the Watney case began to dance in his mind as he sat down at his desk. No matter how many days passed, he could never seem to get away from what happened. It haunted him. The looks and comments uttered by the other cops were stuck to him like a bad stench. But it was *his* doing. He chased a theory. His pursuits ended up freeing Randall Watney of all charges.

Ford slipped off his blazer and proceeded to fine-tune the paperwork on Morris. The entire time, he couldn't stop dwelling on the fact that something wasn't adding up. It nagged at him like an itch he couldn't seem to scratch. Doing his best to shake it off, he was sorting through his files when something caught his eye.

Ford pulled out a photo taken of Rene Stansfield's body. His focus shifted to the laptop resting on the desk in the background. Curiosity lingering, he pulled out his cellphone and dialed Detective Weintraub.

"Weintraub."

"It's Ford. I've got a question."

Weintraub sighed. "Go ahead."

"The evidence collected at the Stansfield crime scene."

"What about it?"

"There was a laptop in Rene's room with a bunch of papers beside it. Did we collect that?"

"Yeah, we did."

"What was on the laptop?"

"We haven't gone through all the files yet."

"But was there anything that stood out?"

"Like what?" Weintraub asked with a long sigh.

"Like an open document, a photo, an email."

"Wait," Weintraub said. Ford heard items being shuffled on the other end. Weintraub came back on the line. "Yeah, an email."

"Email?" Ford asked.

"It was open when the tech guys managed to unlock the laptop."

"What was on the email?"

"It looked like Rene was in the middle of drafting it."

Ford said, "An e-mail to who?"

"I have it right here." It sounded like Weintraub was lifting a piece of paper to read off of. "It was addressed to someone named Richard."

Ford knew who it was.

Richard Kellerman. The CFO of Stansfield-Kellerman.

FOURTEEN

Jo drove up to the field office off 3rd Avenue. The building was situated amongst dozens of others in Downtown Seattle. Jo proceeded to pull the Jetta Sam had loaned her into the parking lot. She signed in at the front desk, pinned her laminated security badge to her blazer, and waited in the lobby to be greeted by a fresh-faced agent.

"Agent Pullinger?" the young man said. "I'm Agent McKinley."

Jo shook McKinley's hand as she took in his appearance. He looked just north of his mid-twenties, and based on the lack of malaise he had about him, he was probably only a year or two into his tenure with the Bureau. "Pleasure to meet you," she said.

McKinley moved toward a bank of elevators. "The SAC is in his office waiting for you. How was your flight in?"

"Quick and easy," Jo said.

"Very good. It's nice to have a new face around the office."

Good heavens, she thought. *This kid is an eager beaver.* Checking her watch, she then looked up and saw the counter tick off the floors above the doors.,

"So, um," McKinley said as he cleared his throat, "I, um... I wrote a paper on you."

Her brow furrowed. "On *me*?"

McKinley flashed a toothy smile. "Oh, yeah. I wrote a dissertation on the Bridgeton Ripper case when I was in college."

"How old are you?"

"Twenty-eight."

Depression settled over Jo for a brief moment as she realized she was already in grade school by the time McKinley was born.

"Anyway," McKinley said, "the Bridgeton Ripper was what made me want to become an agent. You're, well, kind of a rock star around the Bureau."

Jo waved him off. "No, not really."

"Oh, nonsense! Anyone who's been around long enough knows the story of Jo Pullinger."

"Most of what you heard was probably rumors."

Leaning in, McKinley asked, "Was it true? I mean, about the whole heart transplant thing? Did you really receive the Bridgeton Ripper's heart?"

The comment made Jo's heart flutter. She understood why McKinley was being so inquisitive. She just wished the kid would ease up a bit. "If you remember the case," she replied, "then you'd know that's not *exactly* what happened."

Jo's slightly vexed tone caused McKinley to stand back. "I'm sorry. I don't mean to be so persistent."

"It's okay, Agent McKinley. I understand. It's good that you ask as many questions as you do. Inquiries are half the job."

"Well," McKinley said, clearing his throat once again, "I was curious if I could ask you another question."

"Shoot."

McKinley said, with a slight hesitation, "Have you ever shot anyone before?"

Jo could almost hear the sound of the gunshots she had fired in her career playing back. "Yes," she said. "I have."

"Is it…" McKinley shifted his weight. "Well, scary?"

"Very much so."

"Do you ever get used to it?"

Jo shrugged. "In a way, yes. But not the bodies. You never get used to that. But that's a good thing."

His brow furrowing, McKinley asked, "Why?"

Jo looked at him. "It reminds you that you're human."

McKinley nodded as if she'd made a profound statement. "I look forward to working with you, Agent Pullinger."

Jo said, "You can call me Jo."

McKinley replied, "Right. *Jo.* My name is Lewis."

Shaking his hand, Jo said, "Pleasure to meet you, Lewis."

A ping rang out, and the doors slowly slid open.

FIFTEEN

The elevator had taken Jo and McKinley up to the tenth floor. Upon stepping out, Jo was met by the familiar sounds of telephones ringing as if on an endless loop, by the sight of agents and support staff marching to and fro throughout the floor as they spoke as quietly as bankers.

McKinley gestured to the back. "The SAC's office is down the hall."

"Tell me," Jo said, "what's the biggest case that's floated through here recently?"

"Mostly white-collar fraud," McKinley said. "Nothing as noteworthy as the stuff the L.A. or New York offices have."

Jo examined the agents moving about the area, all of them too preoccupied with their duties to take note of her presence. As she strolled alongside McKinley toward a room with the shades drawn in the back, she felt the same revitalizing energy that instilled her with a sense of purpose any time she reported for duty.

McKinley motioned to a door with the name "Special Agent in Charge Robert Grantham" etched into a nameplate. He raised his hand and knocked with two fingers on the glass.

"Come in," a commanding voice replied.

McKinley opened the door. Jo stepped into the room. Seated behind a polished oak desk was a barrel-chested man with raven-colored hair and a pair of cobalt eyes. His eyes were leveled in her direction. Every inch of his wardrobe was pressed and wrinkle-free. Framed credentials were on the wall behind the desk. A few photos of the SAC shaking hands with prominent political figures flanked them. A wanted poster of John Dillinger was nestled amongst the displays.

"Sir," McKinley said, "this is Agent Pullinger."

The SAC nodded. "Thank you, Agent McKinley."

McKinley quickly ducked out of the room and closed the door behind him. Grantham gestured to the chair across from him.

"We're glad to have you here, Agent Pullinger," he said.

"I'm glad to be here, sir," Jo said, taking a seat.

"Unfortunately, no one on the Hot List was eager to transfer over here."

Jo said, "Can I ask why that is?"

Grantham steepled his fingers. "Simply put, the current focus of our efforts has been on local terrorism."

Jo furrowed her brow. "Local terrorism?"

"Indeed," Grantham said. "After the riots that took place in the city during the past twelve months, and coupled with the slew of officers resigning from the Seattle P.D. because of the anti-police climate, we've been, in essence, assisting the PD in picking up the slack. Seattle, putting it lightly, isn't a hub for illegal activities at the moment. Needless to say, your request was a welcome one."

"Well, I'm happy to come on board, sir."

Grantham flexed his brow. "You've had quite the career, Agent Pullinger. I also knew your father, Bill."

Only took a minute for him to mention Dad, Jo thought. "I'm sorry to say he never mentioned you, sir."

The SAC nodded. "We worked together a few times. We were actually on the ground together in April of nineteen-ninety-five."

The comment made Jo sit up straight. It was news to her that Bill Pullinger had been part of the Oklahoma City Bombing investigation. "Really?" she asked.

"We were," Grantham replied. "Quite a hectic time. Your father was a good man. I was sorry to hear what happened to him." He then waved his hand through the air. "But enough about your father. Let's talk about you. Your record is commendable. I'm surprised you're not in a Field Supervisor or ASAC position by now."

"To be honest, sir," she said, "I enjoy being on the ground. The idea of being stuffed behind a desk doesn't sit well with me."

"I can understand that." Grantham's eyes glimmered. "Either way, your talents will assist us greatly." He leaned forward in his seat. "But there is one issue I wish to bring up."

Jo knew what was coming next, and she braced herself with her head held high. "Yes, sir?"

Grantham spoke as if measuring each word. "Your dedication and your ethics are not of any concern. But certain, well, *health issues* do raise some red flags."

"You're asking about my heart condition, sir?"

With a nod, Grantham said, "Yes. Given the history, which I have made a point to familiarize myself with, you can understand why a man in my position would want to seek out any potential problems that may arise from this particular issue. You've been cleared medically as well as psychologically. But the word of third parties only goes so far. I want to hear what *you*, Agent Pullinger, have to say on the matter."

Drawing a breath, Jo composed herself. "I can assure you with absolute certainty that my heart condition will not affect my duties. The job, sir, comes first and foremost, and if I had the slightest indication that my performance would be altered in any way by this, I would have resigned a long time ago."

For several minutes, a dead silence hung in the air.

"I'm inclined to believe you, Agent Pullinger," Grantham finally said with considerable resolve. "But should this change, I want to be notified without hesitation. To say I run a tight ship may be cliché, but it nonetheless stands."

"I will, sir," Jo replied dutifully.

"Very good." Grantham flattened his palms on the desk. "Then you might be pleased to hear that you'll be hitting the ground running." He stood. "In fact, I have the Governor waiting to speak with us."

"Now?" Jo asked.

Grantham nodded. "I've informed him that you'll be taking the case. He's waiting to speak to you."

"What about a squad assignment, sir?" Jo asked. "Shouldn't I be assigned to one first before taking this case? I know you said we're assisting the Seattle P.D., but still, that's normal procedure."

Grantham shook his head. "A squad assignment will come after this case, Agent Pullinger."

He started for the door.

Jo followed after her boss. *He wasn't kidding when he said, "hit the ground running,"* she thought.

SIXTEEN

Jo followed Grantham into a conference room. Waiting inside was a man in a three-piece suit. He was shorter. His hair was lazily combed over. He pushed the wire-rim spectacles on his pointed nose back and smiled forcefully.

"Governor Landsman," Grantham said to the man, "this is Special Agent Johanna Pullinger. She's just started with us today."

Landsman stuck out his hand. "A pleasure, Agent Pullinger."

Jo shook his hand. "Likewise."

Landsman said, "You come highly recommended by your boss."

"I'm honored, sir."

Landsman pushed back his glasses. "I took the liberty of pulling your file." He wagged his finger. "Quite impressive. The Bridgeton case made your career."

Jo held back a frown. *That case will always follow me.* "I'm just doing the best I can, sir," she said instead

"Well," Landsman said, "when I was told that you were going to be taking on this case, I was quite pleased. You probably aren't aware, but what has transpired in the last twelve hours is of great concern to me."

"I'm afraid," Jo said, "that I haven't been told the details, except that there is a case waiting for me."

"It's not just any case," Landsman said. "It's a case involving a very prominent family—one that I had the privilege of meeting on several occasions. Let's just say the head of the family was a big donor during my last re-election."

"All right," Jo said.

Landsman let out a long sigh. "Rene Stansfield was killed inside his home in Broadmoor along with his entire family. Are you familiar with the name?"

Jo shook her head. "I am not."

"Rene Stansfield," Grantham chimed in, "is the co-founder of Stansfield-Kellerman pharmaceuticals."

Jo nodded. "I've heard of *them*, yes."

"Well," Landsman said, "it appears that a young man broke into their home and murdered them, apparently, as a result of a soured relationship the suspect had with the daughter."

Grantham said, "The case is seemingly open-and-shut, but the fact that it is a high-profile matter has forced us to take a look at the case and offer up our opinions on the matter."

Jo said, "Understood."

"This is a big deal," Landsman said, wagging his finger. "If people like the Stansfield's are gunned down in their homes, it puts others on edge—important people. People with deep pockets, if you know what I mean."

It never sat well with Jo that only the rich could be afforded the chance to have the government step in when they were in harm's way and not the other way around. She could tell that Landsman was only worried about his next re-election. It was bad for business when prominent people started asking what the Governor was doing to keep them safe. People who could have an influence during a campaign. But Jo kept her thoughts to herself.

"This is a simple case, Agent Pullinger." Grantham pointed at Jo. "Seattle P.D. is certain they have the right person in custody, and all the evidence on hand points to that being the case. All we need you to do is take a look into the matter and confirm their findings. That's all."

Jo nodded. "Consider it done, sir."

"We're counting on you," Landsman said with a grave tone. "Make sure this is wrapped up as soon as possible."

Jo didn't like being told how to run an investigation, but as this was her first day in a new city and a new office, she didn't want to start off on the wrong foot. "I'll do my best, sir," she said.

Landsman smiled. "We know you will, Agent Pullinger."

SEVENTEEN

Six o'clock hit by the time Ford walked onto the main floor of Stansfield-Kellerman Pharmaceuticals. The headquarters resided in a high-rise in Downtown Seattle that offered clear, unobstructed views of the Seattle skyline and all of its landmarks. Ford noted an air of discomfort about the employees as he walked inside, one that he assumed was brought on by the untimely death of their CEO.

A young woman behind the reception desk looked up at Ford as he made his way toward her. "Can I help you?" she asked.

"Detective Ford. Seattle P.D.," he said, flashing his badge.

Her eyes went wide. "Oh, goodness, is everything all right?"

Ford nodded. "Everything is fine. I was just hoping to have a word with Richard Kellerman."

The woman looked around nervously. "Oh, I'm, uh…" She blinked several times. "Yes, of course."

Ford followed the woman down a hallway that led to a conference room made of glass. She looked sheepish as soon as they arrived at the door. Ford spotted three men in suits being addressed by a toned, tanned, and refined man with grey streaks in his hair. Bags were under his eyes. He gritted his teeth as he spoke with passionate swipes of his hand. Behind him, seated in a chair, was a young woman in a suit who was taking notes.

The conference room was soundproof, but it was easy to tell the man was angered, disturbed by something.

"Is that him?" Ford asked, pointing to the man speaking at the head of the table.

"Yes," the woman said. "That's Richard." She held up a finger. "One moment, please."

Ford watched the receptionist enter the room. She interlaced her fingers and hung her head, saying something to Richard Kellerman, who took a furtive glance at Ford. His eyes were wide. He appeared vexed by the fact that Ford was there.

Kellerman turned to the woman scribbling notes. He whispered in her ear. Whatever he said forced the young woman to stand and walk briskly out of the room.

"Hello," she said, forcing a pleasant smile. "I'm Claudia. I'm Richard's assistant. He's quite busy at the moment."

"I see," Ford said, spotting Kellerman making the occasional glance in his direction. "Well, I just need to ask him a few questions."

The assistant showed Ford her palm. "I'm so sorry, detective, but this isn't a good time," she said in a strained voice. "We're in a bit of a scramble right now."

The answer was not good enough for Ford. He stepped around the assistant, knocked on the glass, and motioned for Kellerman to come outside.

Kellerman's eyes narrowed. He approached and poked his head out the door. "Yes?"

"Mr. Kellerman," Ford said, "I'm Detective Bryan Ford from the Seattle P.D. I need a moment of your time if you don't mind."

"It'll have to wait, I'm afraid," Kellerman replied.

"It's in regard to the murder of your partner."

Kellerman cleared his throat. "I see. Well"—he glanced at his watch—"make an appointment with my assistant, and I'll make sure to speak to you when I have a moment." He turned back into the room.

Ford's face turned beet red. *Unbelievable*, he thought.

He took a step forward. The assistant blocked his path. "My apologies, Detective. As you can imagine, Richard is under a lot of stress. We all are. Rene's death has shaken everyone at Stansfield-Kellerman. I promise you, when the meeting concludes, I will have Richard give you a call."

Ford knew he couldn't barge in and force Kellerman to speak to him. Kellerman was a person of interest, not a suspect. Kellerman was also head of a large pharmaceutical firm—one that employed hundreds, if not thousands, of the city's citizens. Harassing him would not be a wise career move on his part, especially now that he was on thin ice because of the Randall Watney fiasco.

"Okay," Ford said as he pulled out a business card and handed it to the assistant. "Tell him to call me as soon as he can."

Saying nothing more, the assistant took the card and went back into the room.

Ford proceeded to head back to his car, fully content with the fact that he wouldn't be receiving a call from Kellerman anytime soon.

EIGHTEEN

Ford watched the rain splash against the windows of his office with a view of the Pike Place Market. He rubbed the back of his neck and took a deep breath. Kellerman still hadn't called and likely wouldn't anytime soon. The visit from the FBI agent had yet to occur, and it was not something he was looking forward to. Needing to kill time, he indulged himself by plugging in his earbuds and listening to his daughter's favorite song, "Don't Worry Baby" by The Beach Boys.

Ford closed his eyes. He had heard this song so many times that he could recite the lyrics backward. His daughter, Hazel, was a fussy sleeper since the day she was born, but Ford discovered that the sounds of The Beach Boys put her at ease better than a high dose of melatonin.

He was desperate to see his little girl more than anything else in the world, but his estranged wife, Kelly, told him many times over that she "wasn't ready to talk." Sighing, Ford tried his best not to focus on his heavy heart. Instead, he let the melodic sounds in his ears sweep him away.

He wasn't sure how much time had passed, but a sound snapped him out of his reverie. In the distance, he spotted Griffin making his way towards his desk.

Ford removed the earbuds and immediately stood up.

Griffin motioned to the woman next to him. She had striking features and long blonde hair. "This is Special Agent Johanna Pullinger of the FBI," he said.

"Detective Bryan Ford," he said with a nod. "You must be here in regards to the Stansfield murders."

"I am," Pullinger replied.

Griffin crossed her arms. "I'm sorry that the Bureau feels the need to look into this. All signs point to the suspect we have in custody."

Pullinger nodded. "That was the message that was relayed to me. I simply wanted to confer with you and your people and pass my findings to my SAC." She looked at Ford. "What can you tell me about the suspect?"

Ford said, "His name is Tim Morris. Eighteen. He had a relationship with the youngest victim that soured recently. It appeared that he broke into the Stansfield's home and executed the entire family because he wanted her back."

Pullinger said, "Have you spoken to him?"

"Several times. He insists that someone else is at fault."

"Has he requested a lawyer?"

Ford shook his head. "He's refusing despite the fact that he's been counseled by his parents and us on the matter."

"Interesting."

"To say the least."

"What evidence do you have on hand?"

"Morris was found with a gun on his person when the arriving officers entered the house. We found eight shell casings at the scene. Half of the rounds in Morris' weapon were depleted. Morris was also found with GSR on his hands, and the medical examiner pulled matching slugs out of the bodies."

"Any witnesses?"

"The neighbor that lived next door. She said she heard everything. Frankly, there isn't anything that doesn't point to Morris being the culprit."

Pullinger nodded. "I see." She looked at Ford. "Would you mind if you took me to the Stansfield residence so I can walk through the scene?"

Ford stared at her for a moment.

"Sure, no problem," he said, grabbing the corduroy jacket that was draped over the back of his chair.

So much for the hope that she'd confirm the facts and leave, he thought.

Griffin said to her, "Detective Ford will make sure you have access to everything. The Seattle P.D. has always had a good relationship with the Bureau. And we'll make sure it stays that way."

"Thank you, ma'am," Pullinger replied.

Ford said, "Follow me."

They made their way to the elevator.

Not a word was passed between Ford and Pullinger. They entered, and the doors slid shut. The tension was so thick it could have been cut with a knife. Finally, Pullinger broke the silence by saying, "Is this the first time you've had to deal with the Bureau?"

Ford replied by holding up two fingers.

Pullinger said, "I'm not here to step on any toes."

"That's what the last FBI guy said when he came around to stick his nose in everything."

"Well, the facts seem to line up. This case appears to be open-and-shut."

Ford replied, "The latest story that went out was that Stansfield's daughter, Lindsey, may have been the one responsible."

"Isn't she one of the victims?" Pullinger asked.

"She is, and that's what makes it a wild theory not grounded in facts. The media will come up with anything to sell papers or get viewers."

"I can't imagine the kind of pressure this puts on your department."

"Late nights are a common occurrence." He scoffed. "Especially when the FBI becomes involved."

"Look," Pullinger said. "I don't want you to feel like I'm some sort of spell-checker who came in to proofread your work. I'm just going to take a look at everything, report what you have, and then I'm out of your hair. We all have families we're trying to get home to."

Had, Ford thought. *Past-tense.* "I appreciate your candor, Agent Pullinger," he said. "But in the interest of full transparency, I'm not exactly a fan of the FBI. No offense."

With a nod, she said, "Fair enough, but why don't you call me Jo?"

NINETEEN

Jo took note that Ford was a handsome man—but she was certain that he was either divorced or in the midst of a separation. She had interviewed and crossed paths with enough people in her life that she was well aware of the signs: Ford looked fatigued, but he had a longing in his eyes, a yearning that only came as a result of heartache.

The Crown Vic was two minutes out from arriving at the Stansfield residence. Jo eyed the wealthy homes that were spaced out from one another. They were impeccable in their design and were maintained according to the demography. Manicured lawns. Painted fences and gates. The driveways laid in marble stones. She couldn't help but think that no matter how much she saved, she would never be able to afford such a place.

"Pretty gratuitous, aren't they?" Ford asked as if reading her mind.

"A little bit," Jo replied. "I was never one for big houses."

"Same. My family was blue-collar. We learned how to stretch a dollar."

"Likewise."

Ford said, "People with money seem to think that they need an abundance of rooms that they'll never set foot in."

"Well," Jo said, "square footage is the trophy people flaunt when they have the means."

"My father said something similar. He just phrased it a bit differently. He said, 'The bigger the house, the bigger the a-hole who lives inside of it'."

"Poetic."

"I'd like to think so."

"So," Jo said, "I'm curious to know more about this company, Stansfield-Kellerman."

Ford said, "They're not on par with Pfizer and J&J, in terms of standing and overall profits, but they are the largest in the state, that's for sure. From what I've read, the company started out in Rene Stansfield's basement back in the early nineties when it only comprised him and Richard Kellerman. The two of them met in college, apparently, and they set about selling medical equipment door-to-door right after graduating. Thirty years later, they're one of the leading pharma companies in terms of cancer treatments."

"What's the company's reputation?"

"Pretty good overall. They've had a few lawsuits and litigations here and there, the usual run-of-the-mill kind of problems that a company of their size experiences. Nothing strange or sinister, though."

"Until now," Jo said. "I can't recall the last time a CEO and his entire family were gunned down in their home."

"Quite true," Ford said. "It'll be interesting to see what happens to the company after the fallout. I saw a bit of it myself when I stopped by to ask Richard Kellerman some questions a few hours ago."

Jo's brow furrowed. "What did he tell you?"

Ford said, "Nothing yet. His assistant stepped in. The man looked a little on edge."

Interesting, Jo thought.

The Crown Vic pulled up outside the Stansfield residence. A strand of yellow police tape covered most of the driveway. Ford parked just behind the tape.

A patrolman got out of his cruiser and approached them.

"Sir, you can't park here," the patrolman started to say before realizing it was Ford behind the wheel. "Sorry, I thought you were someone from the media."

"They've been giving you trouble?" Ford asked.

"There were half a dozen news vans parked in the driveway. It seemed like everyone wanted a photo-op in front of the house."

"It is a major story in the city," Ford said.

"Yeah," the patrolman said, adjusting his police cap. "It took a lot of effort to get them to leave."

"I'm surprised they left," Ford said with a laugh. "They're parasites if you ask me. They won't hesitate to contaminate a crime scene if given the opportunity."

"I won't let any unauthorized personnel inside," the patrolman said with pride.

"Good man." Ford then forked his thumb at Jo. "This is Special Agent Pullinger with the FBI. We're here to walk around the crime scene." Ford glanced toward the upper floors of the house. "Is there anyone else inside?"

The officer shook his head. "Forensics left about a half-hour ago. I guess they wanted to make sure they didn't miss anything."

"Any problems from the neighbors?"

The patrolman gestured to the street. "A few joggers keep making loops around the house. I guess they are just curious."

"Yeah," Ford said. "That's going to happen for a few days."

"Well, it's all yours." The patrolman stood aside. "I'll be out here if you need anything."

"Thanks."

Ford strolled toward the house. Jo walked next to him. "You need any gloves?" he asked.

"I do, yeah," Jo replied.

Ford produced a pair of latex gloves from his blazer and handed them to Jo. As she slipped them on, he donned a pair as well before pushing open the front door and leading Jo inside.

TWENTY

Jo scanned the foyer. The first thing she spotted was a portrait of the Stansfields displayed proudly on the wall. They were happy. Bright smiles all around. She examined the home's interior. It was immaculate. Pristine. Some of the furniture looked as though it had never been touched.

Jo took a deep breath to clear her mind. She didn't want anything to cloud her judgment as she walked the scene.

"Where did it happen?" she asked.

"Upstairs," Ford replied. "Second floor. Lindsey Stansfield, the daughter, was found in her bedroom with Tim Morris, the suspect, holding her. Shell casings were near the window. Rene Stansfield was found in the study. Justine Stansfield's body was discovered in the master bedroom."

Jo slowly made her way across the polished floors. "Where did you say Morris entered from?"

Ford pointed with two fingers toward the room on the second floor. "He came in through Lindsey's bedroom. What's funny is when I asked Morris about it, he claimed the window was already open."

"I'm sure that he did," Jo said.

The two looked around the kitchen. Then the living room. Finally, they made their way upstairs. Jo took her time ascending the staircase. She arrived at the door leading into Lindsey's bedroom. Pushing the door ajar, she drew a breath as she laid eyes on the pool of blood on the wooden floors; it had turned from a crimson to a shade of black. "This is where you found her?"

"Three shots to her sternum," Ford said. "We figure she was in her bed when she saw the suspect coming in through the window." He pointed to the window, which was now shut but was likely dusted for fingerprints by the crime scene unit. "And she was shot as soon as she turned around to face the suspect. The shell casing by the window and blood splatter analysis confirms the theory."

Crouching at the foot of the bed, Jo examined the bloodstain. "How old was she?"

"Sixteen."

Jo sighed. She stood up, hands on her hips. "And this was where Morris was when the units rolled up?"

Ford nodded. "Arriving officers found him cradling Lindsey in his arms. When they ordered him to raise his hands, the gun he had on him fell out of his lap."

"You tested the weapon?"

"It was hot. Morris definitely fired it, but he insisted that it was because he went to the gun range earlier that day. That's also why he says half of his magazine was empty."

"Did you go to the range?"

"I did. Morris was there. But it still doesn't clear him of all of this."

After taking one last look around Lindsey's bedroom, Jo focused her attention on Ford. "Walk me through the rest."

Taking the lead, Ford stepped out into the hallway. "After the suspect killed Lindsey," Ford said, motioning down the hall, "he made his way to the study on the left." Ford stopped at another door, where Jo's eyes fell on the black stain just inside the room.

She appraised the massive and ornate study. High-backed leather chairs flanked each other. A shelf filled to the brim with leather-bound books was behind it. In between the leather chairs rested an end table with a T.S. Eliot book on top of it. The scent of dried bourbon hung in the air.

Ford pointed to the chairs. "Rene was probably in here reading. We figured he heard the shots go off in Lindsey's room, got up, and ran to the door. He was most likely taken down from between eight to ten feet away. His body was found just inside the doorway."

"The killer was moving quickly."

"Very quickly. And Rene was a big guy. Two-hundred-and-ten-pounds, so he moved slowly. That's why he never made it out of the room in time. The killer ran to the study and dropped Rene before Rene could make his way out into the hallway."

Jo looked at Ford. "What about the wife?"

"The killer turned his sights on her next." Ford moved toward the room at the far end. "Our suspect rushed his way to the master bedroom after shooting Rene." Jo and Ford walked inside the master bedroom. "And he shot Justine before she got off of the bed."

Jo spotted bloodstains on the silk sheets of the king-sized bed. "How old was Justine?"

"Forty-one."

"Good health?"

"Far as we know. Why?"

"Because," Jo said, "an awful lot of time passed between the first shots being fired and her getting out of bed. A gunshot is going to wake anyone up."

Ford said, "Maybe she panicked and didn't know what to do."

"It's possible." Jo took another scan of the room. "So," she said as she headed back toward Lindsey's room. "The suspect shoots Lindsey, walks down the hall, shoots Rene, moves to the master bedroom, shoots Justine, and he comes back"—she pointed to the stain at the foot of Lindsey's bed—"*here*."

Shrugging, Ford said, "That's the story."

Biting her lip, Jo processed the information. "I'm curious," she said.

"About what?"

Jo moved back to Rene's study and pointed to an alarm panel on the wall. "None of the reports or witness statements said anything about the alarm going off."

Ford shook his head, "No, they didn't."

"Why?"

"We just assumed that the alarms were off. Maybe Rene forgot to turn them on. He was drinking that night. A half glass of bourbon was found next to the leather chairs. It's logged into evidence."

Jo said, "Did you call the company that installed the alarm?"

"No," Ford said. "Haven't gotten around to it yet."

Jo pulled out her phone and dialed the number listed under the company name. She held the phone to her ear. It rang twice before someone answered.

"Secure & Safe," a female voice said.

"Hello, my name is Agent Jo Pullinger with the Federal Bureau of Investigation. I'm calling in regard to a case we are currently working on. Your company installed the security system at the home of Rene Stansfield. I need to ask you a few questions."

The woman transferred Jo to her supervisor. After Jo haggled with the supervisor for a few moments, the supervisor pulled up information on Rene's account, and one item, in particular, stood out: Rene Stansfield had deactivated the security alarms one hour before the murders occurred.

Jo asked, "You didn't find that odd?"

The supervisor replied, "Well, we call every time the alarm is deactivated. Mr. Stansfield said that it was a lapse in judgment—he did it by mistake."

Jo asked a couple of follow-up questions, thanked the supervisor for his time, and hung up. "Rene," she said to Ford, "shut off the alarm *several* times in the weeks leading up to the murders."

Ford said, "That could mean anything."

"It could," Jo said, mulling it over. After a brief pause, she clapped her hands together and said, "Let me get this straight. Our suspect, if it is Tim Morris, heads back to Lindsey's room and proceeds to cradle her in his arms. And the narrative at this point, if I'm assuming correctly, is that he probably felt some sort of remorse over what he had done and felt inclined to hold his dead girlfriend one last time."

Ford said, "Everything we pulled up indicated that the relationship between Tim Morris and Lindsey Stansfield had been terminated by Lindsey. By Morris's own admission, he came here the night of the murders to scare her by wielding a gun."

"So," Jo said, "your Lieutenant believes, as do you, that it's an open-and-shut case." She cocked her head and looked at Ford curiously.

Ford said, "You're inclined to think otherwise?"

"It's best to explore all narratives for the sake of being thorough."

Ford laughed. "Morris did it. Don't kid yourself."

Jo gestured to the bloodstain by the foot of the bed. "You don't think it's odd that Morris killed everyone and then decided to weep over Lindsey's body?"

Ford shrugged. "He was feeling guilty."

Shaking her head, Jo said, "He was high on emotions, possibly, blinded by rage and resentment that Lindsey had dumped him. It doesn't make sense to me that he would kill everyone and then regret it in the blink of an eye. If he was broken up about his actions, it would have caught up to him much, much later. Maybe when he'd gotten home, and the adrenaline had worn off."

"You're reaching, Agent Pullinger," Ford said defensively. "Morris is our guy. I'm convinced of it."

"Yet, Morris is sticking to his story that he's not at fault."

"He's got no other choice but to stick to his story. He knows there is overwhelming evidence against him."

"He could have run away after the killing, but he didn't."

Ford said nothing.

"I want to talk to him," Jo said. "I want to talk to Morris."

TWENTY-ONE

Jo and Ford were already seated in the interrogation room at the King County jail when Tim Morris entered the room. Morris looked at them curiously. He appeared frail underneath his beige jailhouse uniform. Hands shackled, he was ushered over to the table by a burly guard who informed Jo and Ford that he would be outside of the room if they needed anything. The noise from the door shutting and locking made Morris shudder.

Jo saw a timid and scared kid. For a brief moment, she felt an overwhelming sense of pity for him. But she had a job to do.

"Tim," Ford said. "Please take a seat."

Tim gingerly pulled up a chair and sat down across from them.

"Hello, Mr. Morris," Jo said. "My name is Jo Pullinger. I work for the FBI. I would like to ask you a few questions."

Morris blew the air out of his lungs and shook his head. "What more do you guys want from me? I've already answered your questions like a million times."

"I just want to have a quick chat."

Morris shrugged. "I don't know how many more times I can keep telling you the same thing."

Jo pulled the file pertaining to Morris in front of her. She had spent the ride over becoming familiar with his story. "Have you talked to your parents yet?" she asked.

Morris replied, "A couple of times."

"Are they doing okay?"

"They're pissed."

"At you?"

Morris shrugged. "I don't know. I guess."

Jo sat back in her chair. "I'm just trying to get a sense of what happened the night Lindsey was killed. According to Detective Ford, you said that you showed up at her house—in your words—to scare her."

"Yeah, that's right."

"With a gun?" she said with a raised eyebrow.

Morris looked away. "I wasn't going to shoot her. Honest."

"Okay, let's say I believe you that you had no intention of harming Lindsey when you went to her house."

"I didn't. I swear."

"How did you get inside the house?"

"I went up the drain pipe to her bedroom window."

"Was the window open or closed?"

"It was open."

"Did Lindsey normally leave her window open at night?"

Morris thought about it. "Not really."

"Not even during the hot summer days?"

He almost laughed. "Her family's rich. They got a central air conditioner, you know."

"Fair enough," Jo said. "But I assume she opened the window to let you inside her room, is that right?"

He looked down at the table. "Yes. She would unlock it so I could come inside."

"Did she unlock the window for you on the night she was murdered?" Jo asked.

He looked up with wide eyes. "She had no idea I was coming to her house that night. I mean, we'd already broken up."

Jo leaned over the table. "But the window was open, yes?"

"It was."

"Why would that be if she only left it open for *you*?"

Morris mulled it over. "Maybe she left it open to get some fresh air."

"But you said they had central air conditioning."

"It was kind of cool that night," he said. "I know her mom was always cold. She even wore a cardigan inside the house when the AC was on. Her dad, on the other hand, was always hot. He was a big guy, you know. Whenever I saw him, he would be wearing a polo shirt even when it was below zero outside."

"What's your point, Tim?" Ford interjected.

Morris looked at him. "I'm saying that it was kind of cool that night. I'm certain her mom must have turned on the heat. Lindsey's room always got hot and stuffy fast. I'm sure she must have cracked open the window to let air in."

Ford stared at him.

Jo said, "All right, sure. So, was the window open a crack, or was it wide open?"

Morris's eyes darted from left to right as if he were thinking. "Wide open," he then said.

"Why do you think that was?" Jo asked.

"Maybe it was the real killer," Morris said matter-of-factly.

"Did you see anyone inside the house when you went in?"

Morris looked at Ford. "I told your friend here that I heard some shuffling in Lindsey's bedroom when I ran down the hallway to check on her parents. Whoever did this must have slipped out through the window."

TWENTY-TWO

Jo knew she wasn't getting anywhere with the window angle, so she changed tactics. "You've gotten into some trouble recently," she said, examining his file. "You skipped out of school several times this semester."

"I turned eighteen in September," Morris said. "I can sign myself out whenever I want."

"You're barely on track to graduate."

Morris' tone turned flippant. "Whatever."

Jo pulled out a police report from Morris's file. "What about this thing at your local pharmacy?"

Morris rolled his eyes. "Who cares."

Jo leaned in. "Tim. You've been charged with a triple murder. Giving me an attitude is only making things worse."

Morris's shoulders slumped. "I got into a fight with another kid from school and knocked some stuff off a shelf," he said. "That was it."

Jo looked down at the page. "Six months ago, your mother called the police after you and your father got into a bit of an argument. She said you swung a baseball bat at him."

Gritting his teeth, Morris said, "I threw a bat at his feet. I didn't *swing* it at him. She overstates stuff all the time."

"Okay, let's go back to the gun. You bought it recently. The same gun found at the crime scene." Jo leveled her focus on Morris. "Why would you do that?"

"I told you already. I was gonna scare her."

"Scaring someone with a gun is pretty extreme, don't you think?"

"It's America," Morris said with a shrug. "Everyone owns a gun."

"So, you weren't planning on using it to shoot Lindsey?"

"*No.*"

"What were you planning on doing with it?"

Morris said nothing.

"Tim," Jo said softly, "you must've had a plan."

Morris threw up his hands. "I don't know! Okay? I wanted her back. I thought maybe, I don't know, that if I…" He shut his mouth, his jaw muscles tensing.

Leaning in, Jo said, "That if you *what*?"

Tears welled in Morris' eyes.

"Tim," Jo said, "if you *could* go home, would you want to?"

"That's a dumb question. Of course, I want to go home."

"You're not telling me everything. Then tell me how you planned on scaring Lindsey. The only way you help yourself is by talking."

"I was going to hold the gun to my head. I was going to tell her I would kill myself if she didn't take me back." The tears flowed freely down his cheeks, and he wiped them with the back of his sleeve.

Ford leaned forward. "Tim," he said, "why didn't you tell me that when I asked you how you planned on scaring Lindsey?"

"Because *I'm scared*," Morris said defeatedly. "I don't know what's going to happen to me. I just want this nightmare to be over. I want to go home."

He lowered his head and began sobbing.

Jo felt the urge to comfort him, but she knew she couldn't. Her job wasn't to comfort a suspect. Her job was to get the facts that would lead to a conviction. And right now, she wasn't sure she was getting that.

"Tim," she said, "let me ask you: if you didn't do this, who do you think did?"

He looked up. His eyes were raw. "I told you I didn't see anyone."

"I know. But play detective for a moment. Put yourself in our position. You were with Lindsey long enough."

Morris furrowed his brow. "What's your point?"

"You had been around Lindsey's parents long enough that maybe you heard something you weren't supposed to."

"I don't know," Morris said. "I know that Lindsey's dad hated the guy he worked with."

"Who?"

"Richard something."

Jo knew Morris was referring to Richard Kellerman.

Morris said, "They were fighting all the time. One night when I'd snuck into Lindsey's room, I heard Rene in the hall yelling into his phone. He said something like, 'You'll never get away with this'."

Jo made a mental note of this. "Tim," she said.

Morris locked eyes with her.

"I want you to tell me to my face that you didn't do this."

With every bit of energy he could muster, Morris said, "*It. Wasn't. Me.*"

TWENTY-THREE

"So," Ford said to Jo as they walked out of the King County jail, "what do you think?"

Moving her way to Ford's Crown Vic parked near the curb, she replayed the conversation she had with Morris. She had done her job long enough, had been through enough training, and spoken to enough suspects that she was able to say out loud to Ford, "It's possible, just possible, that there's something more to this that we are not seeing."

Ford threw up his hands. "You can't be serious."

Jo pointed to the doors leading into the jail. "That kid in there is a punk."

"No kidding."

"He has problems," Jo said, "but I'm beginning to think he was just in the wrong place at the wrong time."

"There's only one problem with your theory."

"And what is that?"

"You don't have any evidence to back it up. You're playing a hunch."

"Which is why I plan on making sure it's not."

"How?"

"By talking to Rene's partner for starters."

Ford rolled his eyes. "Oh, come on."

Jo held out her arms. "What's the problem? You said it yourself. He was being dodgy when you spoke to him last."

"That's a poor lead to work with."

"Why do you say that?"

"Morris telling us about Rene's strained relationship with his partner doesn't mean anything."

"How so?"

"Because *everyone* gets under the skin of the people they work with. I've worked with you for a couple of hours, and I'm starting to get a headache."

"Look," Jo said, "we have to explore every avenue, even if Morris is at fault here, which he may be."

Sighing, Ford rested his arms on the roof of his car. "I don't want to be chasing false leads. I don't want to stir up a hornet's nest. This case is open-and-shut."

Slightly perturbed, Jo ran her fingers through her hair. "I thought you were inclined to do the right thing here, Ford."

Ford pointed his finger and said, "The last thing I want is to cause an uproar. The kid did it."

"You believe that? Wholeheartedly?"

Ford looked away.

"Think about it," Jo said. "It doesn't make sense that Morris killed everyone in cold blood and then cries over it just a moment after he did it. That's not how it works. You must be skeptical, even just a little bit."

The question seemed to cause Ford to slump slightly. He tapped his finger on the roof of the car, staring up at the sky as he did so. "I'm thirty-nine years old," he said. "I should be a sergeant by now, but I've been stuck as a detective, and I probably will be for my entire career."

"Meaning what?" Jo asked.

Ford stared at her for a moment. He then held up a finger. "First thing's first," he said, "I need to know that what I'm telling you stays between us."

Jo shrugged. "Unless it's something illegal, you have my word."

"Randall Watney," Ford said.

Jo asked, "Who's that?"

Ford sighed and said, "Randall Watney was a man charged with killing his wife and daughter. All the evidence pointed to him being the culprit. It was a clear case, but I got, well, sidetracked."

"Sidetracked how?"

"Randall Watney made a call the night of the murder to his brother. No one thought anything of it. When I looked into it, I found out that Watney's brother, Hickson, was a repeat offender who had a penchant for breaking and entering. Hickson was out on parole. He had stopped by his brother's place six hours before the murders."

"So, you looked into him as being a suspect."

Ford nodded. "When we questioned Randall, he tried to convince us that his brother was at fault. He said his brother wanted to borrow money from him. Randall said no, and he claimed that his brother returned when Randall wasn't home and murdered his entire family. I thought there may have been some truth to his story being that the two shared the same DNA, so it was *possible* that it was Hickson Watney that did the killing."

"So, what happened after that?" Jo asked.

Ford shook his head. "I pursued the angle that Randall's brother had committed the murders. Long story short, I listened to my gut and kept pushing that charges be brought against Hickson instead. It turned out that Hickson was miles away when the murders had taken place. By the time we turned our focus back on Randall, he had already fled the country, slipping into Mexico and then making his way into Central America. After that, the trail went cold. We have no idea where he could be, and believe me, I've not stopped looking."

Jo said nothing.

Ford sighed. "Look. The reason I'm telling you this is because the last time I played a hunch, a suspect that killed his wife and thirteen-year-old daughter is right now walking free because, in a lapse of judgment, I thought that someone else might have done it. It's left me with a detective's rank for the rest of my life. The person responsible for my situation is Randall Watney."

Jo had seen many careers ruined because people tried to think outside of the box. The last thing she wanted to do was watch Ford, though she barely knew him, suffer the same fate. "Listen," she said, easing up on her stern tone, "I won't overstep my boundaries here or throw you under the bus. I just need to do a little more digging first. We talk to Rene's partner. Feel out the situation first."

Ford stared at her a moment. He then shook his head. "I'm sticking to my guns on Morris being at fault here. I don't see this thing being pinned on anyone but him. But if you want to follow through with your theory, fine. Just don't drag me down with you if you start taking this investigation to places it doesn't need to go."

"Fair enough," Jo said. She was not expecting that response, but she had not earned his trust yet. "I need to swing by the office. Care to drop me off?"

Nodding, Ford got in the car. No words passed between the two of them the entire drive over.

TWENTY-FOUR

Jo knocked twice on Grantham's door.

"Come in," he said.

Jo entered the room and found that Grantham was in the middle of a phone call. She slipped into a chair across from his desk, waiting patiently for the SAC to finish his conversation.

"Agent Pullinger," Grantham said, hanging up the receiver.

"Sir," Jo replied.

"I assume you're here to provide updates." Grantham checked his watch. "Your previous SAC wasn't kidding about your ability to move quickly."

"Yes, sir," Jo said. "I just finished speaking with the suspect, Tim Morris. I also had the detective running lead on the investigation run me through the crime scene."

Grantham leaned forward, scanning the documents spread across his desk. "Detective… *Ford*," he said upon finding the name. "How was he?"

"A bit bull-headed. A little closed off. But he's a solid investigator."

Grantham shrugged. "So, give me the short version. What did you find?"

"Well," Jo said, "everything seems to indicate that the suspect, Tim Morris, is responsible for what happened to the Stansfields. From the evidence to the eyewitness's testimonies, and coupled with the report from the Medical Examiner, the Seattle P.D. has a slam dunk case on their hands."

"Good," Grantham said. "So, then it's safe to say that you don't need to look into the matter any further."

Jo paused a moment. "Not quite, sir."

Grantham raised an eyebrow. "What's the hold up?"

"Just a few details that I want to look into."

"Such as?"

"Well," Jo said, "the company that installed Rene Stansfield's alarm, for starters. It appears that Rene deactivated the system an hour before the murders took place."

The comment caused Grantham to lean back in his chair. "Interesting."

"I thought so, too. Seattle P.D. was eager to dismiss this particular element. Obviously, they're inclined to overlook such a detail when they have a suspect in custody with a motive for the murders."

"I see," Grantham said as he interlaced his fingers. "What else?"

"People close to Tim Morris are a bit shocked that he could've committed these murders."

"That's merely an opinion. That doesn't supersede evidence."

"Nonetheless, if Morris is at fault, I would like to speak to more people who knew him. It'll assist in building a narrative when the trial rolls around." Jo sat up straight. "I also want to speak to Richard Kellerman, the second half of Stansfield-Kellerman. Again, this is just a formality. He hasn't gone on the record yet."

Grantham nodded. "Well and good, Agent Pullinger. But time is of the essence. The Governor's office just called. They want this closed off as soon as humanly possible. I'll give you three days to square things away before the FBI withdraws all interest in the matter."

Standing, Jo said, "Understood, sir."

***

Jacket off, sleeves rolled up, Jo sat hunched over her desk with all files pertaining to the Stansfield murders in front of her. Checking her watch, she saw that it was just after six p.m. *One more hour*, she told herself, *then cut yourself a break.*

A short while later, she thought it would be good to check in with Sam to let him know her first day had gone well—and then a thought occurred to her:

The cell phone records.

Jo punched in Ford's number. It rang once before he answered.

"Agent Pullinger," he said with a slight hint of irritation.

"Evening, detective," she said. "I was curious if the cell phone records for the Stansfield's have been dumped."

"They came in just under an hour ago. I didn't have a chance to go through them yet."

"Well, if it's all right with you, I'd like to take a look at them."

"I figured as much."

Jo rolled her eyes. *This guy really is a gem,* she thought. "Tell you what," she said, "I'll go through it while I have you on the line. That way, you can tell your Lieutenant that the FBI didn't get to it first."

Ford agreed and forwarded everything he had to Jo's inbox. Moments later, the two of them were scouring through all the calls and texts that had originated from each of the Stansfield's cell phones.

"So," Jo said, looking at her screen, "Justine made several calls to the same number."

"I just ran it," Ford said. "It's a friend of hers. Karen Caldwell. Her name came up in a few witness statements."

Jo squinted as she looked at a series of texts from Lindsey. "Lindsey texted someone two hours before the murders. Based on the comments, Lindsey and Rene had a fight. But she doesn't really say about what."

"I jotted down the number," Ford said. "I'll cross-reference what I have to see who she was talking to."

Jo and Ford spent ten more minutes going over every number, call, and text in the records. At one point, Jo spotted something in Rene's records that made her pause and say, "Look at Rene's call log."

"I see it," Ford said. "He called the same number. Ten times."

"Right. Also, look at the times when the calls were logged. They were all made within forty-five minutes."

"Hold up," Ford said. "Look at the number's area code."

"What about it?"

"I worked Vice for a while."

Jo said, "You wore pastel shirts and loafers with no socks?"

"Unfortunately, no. I worked the drug angle for a while, though. We were trying to locate a few meth suppliers in the city. Most of these guys use burner phones to make calls. They buy some prepaid phones, run out the minutes, ditch the phones, and buy new ones."

Jo said, "Most of these guys use apps now that delete the messages as soon as you send them."

Ford said, "Quite true. And that, right there, is a number for a burner phone."

Jo sighed. "So, it's going to be difficult to trace."

"I'm afraid so."

"Still," Jo said, "it's quite curious that Rene would be putting in a bunch of calls to a burner number."

Ford said, "My thoughts exactly."

TWENTY-FIVE

Nine p.m. rolled around by the time Jo decided to head home. She was weary. Her eyes were red from staring at a computer screen. Her ears were sore from talking to Ford about the Stansfield's cell phone records. Grabbing her coat, she made her way toward the door, and when she was just two steps shy of reaching the elevator, she was intercepted by Lewis McKinley. Despite the hour, he was full of pep. "Agent Pullinger… Um, I mean, Jo," he corrected himself with a wince.

"Evening, Lewis," she said.

"Are you headed out?"

She pointed to the elevator. "As we speak."

"Listen, um—" McKinley lowered his voice. "I was curious if I could assist you somehow. I've been sort of floating through since I got here. I haven't been able to shadow anyone yet. I was kind of hoping maybe there was some work I could do for you."

He's desperate for experience, she thought. "Sure," she said with a sigh, "there might be a few things I can throw your way in the morning. But I'm taxed. I need to get some rest. I'm no good to anyone if I'm running off just adrenaline."

"Oh, yeah, of course." McKinley held up his hands. "No pressure. Anything you could do would be great."

"You got it," Jo said with a forced smile.

"So," McKinley said as she waited for the elevator doors to open, "I was looking at some old case files of yours."

"Like what?"

"The Doyle Murders," McKinley smirked. "Boy, that one was a doozy."

It was, Jo thought. *Six months of my life.* "I remember it, yes," she said.

McKinley's eyes flickered. "I mean, how did you realize that the shoe imprint they found at the crime scene was planted? No one else thought of that."

"It was gut instinct, I suppose," Jo said, jabbing the button on the elevator panel. "The crime scene tech that was on the scene, well, there was just something a little off about him. He was ill-prepared. Careless, in fact. So, I had to do what he failed to do. Make sure whether the shoe print belonged to the suspect or that it was merely placed there to throw us off."

McKinley shrugged. "Well, it's not exactly a secret that you have a penchant for sniffing out things that are, well, unusual."

So I've been told, Jo thought.

"Tell me," McKinley said, "how did you go about—"

Jo held up her hand, "I understand you're itching to get your beak wet, Lewis. But it's late. I'm completely taxed."

"I'm sorry," he said quickly. "I have a hard time turning it off."

"When's the last time you slept? You *do* sleep, don't you?"

McKinley held up four fingers. "That's all I average a night. It's hard to sleep any longer than that. I feel like I'm wasting time that could be better applied."

"That's commendable. But if you operate like that for too long, you'll start to develop grays in your hair prematurely."

"You know," McKinley said, ignoring her comment, "when I wrote my paper on you, I came across an interview that said you were up for seventy-two hours at one point because of the Doyle case. Is that true?"

Jo was a bit vexed at the relentless number of questions, but she understood why the kid was being so persistent. She was the same way when she first started out. *Cut him some slack*, she thought. *Agents like him are the future of the Bureau.* "It's true," she said. "But it wasn't a good idea. I thought I was seeing things that weren't there after being up for so long."

From one of the cubicles, someone said, "The Doyle case?"

Jo turned her head. Another agent, tall and built like a basketball player, looked on curiously as he stepped out of his cubicle. He had thick hair, combed neatly, and a complexion that gave most *GQ* models a run for their money.

"Yeah," McKinley said to the agent as he jutted his chin at Jo. "This is Agent Pullinger. She just transferred here."

The agent snapped his fingers and pointed at Jo. "I heard you were coming." He stuck out his hand. "Tom Westin. *Agent* Tom Westin."

Jo shook his hand. "Pleasure."

"Yeah, you're a bit of a rock star," Westin said.

Jo replied, "If I had a nickel for every time I heard that one…"

"It was a noteworthy case. The Doyle case, I mean. They talk about it over at Quantico quite a bit. It's almost a prerequisite along with those Toolbox Murder tapes they make you listen to."

Jo turned to leave. "Well, I'm happy my cases can assist in rounding out the Bureau's curriculum."

Westin crossed his arms. "Indeed. But to be honest, as good a job as you did with that one, I felt like you made a few, well, *missteps* with your investigation of the Doyle murders."

The comment made Jo stop in her tracks. "I see," she said. "And what do you think those missteps were?"

Westin waved her off. "Oh, who cares what I think," he said, his tone condescending. "Everyone has a different style." He shrugged. "I'm just saying that I would have, well"—he smirked—"done things differently than you did."

Jo's jaw muscles tensed. "You said your name was Westin?"

Westin nodded.

Jo stepped toward him. "Well, Agent Westin, let me ask you this: how many collars have you made?"

The agent tilted up his chin. "Two."

"That's very commendable," Jo said. "But, and pardon me for being rude, until you take on a case that matches the caliber of the Bridgeton Ripper case"—she patted Westin on the shoulder—"keep your comments to yourself."

The elevator arrived on their floor, and the doors opened.

"Um," McKinley said, "have a good night, Agent Pullinger."

"Yes, Agent Pullinger," Westin said. "Have a splendid night. I'd love to pick your brain sometime about the Bridgeton Ripper case."

Jo said nothing and entered the elevator. She made it a point to avoid eye contact with Westin and McKinley. As soon as the doors closed, memories of the heart transplant made the muscles in her chest tighten. Her breathing became strained. She held a hand over her heart and told herself not to think about the past.

The elevator arrived in the lobby with a *ping*. She got out and hurried away before someone else stopped her.

TWENTY-SIX

Jonathan and Deborah Morris didn't care that it was ten at night. It meant nothing to them that they had been running on just a couple of hours of sleep since Tim was arrested. They wanted to see their son, and despite the fact that both of them were weary and worn down, they were escorted into the visitor's area at King County jail by a guard.

Morris, dressed in his jailhouse uniform, began to weep the moment he was escorted into the cold and windowless room. The guard reminded them that touching was prohibited, and after Jonathan and Deborah greeted their son from a distance, the trio sat down at a metal bench and table that was bolted to the floor.

"Hey, Mom," Morris said, looking away from his parents. "Hey, Dad."

"Hey, son," Jonathan said, tears in his eyes. "How are you holding up?"

Morris shrugged. "I can't sleep."

Batting the tears from her eyes, Deborah's posture slackened as she looked at her frail and terrified child. "Oh, *honey*. I'm sorry."

Jonathan said, "Are you eating?"

Shrugging again, Morris said, "Just a little."

"You need to eat, Tim. You're withering away. You look awful."

Morris said nothing.

Deborah flattened her palms on the table. "Your lawyer called us. I'm glad you finally came to your senses and agreed to one."

Fatigued, Morris said, "I didn't know what else to do."

"Did he tell you the game plan?" Jonathan asked.

Morris nodded. "He said I should confess. If I do, I could get life with the possibility of parole. He said there's no point in going to trial." Morris looked down, head in his hands. "But I can't do that."

Deborah leaned toward him. "Tim—"

"I didn't do this, mom," Morris cut in. "I don't know how many more times I can say it. No one believes me. I didn't see who did this, I don't *know* who did this, but it wasn't me."

Jonathan looked at his wife. He was skeptical of his son's narrative. He wanted to believe him—he just couldn't bring himself to do so. "Tim," he said, "we have to be smart about this."

Morris said, "What are you trying to say?"

Jonathan sighed. "I'm worried, son. I think we need to get, well, ahead of the problem."

Morris shook his head. "No, the cops need to find who really did it. I would never hurt Lindsey."

"Then why were you there that night?" Deborah asked.

"I've told everyone why a thousand times. I'm not going to go over it again." Morris slumped in his chair. For a brief moment, he thought he might pass out.

Jonathan, at a loss, leaned back and tapped his finger on the table. "Your arraignment is coming up. We need to figure out exactly what we're going to do, and soon."

"I told you," Morris said as he looked at his father with a pleading set of eyes, "I'm not going to confess to something I didn't do." He leaned toward his parents. Eyes wide. On the verge of tears. "You need to tell the cops to find whoever did this. You have to. It's the only way. Don't let them put me away for something I didn't do. *Please.*"

His father said nothing. His mother followed suit.

Morris said, "You do believe me, don't you? You don't really think that I did this?"

Again, his parents said nothing. A moment later, the guard informed them that their time was up.

TWENTY-SEVEN

Ford met Jo at the curb just outside the Seattle P.D. station a little after eight in the morning. She had two cups of coffee in her hands.

Ford looked at the cups. "What's this?" he asked.

Jo held out one of the cups to him. "I thought we could start with a little peace offering," she replied.

The gesture caused a hint of a smile to form on Ford's face as he took the coffee.

Jo said, "I figured you took it black."

Ford said, "I do."

"I guessed right."

"You're a decent judge of character." Ford held up the cup. "Thanks."

Jo said, "You're welcome."

"Well," Ford said. "I just spoke with your SAC. He's intent on backing up your play of looking into this thing a bit more, despite my objections."

"I figured that would bend you out of shape a little," Jo said. "That's why I brought you the coffee."

Ford sighed. "Well, if we're going to do this thing, then let's do it. You said you wanted to talk to Richard Kellerman."

"I just want to be thorough."

Shrugging, Ford said, "Your call." He then pointed to the Bureau-issued sedan behind Jo. "I assume you're driving?"

She nodded. "Yes, indeed."

The two got in the car. Jo started the engine and pulled away from the curb.

"Well," Ford said, "if this is going to be a waste of time, then I guess the silver lining is that it will be a waste of the Bureau's gas."

Jo glanced at him. "Can I be honest?"

"That doesn't seem to be a problem with you."

"I think you're a good detective. After that story you told me about Randall Watney, well, I had a feeling that you were a good guy, putting it simply."

"Thanks a million."

"Point being," Jo said as she made a left turn, "I don't think you're as stuck to the narrative of Morris being the one and only suspect in this whole thing as you claim to."

Ford laughed. "Is that a fact?"

"Yes, it is. I took a look at your file. You have a knack for doing the right thing, in so many words. You're not just a guy punching his timecard. I'm inclined to think that you do the job because you genuinely believe you can make a difference."

"Yeah," Ford said as he glanced out the window and thought of the Watney case, "I'm a regular Boy Scout."

"I want to ask you a question," Jo said. "Off the record."

Ford said, "I thought FBI agents *lived* by the record."

Jo's eyes narrowed into slits. "Be straight with me. I want to ask you something, and I'll make sure it doesn't get documented."

Throwing up a hand, Ford said, "Go ahead."

"When you hear Tim Morris' version of events," Jo said, "despite the fact, there are gaping holes in it, and despite the fact that the evidence points to the contrary, tell me: do you think he's telling the truth?"

Ford stroked his upper lip with his finger, his focus fixated on the street. "You promise to keep it off the record?"

With two fingers held up, Jo said, "You have my word, Boy Scout."

Ford shifted his weight. "I think there's something missing here. I just can't put my finger on what that is. That's not to say that I think Morris is innocent—I just think there are a few things we still haven't learned." He looked at Jo. "Good enough?"

She nodded. "Good enough. Look, I know that the brass is pulling the strings on this. It's a high-profile case, and the last thing someone in your position would want to do is rock the boat."

"Precisely," Ford said. "But I'd lose sleep over this if the wrong person got pegged for the murders."

"I understand," Jo said. "I'll make sure that doesn't happen."

They continued their drive to Richard Kellerman's residence. After a minute, Ford said, "Your Boy Scout comment."

"What about it?"

"I'm just curious. Were you in the Girl Scouts?"

Jo shook her head. "No, but I played volleyball."

"Interesting."

"How so?"

Ford shrugged. "You have more of that chess club nerd vibe."

Laughing, Jo looked ahead and saw the home of Richard Kellerman.

TWENTY-EIGHT

The lofty home of Richard Kellerman resided in a gated community not too dissimilar from that of the Stanfields: expensive, lavish, multi-storied. The house had a carport with a Ferrari, Tesla, and Bentley in the driveway.

Jo and Ford approached the front of the house. She pressed a buzzer next to the gates and waited.

A moment later, a voice said, "Yes?"

Jo spotted a camera just above the gate. She produced her FBI credentials. "Sorry to disturb you. Are you Richard Kellerman?"

"I am," came the reply.

"Mr. Kellerman, my name is Special Agent Johanna Pullinger of the Federal Bureau of Investigation."

"The FBI?"

"That's correct."

"And this is my partner, Detective Bryan Ford of the Seattle Police Department," Jo said, introducing Ford.

Ford glared at the camera. "We met at your office, but you were too busy to speak to me."

There was a moment of silence. "Um, yes, I remember. I'll buzz you in."

They heard a loud noise, followed by the gates unlocking.

They walked up the long driveway, and when they got to the door, they found Kellerman waiting for them.

He was wearing a sweater and light-colored pants, and his feet were clad in loafers.

Kellerman smiled at Ford. "My apologies, detective. I didn't mean to brush you off the other day. Things have been a bit hectic, as you can imagine."

"I'm sure," Ford said

"Please, come in."

Jo and Ford went inside. The foyer was grand and covered in white marble.

Kellerman motioned them into the living room. "Can I get you anything? Water? Sparkling? Tap?" he asked.

"No, thank you," Jo said, looking around. The walls were painted in brightly colored tones. Expensive furnishings were scattered throughout the space.

Kellerman lingered near the foyer with a weary look on his face. "I trust you're here to discuss what happened to Rene."

"We are," Jo said. "Have you spoken to anyone else yet?"

He shook his head. "I'm trying to come to terms with this..." His breathing became labored. "*Tragedy.* I can't believe that Rene and his family were killed. It's a shock, to say the least."

Ford and Jo exchanged a subtle glance. Jo jutted her chin at Ford, silently telling him to take the lead.

"Mr. Kellerman," Ford said, "I hope you'll be forthcoming in your answers to our questions."

"I have nothing to hide," Kellerman said, spreading his arms. "Do you mind if *I* have a drink? It calms my nerves."

"Go right ahead," Ford said. "It's your house."

Kellerman made his way to a cabinet in the corner. He produced a bottle of scotch and poured himself a drink.

Ford said, "Mr. Kellerman…"

"Please"—Kellerman held up his hand—"call me Richard. Mr. Kellerman was my father."

"Well, Richard," Ford said, "Where were you on the night of the murders of Rene, Justine, and Lindsey Stansfield?"

Kellerman brought the scotch to his lips. "I was at the opera."

"What show?"

"*La Traviata.*"

"I've never heard of it."

"I'm not surprised," Kellerman said with a snicker.

Ford crossed his arms over his chest. "Please enlighten me."

"It's a tale of love and heartbreak set in 1850s Paris. A lavish production. All the showings are sold out, but I know the owner of the theatre where it's playing, and if you're interested, I can get you tickets."

"I'll pass," Ford replied.

Jo coughed, cutting through the tension in the room. "I'm sure you've been keeping up with the investigation," she said. "I mean, after all, it was your partner that was killed."

Kellerman turned to her. "I know only what I've heard on the news. And according to them, a young man, a man who was involved with"—he sighed—"the *daughter*, is at fault."

"He's in custody," Ford said. "Yes."

"His name is Tim Morris," Jo added. "Do you know him?"

127

Kellerman shook his head. "No, I don't. The first time I heard about him was when he was arrested."

"How close were you with the Stansfields?"

"Rene and I were best friends. Not so much in the past year, I'm sorry to say."

Jo said, "Can I ask why that was?"

"Well," Kellerman said, "we didn't see eye-to-eye on certain matters. I suppose that comes with the price of maintaining a professional partnership for almost twenty-five years."

"Yours was quite the success story," Jo said. "Most companies fail within the first three years, and most friendships end as a result of that failure. But not in your case."

"Rene and I were a success story until recently, I'm afraid," Kellerman said as his smile melted into a frown.

"Can you speak about that?"

"In broad strokes, yes. Rene wanted to take the company public. I didn't. So, we butted heads quite a bit about it."

Jo said, "But you still remained on friendly terms, is that correct?"

Kellerman's eyes went wide. "Of course. We didn't hang around each other as we once did. But hearing that Rene passed in the midst of us squabbling just... Tears me apart." He took a sip of his drink. "I regret that I left our relationship on such terrible terms before he passed." He dabbed at the moisture under his eyes.

Jo said, "I know this must be difficult on you."

Kellerman nodded. "It is."

"We just want to make sure we're being thorough," she said. "Was there anything, anything at all that you might know that could shed some light on this whole situation?"

Downing his drink, Kellerman went about fetching another. "I don't know what I can tell you that you don't already know."

"Richard," Ford said, his tone more inquisitive, "when you say you were butting heads with Rene recently, what do you mean by that, exactly?"

Kellerman glared at Ford. "I told you: we were at odds at taking the company public."

Jo took a step toward Kellerman. "But how badly did you, well, *butt heads*? Were there arguments? Anything along those lines?"

"Are you asking if we *threatened* one another, Agent Pullinger?" Kellerman asked in a defensive tone.

"We're just trying to—"

"I," Kellerman cut in, "have survived in this business for a long time. Do you know why that is, Agent Pullinger?"

Jo kept her mouth sealed.

Kellerman held up the glass to emphasize his point. "Because," he said, "I have tough skin. I learned to take hits, insults, and incessant inquiries since the day I turned a profit. The point being, I know when I'm being put in the hot seat."

Jo said, "You're not in the hot seat."

"But you still feel inclined to question me on my relationship with Rene."

"It's a matter of being thorough."

"You keep saying that," he said. "But you can understand why me being questioned like a suspect would make me hot under the collar."

"I can."

Kellerman pointed a finger at Jo. "Then I will make this as painless and straightforward as possible. My relationship with Rene was dissolving. But I am up every night reeling over the fact that we never made amends. This entire matter sickens me, and I don't know how I'll be able to live with myself knowing that I wronged him in the way that I did."

"I'm sorry that you feel the way you do," she said. "We're not here to attack you. We just want answers."

Kellerman stared at her. He then sighed. "No. *I'm* sorry. I'm just upset. My partner is gone, and I'm unsure how to proceed forward with the business without him."

"I understand." Jo produced a business card. "I'm going to leave this for you. If you can think of anything that might be pertinent, please don't hesitate to call."

Kellerman took the card. "I'll make sure to do that if I think of anything."

When Jo and Ford were walking back to their car, Ford turned to her and asked, "What do you think?"

Jo said, "He's had the same look on his face that I've seen before."

"What look would that be?"

"The same look my niece has when she's caught with her hand in the cookie jar."

"I don't get it," Ford said with a frown.

"She'll say anything to stay out of trouble."

TWENTY-NINE

Jo returned to the field office, updated Grantham on her status, and then headed home. The entire drive back, Jo thought about the facts of the case: *Tim Morris is being pegged for the murder. I'm just not convinced that he is the killer, but nothing points to him* not *being the one responsible either.*

Jo replayed the conversation she had with Richard Kellerman. It was clear that there was something going on at Stansfield-Kellerman that he was not revealing. She just couldn't put her finger on what.

As soon as Jo got closer to Sam's house, she found him rolling a garbage bin down the driveway.

He smiled when he saw her. She waved and then parked behind his Jetta.

"So," Sam said, "how'd it go?"

"How did what go?" she replied, getting out.

"Your first day at the new office."

"Not bad," Jo said.

"I assume you can't talk about it."

Jo shook her head. "Maybe once I get some facts sorted out first."

Sam grinned. "Wink once if it has anything to do with those murders in Broadmoor."

Jo winked.

She moved toward the house. Sam put his hand out to stop her. "It's Chrissy's bedtime, and if she saw you now coming through the door, she'll be excited and hyper for the next couple of hours. Good luck trying to get her to fall asleep then. And she's got school in the morning and…"

Jo smiled. "Don't worry, Sam. I understand."

Sam looked up at the sky. The moon was full and bright, surrounded by a twinkling sea of stars. "Why don't we go for a stroll? We can talk while we walk."

"Sounds good to me."

They weaved their way through the neighborhood. Jo took in the sights, amazed at how lush and green the state of Washington was. Sam caught her up on the events of the day.

"Also," he said, "we're going to the art museum this weekend. If you want, you can join us."

Jo perked up. "That's so funny. I drove past there today, and I thought it might be fun to go there with Chrissy."

"Well, fate has swung in your favor. Where were you driving to, if you don't mind me asking?"

"To question a lead. I was riding shotgun with a Detective from the Seattle P.D. We're working together on the case I was telling you about."

Sam said, "Was he a man?"

Jo rolled her eyes. "You're such a dolt, you know that?"

Her brother laughed. "I'm just curious when you might dabble in the romantic arena again."

"When I'm in my grave."

Sam groaned. "Oh, come on. Quit being such a downer."

"I'm not a downer," Jo said. "I'm a realist."

"Says the girl who wrote a love letter to Danny Ambrose when she was in the sixth grade."

Jo sighed. "I should have never told you about that."

"You never think about it?" Sam asked. "Being in love? Getting married? Having kids?"

Jo shrugged. "Maybe every once in a while. But I'm just not ready. You know the history of my disastrous romantic life as well as I do."

Sam frowned. "Well, was this detective a *handsome* detective?"

He is, Jo thought and replied, "A little bit."

"Did he have a ring on his finger?"

"No. But he's held up on someone. I can tell."

"Did you ask him about it?"

She glared at him. "It's none of my business."

He stopped. "I'm sorry, Jo. I'm just giving you a hard time."

Jo nudged her brother playfully. "I know," she said as she thought back to the men in her life. Reflecting on it all, she felt her heart begin to race, and she slowed her walking pace.

"Hey," Sam said, "are you okay?"

Jo felt like she was out of breath. "Yeah, I'm okay."

"Is it your heart?"

Jo nodded. "Yeah, but I'm fine."

A concerned look overcame him. "Jo, you're worrying me."

Just talk, Jo thought. *You'll feel better if you do.* "I've been having dreams. Nightmares, really."

"About what?"

Jo flattened her palm and placed it over her chest. "It started not that long ago. It happens a few times a month. I keep reliving the memory of being in the hospital. I feel like I can't breathe, and when I wake up, my heart is racing."

Sam said, "That wasn't a problem before?"

Jo shook her head. "No. It just snuck up on me. I'm not losing sleep, but every time I wake up, I feel like I just ran a marathon. I just don't know why I have these nightmares so long after the fact. It's strange."

"Have you thought about talking to someone about it?"

"I don't need a therapist," she replied. "They're just dreams."

"You know," Sam said, "I talked to a therapist right after Mom passed. Sometimes it helps to have an unbiased third party speak on the subject."

Jo wasn't convinced that she needed the help. "I don't know," she said. "Maybe."

"Jo"—Sam rested his hand on her shoulder— "I'm your big brother. I'm always going to worry about you. You've been through a lot. We all have."

"Which is why I'm having these dreams," Jo said. "It's just stress. It'll pass."

Sam said, "I might be inclined to dismiss it all if it was coming from someone who *didn't* have major heart surgery. I mean, it's a miracle you're still working at the FBI."

Jo's nostrils flared. "I'm *fine*, Sam."

"I know you are. You're superwoman, but you're not indestructible. You push yourself to your limits, and it's commendable." He slumped his shoulders. "I'm just worried that you'll push yourself to the breaking point like Dad did."

"I'm not Dad," she said. "I've learned from his mistakes."

Sam said, "This family needs you around, Jo. I don't know what we'd do without you."

Jo smiled. "Thank you, Sam. I'll think about it."

His eyes brightened. "So, you'll speak to a therapist about your nightmares?"

"I said I'll think about it, okay?"

"That's all I ask." He then nudged her. "We want to keep you around for a while, you know. All *four* of us."

Jo squinted. "*Four* of us?"

A proud smile crossed Sam's face. "Kim's pregnant."

"Oh my God!" she nearly screamed.

She jumped up and hugged her brother.

"I'm so happy for you guys," she said.

For a brief moment, all her worries had disappeared. And all she thought about was cradling the next generation of Pullingers in her arms.

THIRTY

Ford rubbed his eyes as he slipped his key into the locks of his apartment and shuffled inside. He tossed his coat on the kitchen table, along with his keys. After cracking open a can of beer and sifting through junk mail, he rubbed the back of his neck and took a moment to breathe. He thought about Jo Pullinger. He worried she had a habit of sticking her nose into things. He just hoped she didn't pull him down with her when her hunch, ultimately, turned out to be wrong.

Leave it to the morning, he told himself. *Look at it with a fresh pair of eyes.*

After downing what was left of his beer, he heated up a meal in the microwave and plopped down on the couch in his scantily furnished apartment. He sighed. He had never gotten used to living by himself, even though it had been six months since Kelly asked him to move out. Vying for a shred of comfort, he fished out his cell phone and called her up.

"Bryan," she said, her voice sounding tired and annoyed.

"Hey," he replied. "Sorry, I know it's late."

Kelly said nothing.

Ford cleared his throat. "You two doing okay?"

"Yeah." Ford could hear what sounded like bedsheets being peeled off. "She had her first dance class today."

The notion of seeing Hazel spinning around in a tutu warmed Ford's heart. He wished he could have been there—but it wasn't his choice to make.

"That's great," he said. "How'd she do?"

"She fell a couple of times, but she did great."

"I wish I was there to see it."

Kelly, again, said nothing.

"Listen," Ford said as he perched forward on the couch, "would it be all right if I talked to her for a moment?"

A sigh came over the phone. "It's late, Bryan," Kelly said. "I have to get up early for work in the morning."

"I just want to say goodnight."

"I just put her to bed."

Ford's brow furrowed. "She's not sleeping in the bed with you anymore?"

"No, she has a big girl bed now," Kelly replied. "She was insistent that she get one."

Closing his eyes, Ford reeled at the fact that he was missing out on so much: big girl beds. Recitals. Everything else in between. "Can I just say goodnight?" he asked.

Kelly's voice became strained. "Bryan, it's late."

"I know."

"I told you I needed time."

"I know."

"Do you know how hard this is for us?" she asked. "It's tough enough having you call up in the dead of night. But it's worse when you ask me to wake our daughter up so you can talk to her."

"I miss her."

"I know you do," Kelly said. "And she misses you too. But each time she talks to you, she gets really upset and emotional afterward. She asks why you're not at home and why we're not a family like the other kids at school. I can't deal with that right now. I just can't."

Ford was at a loss. He wanted to go home. He wanted to be with the people he loved. "How long is this going to last, Kelly?" he asked. "How long are you going to keep me away?"

"*Bryan*," Kelly's voice trembled, "how can you forget what happened?"

It was impossible for Ford to forget the rainy night when a man with a knife showed up at Ford's doorstep to rectify the ten years Ford had put him away for. The memories of Kelly screaming, of Ford pushing the man out of the way, throwing him to the ground, and breaking his arm as little Hazel watched from the foyer.

"I don't feel safe," Kelly said. "I love you. We both do. But I need time. And I need you to respect that."

Holding his head high, Ford said, "I understand."

"Goodnight, Bryan."

"Goodnight, Kelly."

Ford hung up. He leaned back on the couch, playing back the memories he shared with his family and hoping that one day he would be able to make more.

Sleep evading him, he decided to scour through the files pertaining to the Stansfield case. The more he worked, the more he began to think: *Jo could be right. Someone other than Tim Morris might be responsible for the murders.*

THIRTY-ONE

The heart monitor was beeping. Jo, fluttering her eyes, could see the scalpel being pressed against her chest. She felt the steel against her skin. Dr. Cohen nodded to a nurse as he prepared to make an incision. *No!* she tried to scream. *I'm still awake!* Jo couldn't move or speak as the scalpel began to cut. She felt a searing pain strike through her torso like a bolt of lightning...

She shot up, opened her eyes, and realized, once again, that it had been nothing but a bad dream.

Jo clutched her chest. Perspiration clung to her body. She looked around Sam's guest bedroom, the clock on the nightstand reading eleven-thirty. Rain dotted the windows outside. She felt a chill settle over her body as she peeled off the sheets and swung her legs over the bed.

This has to stop, she thought. *I can't keep living like this.*

She caught her breath, stood, and began pacing the floor. The nightmares were becoming more frequent. Every time she awoke, her heart would beat faster than it had the time before. After a few moments of pacing, she sat down on the edge of the bed. Memories of the Bridgeton Ripper played in her mind. She felt like she did back when the case was in full swing: uncertain, terrified, searching for answers.

A soft knock came at the door. Jo, composing herself, answered it to find Sam standing in the doorway in his pajamas with a look of concern on his face.

"Hey," Sam whispered. "You okay?"

Jo forced a smile. "Yeah, why?"

"I thought I heard you tossing and turning in here."

She waved him off. "I'm okay. Just having a hard time sleeping in a new bed."

"You sure?"

She nodded. "I'm sure."

Sam turned to leave. "Okay. Sleep tight. There's some tea in the kitchen if you need it."

"Thanks, Sam."

"Goodnight."

"Goodnight." Jo closed the door and walked back over to the bed. She couldn't do this to herself anymore. She also didn't need Sam or his family to deal with whatever afflictions she was suffering from. *I need to get my mind right*, she told herself. *I need to pull it together.*

Resolved at catching at least a few hours of sleep, Jo slipped back under the covers and closed her eyes. Her mind drifted to Tim Morris and the fact that she felt he was innocent, no matter how much Ford thought otherwise.

She knew she had an uphill battle in front of her. She not only had to prove to her superiors her belief, she also had to convince her new partner. She felt the latter might be harder to do than the former.

She wasn't sure when, but eventually, she drifted off to sleep.

THIRTY-TWO

Jo caught McKinley approaching her desk with two cups of coffee in his hands and that same eager grin on his face. She drew a breath, certain that the kid was going to ask about some case from her past or fish for tidbits of advice. She liked McKinley well enough, but his incessant nature was worse than dealing with her niece during a sugar high.

"Good morning, Jo," he said warmly.

She forced herself to smile. "Good morning, Lewis."

He forked a thumb over his shoulder. "The courier just showed up. Guy downstairs says he has a bunch of boxes from your old field office."

The lightbulb clicked on in Jo's mind. "Oh, shoot," she said. "I completely forgot about that." She stood. "Has anyone let him up?"

"I signed for the boxes," McKinley said. "I thought it might be a bit of a trek for you to go back and forth like that. He's bringing it up as we speak." He extended one of the cups in his hand. "Also, you looked like you could use this." He winced. "Sorry, I hope I'm not overstepping any boundaries. I know I can be a bit—well, tenacious."

Jo paused, but then she smiled and took the cup. "Thanks, Lewis," she said.

"My pleasure."

"Tell you what. I could use some help scouring through cell phone records for the Stansfield case. We're trying to figure out the owner of a certain telephone number that keeps popping up. I can forward the information to you now. Think you can handle it?"

The question caused McKinley's eyes to go wide. "Oh, yeah, of course! I'll get right on it."

Jo quickly forwarded the necessary information to McKinley's inbox. She then hurried to the elevator, where she met the courier who wheeled four boxes over to her desk. Most of the materials were old case files—but one box, marked "Personal," contained mementos from the past.

Jo grabbed a pair of scissors, cut the tape, and peeled open the flaps. Inside were a few framed photos of her and her mother. One of her and Sam. A few knick-knacks she had accrued during her tenure, novelty items like drink coasters, mugs, and even her old credentials from Quantico.

Jo nearly lost her breath as soon as her hand grazed the framed photo of her father, Bill, standing proudly next to her at her school track competition.

Photo in hand, Jo sat down in her chair. The shot of her and her dad was a moment she would never forget. She could still smell the cologne Mom had purchased him from Macy's for Christmas. His arm around her in the photo was a physical display of affection that Bill was not known for doing.

In the photo, she was smiling from ear to ear. She'd just come in first place in a race, and a medal was hanging around her neck. Her cheeks were flushed with excitement. Not only because she had won but also because her father was there to see her do it.

"I'm so proud of you, Jo," she remembered him saying.

It was the first time he had ever uttered those words. It would also be the last. A few short months later, he was killed by the Bridgeton Ripper.

She snapped out of her reverie when she heard McKinley call out, "Jo?"

Placing the photo back in the box, she blinked away the memory. "Yeah?"

McKinley, seated at a desk to the right of her, pointed to his computer monitor. "This could be something you might want to take a look at."

She stood and walked over. "What have you got?" she asked as she saw the Stansfield phone records displayed on the screen.

"Texts between Richard and Justine," McKinley replied. "It's not part of the timeline of the murders, but it still looked interesting at first glance."

Jo shook her head. "You mean *Rene*. Richard was his partner."

"No," McKinley said. "Justine was texting Richard Kellerman."

Leaning into the screen, Jo laid eyes on an exchange between Richard Kellerman and Justine Stansfield eight hours before the murders had taken place:

> RICHARD: We need to talk, Justine.
> JUSTINE: No. We don't.
> RICHARD: Please. Just for a moment.
> JUSTINE: It's OVER, Richard.

McKinley looked up at Jo. "Is this something to note?"

Jo's eyes narrowed. "It is *definitely* something to note."

THIRTY-THREE

Three coffins of varied sizes were lined up side by side in front of the pulpit. Behind them were pictures of Rene, Lindsey, and Justine Stansfield on separate easels. Flowers were in ripe supply, along with the tears flowing from those in attendance. Funerals were never something that Jo could get used to. It didn't matter how many of them she attended in both a professional and personal sense.

Funerals are a bleak affair, but it does corral every person of interest into the same area, Jo thought.

Trying her best not to fidget, she stood at the back of the church, a towering structure made of stone and stained glass. Ford stood beside her. What seemed like every citizen of Seattle was in attendance, a sea of black-clad mourners packed shoulder to shoulder with half the cameras in the western hemisphere waiting outside to snap a photo of one of the most high-profile murder cases in recent memory.

Jo, tight-lipped and doing her best not to highlight her presence, watched as the priest set about reading scripture and consoling all those in attendance. But Jo wasn't listening to the priest's words. She was watching the mourners, specifically Richard Kellerman, as he sat in the front row with his head hung and his shoulders slumped. Jo couldn't help but dwell on the texts that were exchanged between him and Justine.

Scanning the faces in the crowd, she spotted a woman in the front row: blonde, forty-to-fifty years old. The amount of cosmetic surgery she had probably cost north of six figures. As if reading her mind, Ford nudged her and whispered: "That's Karen Caldwell, the woman Justine was texting on the night of the murders."

Her eyes narrowed, thinking.

Ford said, "Justine was telling her that Rene and Lindsey had had a fight."

Remembering, Jo nodded subtly. The funeral continued for what seemed like a long time. When the priest said his closing statements, an organist buried somewhere in the front started to play a melancholy tune. Everyone slowly began to file out and make their way to the cemetery for the final—and perhaps most solemn—part of the day: the burial.

Ford leaned into Jo's ear. "The procession is going to jam up traffic. They've got over two hundred people here."

Jo nodded. "Let's hang back. We don't need to be front and center."

"People are a bit off guard today."

"Meaning?"

Ford shrugged. "Meaning, maybe it might be good to poke around a bit, you know."

"What are you planning on doing?"

"Not me," he said with a shake of his head. "I was hoping *you* would do something."

She stared at him. "Me?"

He grinned. "If someone got mad that we were asking questions at a funeral, I can blame it on you."

Jo wanted to laugh, but she kept her composure. As she waited in the wings and watched the attendants file out, she caught something out of the corner of her eye: a young woman behind the pews. She was clutching her purse, standing off to the side and looking at Jo with an eager expression. She gave a little wave, her eyes beckoning to Jo to join her.

"I'll be right back," Jo said.

She weaved her way through the pews. She approached the young woman. She was short, with auburn hair, and freckles were painted across the bridge of her nose. She offered Jo a pleasant smile that reflected a warm and welcoming disposition.

"My name is Ellie," the young woman said, biting her lip. "Ellie Kavanaugh." She looked at the crowd filing out. "Could we, uh, speak privately for a moment?"

"Of course," Jo said as Ellie made her way to an area to the left of the confessional booths.

Drawing a deep breath, Ellie wrung her fingers and lowered her tone. "I'm sorry for acting so secretive," she said. "Half of the people from the office are here. I didn't want them to hear me talking."

Jo's brow wrinkled. "You worked with Rene?"

Nodding, Ellie said, "I worked *for* Rene. I was his executive assistant." She peeked around the corner. "Honestly, I was trying to get in touch with someone who was working on the... well, case. I just wasn't sure who to call." She bit her lip. "Also, I've signed so many NDAs at this point that I'm worried I might get in trouble. I figured since you were an FBI agent, that might make things easier, I guess."

Jo's eyebrows turned up. "How do you know I'm an FBI agent?"

"Word got around that the FBI was looking into the case." Ellie pointed to the chapel. "I recognized that man you were standing with. He's a cop. I saw him walking through the offices the other day." She shrugged. "When I saw you two talking, and based on the way you're dressed, I kind of put two and two together."

"Well," Jo said with a smirk, "you're not wrong. My name is Agent Pullinger."

"Agent Pullinger, I don't want to linger here long. I just"—she squinted—"feel like, I don't know, the company is doing its best to sort of keep their mouths shut during this whole thing."

Jo asked, "What do you mean?"

Ellie, appearing more nervous than she did at the start of the conversation, leaned in closer. "Richard," she whispered. "Richard Kellerman. He's not being forthright, Agent Pullinger."

"How so?"

"Well—" Ellie's eyes began to dart to-and-fro. "I was Rene's assistant, as I said before. And to be honest with you, things weren't going well between Richard and Rene."

Jo nodded. "That's what Richard told me."

Ellie shook her head. "He's not telling you everything. I can guarantee it." She held up her hand. "Listen, I can only tell you so much because of what I know and what I've been told. But Richard and Rene had been fighting a lot lately."

Jo remembered what Tim Morris had told her. "What were they fighting about?"

"It had something to do with"—Ellie lowered her voice to the faintest of whispers—"the cancer trials."

"Cancer trials?"

"It was the next big thing Richard and Rene were working on. Rene always played his cards close to the chest, but for some reason, right before he died, he seemed on edge, suspicious of Richard. Again, he never said much to me about the trials. But I know that he was worried."

"Worried about Richard, you think?" Jo asked.

Ellie nodded. "Rene told me a couple of weeks ago that if something happened, it was Richard's fault."

"What did he mean if something happened?"

"I don't know. He never elaborated, but do you think he meant…?"

Ellie swallowed, looking apprehensive.

Jo handed her a card and said, "Listen, Ms. Kavanaugh, if you can remember anything else, please call me."

Stuffing the card in her purse, Ellie said, "Thank you. I have to go." With that, Ellie quickly made her exit and joined the back of the line, filing out of the church. Jo, mulling over the information Ellie had given her, stood beside Ford as they waited for the church to empty out.

Ford said, "What was that about?"

Jo caught Richard Kellerman taking a furtive glance at her over his shoulder. "We need to get a room ready," she said. "I have a *lot* of questions for our friend Richard Kellerman."

THIRTY-FOUR

When Jo requested another interview with Kellerman, it was quickly shot down. But when she mentioned warrants, judges, and official inquires, it landed her and Ford in Kellerman's living room with an attorney that charged four hundred dollars per hour.

Ron Coleman, a slick and athletic man with a penchant for brand-name suits, showcased a toothy smile and twirled the ring on his pinky. "This is a waste of time, Agent Pullinger," he said, speaking like a parent talking down to a child. "I should state for the record that this little sidebar is quite unnecessary and a bit, well, *distasteful*."

Talking with Kellerman's lawyer gave Jo the same sickly feeling that a case of food poisoning did. Kellerman, on the other hand, was seated beside Coleman on the couch with his head down and his mouth shut.

"I'm sorry you feel that way, counselor," Jo said. "But as you know, investigations of this caliber require us to be thorough."

"My client has cooperated every step of the way. He's already answered all your questions." He shrugged. "What more could you possibly want from him?"

"Then I'll be frank," she said, "for the sake of your time and that of your client."

Coleman picked at his manicured fingernail. "That would be greatly appreciated."

Jo centered her focus on Kellerman. "Richard... We found texts between you and Justine Stansfield."

The statement caused the vein on Kellerman's head to bulge out. His mouth opened—but Coleman clapped a hand on his client's shoulder and proceeded to intervene. "Don't answer that, Richard."

Ford, standing in front of Kellerman's grand piano, scanned Coleman from toes to temples. "You don't feel that's relevant information?"

"No," Coleman said. "Richard was friends with the Stansfields. I find it a bit obtuse of you to think it's odd that they would be in contact with one another."

Ford crossed his arms. "It's the context of the exchanges that raises questions."

Coleman sighed. "Show me the texts then."

Jo pulled out her phone and held it out before placing it gently into Coleman's palm.

The lawyer sighed and glanced at the texts. He shrugged and handed the phone back to Jo. "I'm not sure what you're insinuating by showing me that."

Ford said, "It's quite clear."

Coleman shook his head. "No, it's not."

Jo said, "Richard and Justine were engaged in some kind of affair."

Coleman pointed a finger. "Careful, Agent Pullinger. That kind of statement is outrageous and unfounded. You know, part of me is inclined to—"

Kellerman held up his hand. "That's enough, Ron."

Coleman patted his client on the arm. "Richard, you don't have to answer them—"

"I said," Kellerman grumbled, "that's *enough*, Ron."

With a huff, Coleman sat back. Jo, inching closer, watched as Kellerman interlaced his fingers and perched forward on the couch.

"Listen," Kellerman said, "you're not wrong." He pinched the bridge of his nose. "Justine and I *did* have an affair."

Jo felt like she had hit the winning lottery number. "Tell me more about it," she said.

"Richard," Coleman said, "I should advise you..."

Kellerman's face turned beet red. "I'm not going to tell you again, Ron. I pay you by the hour, not the minute. If you want to stay on retainer, just stop talking for a minute."

Coleman stood and held up his hands. He moved to the corner of the room and stared at Kellerman like a kid who had just been kicked out of the party.

"The affair was a one-off. It happened a long time ago. I can't even remember how long ago it was," Kellerman continued. He gestured to Jo. "Those texts were the result of a night out drinking."

"When?"

"What do you mean?" Kellerman replied, confused.

"When did you go out drinking with Justine?" Jo asked.

"It was a couple of weeks ago. Rene was busy with work—and she was feeling lonely, so she asked me to drop by. But nothing happened that night. After that, I never sent her another message. I'm sure you can confirm that."

Jo nodded. "We have."

"Then I don't know what else to tell you."

Ford said, "Did Rene know?"

"No," Kellerman said. "He didn't. And it killed me that I never confessed to him what happened between Justine and me all those years ago. That's just another reason why all of this has been so hard."

Jo asked, "When exactly did the affair occur?"

"I told you," Kellerman grumbled through gritted teeth, "I don't remember."

"And how long did—"

"*Stop*," Coleman interjected. "I've had about enough of this." He moved toward Kellerman. "My client is done talking."

This time Richard didn't protest.

Coleman took this as a sign to continue and said, "Unless you guys want to lay some kind of charges that would allow you to incessantly quiz my client the way you have been, we're done here."

"Richard," Ford said, "be smart."

Richard, his eyes looking up slowly to meet Ford's, said, "I have nothing more to say."

A smug grin radiated across Coleman's face as he buttoned his blazer and gestured like a bellhop to the door. "You know the way out."

As Jo and Ford walked out the door, she shook her head and fished out the keys to her sedan. "Well," she said, "that went as expected."

Ford nodded over his shoulder. "We never got to ask him about the cancer trial stuff. Probably too soon for that anyway."

"Exactly. Kellerman is sweating a bit. Let him. When the time comes, we can squeeze him then."

Ford sighed and said, "So, what do we do next?"

"Even if we couldn't ask Richard about the cancer trials, that doesn't mean we can't look into it ourselves," Jo replied. "Whatever it was, it caused a rift between Richard and Rene."

Before Jo slipped behind the wheel, she looked up and saw Richard Kellerman standing by the upstairs window. His face was pale, and he was staring at her through a narrow set of eyes.

THIRTY-FIVE

After Jo and Ford left Kellerman's residence, she placed a call to McKinley back at the field office. She told him to pull up all the information he could on Stansfield-Kellerman pertaining to lawsuits, workman's compensation claims, and anything else that stood out in a legal sense. As soon as she and Ford arrived, they found McKinley waiting for them by the elevators.

"Agent Pullinger," McKinley said as he eyeballed the visitor's tag clipped to Ford's jacket.

Jo said, "This is Detective Bryan Ford."

Ford shook McKinley's hand. "Seattle P.D.," Ford said.

"Pleasure to meet you," McKinley said, and then he turned back to Jo. "Listen, it took a bit of searching, but I forwarded everything I could find on the company so far. There're a few things you might want to take a look at."

Jo proceeded to her desk with Ford in tow. She sat in front of her computer and opened the documents McKinley had just sent her. She and Ford sifted through them one by one. Twenty minutes of scouring and perusing through the company's legal history eventually led them to a series of court filings that read "Stansfield-Kellerman v. Tully."

Jo opened the document. It pertained to a lawsuit filed by a former employee named Mark Tully. "This guy filed a suit against the company," she said. "Citing gross negligence in regard to a drug trial called Comoxin." She glanced at Ford. "That could be the drug trial Rene's assistant was referring to."

"Do they mention anything particular about Comoxin in these documents?"

Jo shook her head. "They don't say what it is." She opened a search page and typed in "Comoxin". Nothing was listed on the company's website, but an independent news article she discovered caught her attention. She clicked the link.

Ford squinted at the screen and summarized it out loud. "Comoxin was being pushed by Stansfield-Kellerman as a revolutionary, alternative therapy for cancer patients. During a meeting with the CFO of Stansfield-Kellerman back in August, Richard Kellerman made the claim, and I'll quote from the article: 'Comoxin had the promise to replace chemotherapy as the standard for cancer therapy'."

Jo scrolled. "The author said that Comoxin never saw the light of day. It gets cryptic from there." She did another search. "I can't find much else."

"So," Ford said, "who's this Tully guy that filed the lawsuit naming Comoxin?"

Jo pulled up the court document again. "He was a lab assistant. Apparently, he tried to sue the company for a little over two million." She pointed to the screen. "Rene and Richard are named in the lawsuit."

Ford read the file. "Looks like it was dismissed two months after it was filed." He pointed to another page. "After that, the company filed a countersuit."

Clicking the mouse and scrolling, Jo found follow-up documents. "Tully was hit with a cease-and-desist order." She scrolled. "Looks like the judge voted in favor of Rene and Richard."

Ford asked, "Any information on Tully? Address? Where's he working now?"

Jo shook her head. "No, everything listed on file pertains to his attorney." She looked over her shoulder. "McKinley?"

He swooped in as if on standby. "How can I help?"

"Pull me up everything you have on a Mark Howard Tully. He worked for the company as a lab assistant."

McKinley clapped his hands together. "I'm on it."

Ford smiled as he watched the kid leave. "Tenacious, isn't he?"

Laughing, Jo said, "Very."

"Were you ever like that?"

"At one point," she replied. "Not so much anymore."

Ford said, "Same." He glanced at his watch. "How long do you think it'll take to pull up Tully's information?"

"Probably five minutes faster than Seattle P.D."

"Are you throwing shade at my department?"

"Of course not," Jo said with a flicker of her eyelids. "The FBI just has all the cool toys."

"Noted," Ford said. "So, assuming this Tully angle pans out, what's your theory?"

Jo wanted a few more pieces of the puzzle before she began with the theories. "Not sure," she said. "Maybe Tully can shed some light on that."

Ford said, "One thing we can say with certainty is that Kellerman and Justine had an affair."

Jo nodded. "Correct."

"So," Ford said, "the question I have is how accurate Kellerman's timeline is in regard to that fact. Which way are you leaning?"

Jo's conversation with Kellerman had left her unsatisfied. "I don't think he's telling the truth. And that might end up being significant."

"Love can make people do some crazy things," Ford said.

"Yes, it can," Jo said, worried that something fouler was at play.

McKinley returned to the desk ten minutes later. "I just forwarded Tully's current address to you."

Jo stood up. "You driving?" she asked Ford.

Ford replied, "Only if you cover lunch after we question Tully."

Jo replied, "Deal."

THIRTY-SIX

It was clear to Jo as she appraised Mark Tully's apartment complex that he didn't have much money. The beige, multi-story complex near midtown looked like a cinderblock. Graffiti was sprayed on the walls. A car with flat tires and faded paint rested on the corner.

Ford hopped out of the car. "Not exactly the Ritz," he said.

"No," Jo said. "It certainly isn't."

"Reminds me of my first apartment," Ford said. "I shared it with this guy who was trying to be a musician."

"I bet that was loud."

"Very. You remember your first apartment?"

Jo nodded. "I had a crazed roommate who stole things from me. Had to change the locks."

"I feel like crazed roommates are a rite of passage."

"Agreed," Jo said. "It was almost impossible to get her out of there. I ended up blasting my stereo from my room and locking the door for a week before she finally caved and left."

The story made Ford flex his brow. "Impressive."

Jo said, "Psychological warfare."

They walked toward the front door; Jo eyed the call box beside it. She scanned for Tully's name next to the button that read: "201." She pressed it. It rang three times before a groggy voice answered: "Who is it?"

Jo said, "Am I speaking with Mark Tully?"

A pause. "Yeah?"

"Mr. Tully, my name is Agent Pullinger. I work with the FBI."

Another pause. "What do you want?"

"I wanted to ask you a few questions in regard to your time at Stansfield-Kellerman."

The front door buzzed. The locks disengaged. Ford looked at Jo curiously.

"That was easy," he said.

"Too easy," she replied.

They entered the complex and ascended the staircase that led to the second floor. The front door was open. Standing in the doorway was a rangy man with shaggy hair, three-day stubble, and a glossy look in his eyes that was likely from a day of binge drinking.

"Mr. Tully," Jo said. "This is my partner, Detective Ford of the Seattle P.D."

Tully nodded in Ford's direction and said, "Please, come in."

Jo entered. Ford followed behind her. She took a scan of the room and saw that Tully lived in a studio with stained carpets and used furniture that sagged from overuse.

"I must say," Jo began, "that you seemed more eager than most people to talk to a federal agent."

Tully, peeling open his fridge, snagged a bottle of beer and nodded. "Those bastards at Stansfield-Kellerman ruined my life. If they're being investigated, then I'm happy to assist in whatever way I can."

"I see," Jo said. "Well, your name came across our desk during our investigation into Rene Stansfield's murder."

Tully thumbed off the cap on his bottle. "How so?"

Ford said, "Comoxin, for starters."

Tully's lips drew into a tight line as he took a swig of his beer. "That name will stay with me until the day I die."

Jo said, "You filed a lawsuit against the company regarding the drug trials that took place. You claimed 'gross negligence' in the statements that you made."

"It's no secret," Tully said. "And after I filed that lawsuit and attempted to put a spotlight on what happened, I ended up losing everything I had just trying to pay my legal fees." He clenched his jaw. "They made sure I never worked again. They even went so far as to say I was a 'lab assistant' in their deposition. They made it sound like I was cleaning the garbage bins." He held up his beer. "Point being, I'm happy to throw shade at them however I can."

Ford said, "What was your role at Stansfield-Kellerman?"

Tully motioned with his beer to the framed credentials on the wall above the sofa. Jo eyed them and saw that they were doctorate degrees in biology. From Harvard.

"I'm a biostatistician," Tully said. "Essentially, I spearheaded the trials for Comoxin. I found the patients, gathered the data, and everything else in between."

"What can you tell us about Rene and Richard's relationship? We've been led to believe that it was in shambles after we spoke to Richard."

Tully's eyes flickered with concern. "You talked to Kellerman?"

Jo said, "We have."

Tully swallowed a lump. "I'm sorry," he said as he placed his beer down. "I think I'm overstepping my boundaries."

Sensing something, Jo said, "Mr. Tully—"

"No," Tully said, holding up his hand. "I've had two beers too many. I'm running my mouth. The last thing I need is that wretched company coming back at me because I broke a cease-and-desist order." He closed his eyes. "I'm sorry, but I can't tell you anything else."

Jo and Ford tried a few more times to get through to Tully. Nothing but resistance was offered up in reply. Leaving a card and thanking him for his time, they left the apartment and got back in Jo's car.

Ford asked, "What do you think?"

Jo replied, "He's scared of Kellerman."

"He's worried about reprisals?"

The look Tully had in his eyes was one Jo had seen before: fear, not just for legal reasons but also for his life.

"We need to keep digging," she said. "We need to feel this out more."

Ford put the car in gear and cruised down the street. Fifty yards behind them, a battered Trans Am followed after.

THIRTY-SEVEN

Ford and Jo decided to take a rain check on lunch so Ford could update his lieutenant. They switched cars at the FBI field office.

Jo pulled up to the Seattle P.D. headquarters. She felt a tickle in the back of her neck. She was certain that someone was watching her and took a glance at the rearview mirror.

"You okay?" Ford asked, unclipping his seatbelt.

Something's off, she thought. *Something feels wrong.* She blinked and then shook her head. She hadn't eaten in two hours, so that could be it.

"I'm fine," she said.

"You sure?"

Jo said, "I'm sure."

"Fair enough." Ford opened his door. "I'm going to check in with my lieutenant. I'll call you later so we can figure out our next move."

"Sounds good."

Ford got out and entered the building. Jo spotted a hot dog cart on the corner. She figured it was better to have a cheap meal than no meal at all. She got out of the car and approached the smiling hot dog vendor, and ordered one with all the trimmings.

Twenty yards away, a man with his hands stuffed in his jacket pockets approached her from behind.

***

The man kept his eyes glued on the FBI Agent. Her back was to him as she ordered a hot dog from the vendor at the street corner. She was exposed. Right out in the open.

The man's hands trembled with adrenaline. He shook them. Stuffed them in his pockets to stave off the shakes. His teeth began to chatter. Sweat accumulated on his brow.

He was ready to make his move.

He inched closer toward the crosswalk. The Agent's back was still turned to him as she paid the vendor. He stepped off the curb. He pulled his hands out of his pockets and drew a deep breath.

***

Jo's cell phone buzzed. She fished it out of her pocket. Sam's name flashed on the screen. She held the phone up to her ear.

"Hey there," she said.

"Hey back," Sam said. "Just thought I'd check-in. How's protecting and serving going today?"

"It's going all right. How are things on your end?"

"Easy breezy. We're having chicken cutlet for dinner. I trust you'll be there?"

"I'll let you know soon," she replied. "I might be out and about for a while."

"No worries at all," Sam said. "Talk soon?"

"Talk soon."

Jo terminated the call. She brought the hot dog to her lips—but then she stopped. A sickly sensation began to coat her stomach. She looked over her shoulder and thought with certainty that someone was standing behind her. But no one was there. Not a single soul. She proceeded to take a bite before getting back into her car and making the drive back to the field office.

***

The man watching the Agent was hidden in an alleyway a few paces from where the Agent had stood. He shook uncontrollably. He dabbed the sweat on his brow. He cursed himself for not making his move. He needed to get ahead of his predicament. He was boxed in. He was quickly running out of options. He had to do something—anything—to save his own skin.

THIRTY-EIGHT

Grantham impressed upon Jo that time was of the essence. Slipping down in his chair behind his desk, he mentioned that Morris was going before the judge the next morning, and based on how fast things were moving, his trial and almost certain conviction would happen sooner rather than later.

"I know," Jo said, seated in the chair across from him. "I just need to tie off some loose ends."

"Such as?" Grantham asked.

"Well, it appears that Richard Kellerman was having an affair with Justine."

"Is this information relevant to the case or just trivia about their social lives?"

"It's relevant," Jo said. "Rene and Richard had a strained relationship. Part of it was business-related, and I suspect the other half was personal."

Grantham said, "Go on."

"Ford and I stumbled across something when we looked into Stansfield-Kellerman—more specifically, about a cancer therapy trial that went poorly. A former employee blew the whistle on it. That employee clammed up the moment we mentioned Kellerman's name."

"Why do you think this employee won't speak up?" Grantham asked.

"I think—and this is just my gut instinct—this employee is concerned for their safety."

Grantham's eyebrows shot up. "Are you saying he fears for his life?"

"I'm not sure," Jo said. "But one minute, this employee was ready to talk to us, and the next, he couldn't wait for us to leave."

"And this happened once you told him you'd spoken to Richard Kellerman?"

"Yes."

Grantham paused as if thinking. He then said, "Do you think Kellerman means him harm?"

"I can't say for certain, but the employee does fear some form of reprisal if he spoke up."

Grantham said while interlacing his fingers, "Again, I need to know how this exonerates Tim Morris from being at fault."

"It's something to go on," Jo said. "Plus, the affair between Richard Kellerman and Justine Stansfield. We can't ignore that."

"If only Rene Stansfield was dead, I could see a motive there. Kellerman wanted Rene Stansfield gone so that he could be with his lover. But with Justine Stansfield dead as well, I don't see how that angle is plausible now."

Jo was silent. She then said, "Something is simmering under the current of this whole thing. I can feel it."

"We can't base our decisions on *feelings*, Agent Pullinger," Grantham shot back.

"I know, but allow me some more time, sir. I can't provide an answer that exonerates Tim Morris just yet. All I can tell you is that everything I've uncovered in the past twenty-four hours prompts a closer look."

Grantham tapped his finger on the desk. Fixed his eyes on the ceiling. Jo could sense that the SAC was mulling all the information over.

"Agent Pullinger," he said, "if it were any other agent sitting before me, I'd tell them they were reaching. But your history at the Bureau does allow you some leeway." He held up two fingers. "Two days. Wrap up what you need to. If nothing of relevance is turned up, you move on to the next assignment. Is that understood?"

"Understood, sir," Jo said, standing and moving toward the door.

She needed answers from Kellerman. She needed to find out what he was holding back. Checking her watch, she saw that it was just past eight o'clock. Ford had likely gone home. There was nothing more she could do tonight. Tomorrow, however, was another day. And the first thing on the agenda would be to bring Kellerman in for questioning. She and Ford would put the screws on him. Make him open up about this affair and the situation with Mark Tully. Secretly, she was also hoping to get another stab at Kellerman's lawyer, Ron Coleman. The last time he'd had his way, but the only reason for that was because they were at Kellerman's residence. With Kellerman stuck in an interview room, they would have a home-court advantage.

Jo liked the sound of that.

Unbeknownst to her, three miles away, a man slowly approached the front door of Kellerman's residence.

THIRTY-NINE

Richard Kellerman was seeing double as he took his third swig of whiskey from his glass. Night had fallen. The house was quiet. His mind was spinning because of copious liquor and overthinking.

Seated on his couch, he put his drink down and held his head in his hands. "I'm screwed," he whispered. "It's over. They know." He pounded a fist on the table in front of him. "God help me."

The FBI and the Seattle P.D. working together had put him on edge. He didn't like them snooping around. The thought of them turning over things he had been keeping secret for years was something that did not sit well with him.

He stood. His legs felt like rubber. Walking like a toddler over to the record player near the bar cart, he took out a Rolling Stones vinyl and placed it on the turntable. He brought down the needle. "Worried About You" began to play as he went about fetching another drink from the cart.

He poured two fingers' worth of whiskey. He took a sip and closed his eyes. His head pounded. Images of Justine began to dance in his mind. His eyes began to water. His world felt like it was falling apart. He turned his focus back to the record player. He turned up the volume. Right as he did, two knocks sounded on the front door.

He squinted. "Who is it?"

No one answered.

He stepped closer to the door. "I said, who is it?"

Still, no one answered.

He put his drink down again. Cursed under his breath. He approached the front door, tripping but quickly regaining his balance. He straightened his posture and tried his best to look presentable.

Composed, he palmed the door handle. He disengaged the locks.

He swung the door open and felt his stomach twist as he found himself staring down the barrel of a gun.

FORTY

Seated at the desk in Sam's guest bedroom, Jo couldn't take off her thinking cap. She knew she was close to breaking something in the case, and she was certain that Kellerman was the key. Her laptop was open, the glow of the screen on her face. She checked her watch. It was eight minutes past ten. She rubbed her eyes. Weariness was settling in. Jo told herself it was best to call it a night.

Knuckles rapped on the door. Two small knocks. She stood, opened the door, and found a weary-eyed Chrissy in her pajamas with a teddy bear clutched to her chest.

"Chrissy Bear," Jo whispered. "What are you doing up?"

"I can't sleep," Chrissy grumbled. "I had a bad dream."

Jo wondered if nightmares were a genetic trait passed down by Pullingers from the past. She smiled, taking Chrissy by the hand and leading her to the bed. "Come on. Sit down."

Chrissy sat.

"So," Jo said, "what kind of dreams are you having, little lady?"

Chrissy shrugged. "I keep having one about the big dog across the street chasing me. I can't find Mommy or Daddy anywhere in my dream."

Jo rubbed her niece's back. "Oh, Chrissy. It's okay." She traced her fingers through Chrissy's hair. "They're just dreams."

"I know. They're still scary, though." Chrissy looked up at her aunt with wide eyes. "Do you have bad dreams, Auntie Jo?"

Do I ever, Jo thought. "I do," she said.

"How do you make them go away?"

Jo wondered that very thing herself. "I remind myself that they're not real. It takes a little practice."

Chrissy crawled into a fetal position and put her head in Jo's lap. "What are your bad dreams about, Auntie Jo?"

Jo knew telling Chrissy the truth wasn't an option. She was a child. She didn't need glimpses into what adulthood was like. "I get chased by a big dog, too," she said.

"Really?"

"Yep. He chases me down the street. Just like you."

"Does he ever go away?"

The "big dog" in Jo's dream, the heart surgery, was something she couldn't seem to cut loose from. But again, someone Chrissy's age needed hope, not fear. "He will eventually," Jo said. "He'll go away one of these days."

"Auntie Jo," Chrissy said with a curious tone, "why *do* we have bad dreams?"

Jo smiled. "You are quite curious, aren't you?"

Chrissy nodded.

"Well," Jo said, "bad dreams happen when we feel stressed."

"Stressed?"

"It means tired, exhausted. You know what that means, don't you?"

Chrissy nodded again. "Daddy says those words after he talks to Momma's mom on the phone."

The comment made Jo laugh. "Well," she said, "dreams are your brain trying to make sense of things that happen when you're awake. Do you understand?"

Furrowing her brow, Chrissy said, "Not really." She sighed. "I just hope that big dog goes away soon."

"Me too," Jo said as she kissed Chrissy on the cheek. "*Me too.*"

FORTY-ONE

Ford's heart skipped a beat when he saw Kelly's name flash on his caller ID. Sitting up in bed, he cleared his throat and quickly answered. "Hey, Kelly."

"Hey, Bryan," his wife said. "It's not too late, is it?"

Ford peeled off the covers and swung his feet off the bed. "No, not at all. Everything okay?"

"Yeah, everything's fine." There was a pause. "Hazel's here. She wanted to talk to you."

Ford's heart swelled with emotion. "That's great."

"You're okay to talk? You're not at work?"

"No, I'm home. You can put her on."

"Hang on." Ford made out the sounds of the phone being passed over before he heard his little girl greet him with: "Daddy!"

Tears welled in his eyes. He could practically feel Hazel right in front of him. "Hi, sweetheart! How are you?"

"I'm good," Hazel said. "I'm tired."

"Did you have a big day?"

"Yeah, I got an A on my spelling quiz."

"Oh, that's wonderful," Ford said, wishing he could see the paper that was probably tacked to the fridge with a magnet. "You're going to be a big-time writer one day."

Hazel said, "I hope so."

Ford said, "I know so."

"How was your day, Daddy?"

Thoughts of murder and intrigue were not things Ford wanted to think about at this moment. "I had a good day, sweetheart," he said.

"Did you catch a lot of bad guys?"

Ford huffed. "Yeah. Quite a few."

"I miss you, Daddy."

The strings tugging on Ford's heart pulled tight. "I miss you, too."

"Can I talk to you soon?" she said.

"Of course, you can."

"*Hazel*," Kelly said, "it's time to go to bed."

Hazel said, "I have to go."

"That's okay, honey. You get some rest."

"I love you, Daddy."

Ford swallowed the lump in his throat. "I love you, too, Hazie."

"Bryan," Kelly called out.

"Yeah?" he said.

"Sleep well."

Smiling, Ford replied, "Sleep well." He placed the phone back on the nightstand. Hope began to well inside him.

His joy was cut short when his phone rang again, and Griffin's name lit up the screen.

Ford answered. "Lieutenant."

"Get dressed."

"What's going on?"

Griffin sighed. "Richard Kellerman's body was just discovered by a patrol unit."

FORTY-TWO

Jo approached the double doors leading into Richard Kellerman's house. A uniformed officer stood guard off to the side. Two police cruisers were parked at canted angles along the property. Jo heard the muffled chatter of people inside. A flash from a technician's camera lit up the foyer. Jo made out the smell of cordite as she entered the home. Upon walking further in, she spotted Richard Kellerman's body sprawled out on his couch. A Sig Sauer was on the floor. A pool of scarlet had collected around the back of his head. A gaggle of crime scene techs congregated around the body.

Wonderful, Jo thought. *Our best lead is now a corpse.*

"Jo," Ford called out.

Jo turned around. Ford approached her. "What happened?" she asked.

Ford lowered his voice to a hush. "Next door neighbor called it in. They said they heard a single gunshot. Units rolled up and found the body. Front door was unlocked."

Jo appraised Kellerman's corpse. His skin was blue. His arms were draped at his sides. Based on the position of the body and where the gun rested on the floor, all signs pointed to Kellerman taking his own life.

"There was no note. Nothing," Ford said as if reading her mind.

Jo pointed to the doorbell camera past the foyer.

Ford said, "It was turned off."

"What about the gun?"

"What about it?"

Jo said, "We need to check if it was registered to Kellerman. I don't recall anything in his file mentioning that he owned a firearm."

Ford pulled up his phone and shot a text off to Detective Weintraub, telling him to start looking.

Jo said, "We'll need to dump Kellerman's calls. Maybe he rang someone up before he pulled the trigger."

"I've already made the call," Ford said. "It'll take a few hours, though." He glanced at the body.

Jo said, "What are you thinking?"

"I'm not sure. But something doesn't smell right."

"Does your lieutenant have an opinion?"

"I just called her. She thinks maybe grief got the better of Kellerman in light of everything that's happened."

"Sounds like she's giving a diplomatic answer."

"I thought the same thing."

"And you?" Jo said. "What does your gut tell you?"

Ford shrugged. "I mean, Kellerman was stressed, but I didn't take him as a guy who would kill himself."

"I'm inclined to agree. But either way, Kellerman taking his own life tells me that we were getting close to something."

A technician, dressed in a jumpsuit and booties, pulled off her mask and nodded for them to join her out in the hallway. She was young, possibly just north of her mid-twenties, with striking good looks to match.

"Looks like your guy," she said, "took a handful of muscle relaxers. We found a half-empty bottle under the couch and a bottle of whiskey. You can still smell the booze on him."

Jo and Ford conferred with the tech for a few more minutes, clarifying and going through even more details that confirmed that Richard Kellerman had, indeed, taken his own life.

"Well," Jo said, "with whatever transpired between Rene and Richard, coupled with Rene's murder, I'm guessing it pressured Richard to the point that he killed himself."

Ford was silent.

Jo then added, "But I don't buy it. Not just yet."

"But we know Kellerman was rattled," Ford replied. "We saw it when we interviewed him in this house."

"I know. It just seems too convenient."

Ford raised an eyebrow. "Convenient?"

"Think about it. The moment we put a little pressure on him, he snaps and kills himself."

Ford stared at her. "I don't see anything odd with that."

"Come on, doesn't that feel just a bit off?"

Ford frowned. "Nope. Not to me. Guilt finally got to him."

"He had an alibi on the night of the murders. We confirmed that he was indeed at the opera when the Stansfields were murdered. There were security cameras on the premises that caught him entering and leaving the theatre. The date stamps on the footage one-hundred percent exonerate him of the crime."

Ford was silent.

She added, "With Rene out of the picture, he was now fully in control of a multi-billion-dollar pharmaceutical company. He should've been celebrating. Not drowning his sorrows in liquor. And most definitely, not putting a bullet through his skull."

Ford thought about it. He then said with a shrug, "Maybe he was feeling guilty about something else?"

Jo bit her lip. "This whole thing feels like a jigsaw puzzle. We just need a few more pieces that show the full picture."

"Okay. How do we proceed?"

"We dig deeper," Jo replied as her brain started to work overtime. "There's something we don't know yet, something crucial." She sighed. "And I have a feeling that when we shed light on whatever that is, we're not going to like it."

The technician called out to Jo and Ford. They walked over. The technician then proceeded to tell them that the shell casing they discovered was a 9mm round. It was a common round. Jo knew that. But something about the *same* caliber of rounds found at both the Stansfield crime scene and Richard Kellerman's suicide tickled the analytical side of her brain.

Now that can't be a coincidence, she thought.

FORTY-THREE

The man paid twenty dollars to the woman at the front desk of the fleabag motel. He made it a point not to make eye contact with her before receiving the key and shuffling off to his room. Once inside, he locked the door, closed the curtains, and sat down on the bed that smelled of mildew.

The man pulled the weapon he had used to kill Richard Kellerman from the back of his pants. He looked it over. His hands started to shake. He held his head in his hands. He coughed and felt his chest sear from the pain that it was causing.

I don't have long, the man thought. *I can feel this stuff tearing apart my insides.*

He didn't want to kill Kellerman—but he had to. There was no choice. The police were getting too close. He couldn't risk them sniffing out a trail.

The man's stomach grumbled. It had been close to six hours since he ate anything, but it was becoming harder to keep a meal down. He could feel his energy levels depleting—he needed to eat something, anything if he was going to be able to stay on the move. He fished in his pockets. He had six dollars in change. He had enough money in his bank account to pay for a five-star meal, but for multiple reasons, he couldn't risk touching the cash yet.

He tucked the gun in the back of his waistband and covered it with his jacket. He slunk out of his room and approached the vending machine at the end of the hall. Thunder clapped overhead. It was only a matter of time before the storm arrived.

He put a dollar into the soda machine and punched the button for a soft drink. He took it, moved to the machine dispensing candy bars and chips, and bought one of each. He turned around to head back to his room.

He saw a young boy standing in the hallway, looking up at him curiously. He couldn't have been older than six.

The man froze in his tracks. He stared at the boy and took a look around for signs of his parents.

"You hungry, mister?" the boy said.

The man swallowed the lump in his throat. "Yeah…"

"Are you okay?" the boy asked curiously.

The man forced himself to smile. "I'm fine."

"What's your name?"

The man said nothing.

"My name is Joseph," the boy said.

"Hello, Joseph."

"Don't you have a name?"

The man paused and then said, "It's… It's Daniel."

"You look sick, Daniel," Joseph said. "Are you sick?"

The man nodded. "I am."

"Can't you take something for it?"

The man shook his head again. "No, nothing will help me." With that, he walked around the boy and shuffled off to his room. He never ended up consuming what he had purchased from the machines, and he stayed awake all night staring at the door to his room.

They're coming, he kept thinking. *They're coming for me.*

FORTY-FOUR

Six hours had passed since Kellerman's body had been found, and Jo felt the lack of sleep catching up to her. If sunshine wasn't peeking through the windows inside the medical examiner's office, she would have been unable to tell if it was day or night.

Ford had already introduced David Curtis, and after exchanging a few pleasantries, Jo got right down to the point, "So, what are we looking at?"

Curtis shook his head. "Well, the short version of the story is that Richard Kellerman didn't kill himself."

This came as no surprise to either Jo or Ford.

Curtis, looking at them, said, "That didn't seem to elicit the reaction that I thought it would."

Ford said, "We had an inkling that something might have been off."

"Well"—Curtis grabbed a file from his desk and peeled it open—"it took all of ten minutes of examining the body to know that things were not lining up."

"So," Jo said, "are we safe to assume Kellerman was murdered?"

Curtis nodded. "Most definitely. First off, Kellerman had no GSR residue on his person." He pointed to the file. "Second, he was shot in his left temple, but the angle of the shot is inconsistent with a suicide. But that's just the surface-level stuff. I have a laundry list of items here that support the theory that this was a homicide masked to look like a suicide." He handed Jo the file.

Jo, perusing the items on the ME's checklist, saw that the position of Kellerman's body pointed to the fact that someone had arranged the corpse after he had died. "Well," she said, "now the question remains: who's at fault for this?"

Curtis leaned back on his chair and then said, slowly, "Unlike the suicide theory, what I'm about to tell you next will surprise you. I'm certain of it."

"And what is that?" Ford said.

"It's quite possible that whoever killed Richard Kellerman is also responsible for the deaths of the Stansfields."

Jo's head felt like it was filled with helium. "Can you please repeat that?" she said.

Curtis jutted his chin at the file in Jo's hand. "As I was working, something stuck out to me: the 9mm round that your techs dug out of the wall, the one that was fired into Kellerman's head, was similar to the rounds I found in the Stansfields. I'll need to corroborate with your people, but when I put the rounds that killed the Stansfields under a microscope, I found that there was, essentially, a valley-like depression near the tip of the bullet. In essence, this would indicate that the bullet was fired from a gun that has seen significant usage. The same depression was found on the bullet that killed Richard Kellerman."

Ford said, "This means we'll need to do a recovery test on the gun we found on Tim Morris, plus the weapon we found at Kellerman's home."

"You will," Curtis said, "but I'd bet every dollar in my wallet that when you do that, you'll find that Morris' gun had nothing to do with the Stansfield murders."

Jo's heart was pounding as she turned the file's pages. She looked at the close-up photos taken of the bullets that killed the Stansfields. She did the same with the one that killed Kellerman.

Both bullets were a match.

"We need to call our people," Jo said to Ford as she closed the file. "It looks like Tim Morris just dodged a triple murder charge."

FORTY-FIVE

Tim Morris sat in his cell as he thought about what his fate would be once he went to trial. At this point, his lawyer was all but certain that he would be convicted.

"You take a deal," the lawyer had told him when they'd met, "and you can get life without parole." He'd pressed a finger on the table to emphasize his point. "*That* is the only way."

Morris shook his head now. A tear rolled down his cheek. He wished he could see Lindsey. He wanted to tell her he was sorry more than anything else. He wanted his parents to believe him. He wanted the truth to come out, but it just was not going to happen.

"I'm going to die in here," Morris whispered as he held his head in his hands. "They're going to bury me."

Thoughts of what would happen to him in prison made him shudder. He had heard the stories. He knew the kinds of things inmates liked to do to young men like him. He tried to breathe. He tried his best to resign himself to his fate.

Then he heard the jingling of keys. He forced his eyes open.

He looked up. A guard was looking down at him, and right beside him was his lawyer.

"What is it?" he asked. "What're you doing here?"

The lawyer smiled. "Tim, I'm here to tell you that you'll be going home soon."

He blinked. "What?"

"You'll be going home soon," he repeated.

He stared at the lawyer in disbelief. "Is this a dream?"

"No dream, son." The lawyer's smile widened. "You're going to be a free man."

A wave of euphoria washed over Morris like a tidal wave. He couldn't speak. All he could do was break down and cry.

FORTY-SIX

It took forty-eight hours for Tim Morris to be cleared of the Stansfield murders. The entire time, Jo found only pockets of sleep. She had been running back and forth between both the field office and the Seattle P.D. headquarters. Endless phone calls had been made. The gun found on Morris was not a match to the murders of the Stansfields, and at 5:02 p.m. on Saturday, Jo, standing with Ford outside the King County jail, watched as Tim Morris ran into the arms of his parents.

A flock of news reporters rushed toward the tearful reunion. They snapped and recorded the raw emotions between an exhausted mother and father and their relieved son.

"Feels good, doesn't it?" Ford said.

Jo watched Tim's mother kiss him on his cheeks. "It does," she said. "But I'm afraid this will stick with him for the rest of his life."

Ford nodded. Tim looked gaunt and pale as his father had his arm around his son's shoulders. "I'm sure he'll never forget this. But he's free now. And that's what matters."

"I agree," Jo replied.

"However," Ford said, "it puts the spotlight back on us, and that is, finding out who's *truly* responsible for those killings."

Jo knew he was right, but she said nothing. The Sig Sauer found at Kellerman's home not only did not match the bullet found in the wall but also hadn't been recently fired. *Quite sloppy*, Jo thought. *Any other killer would've used the Sig Sauer to kill Kellerman and then put Kellerman's fingerprints on it.*

Morris caught them standing in the distance. He approached with his parents. The gaggle of reporters and cameras followed with them.

Jo, standing tall, nodded at Morris. "Hey, Tim."

A teary-eyed Tim extended his hand. "Thank you," he said. "Thank you both for believing in me."

Jo shook Tim's hand. "I'm sorry you had to be locked up, but we had to make sure."

He looked over at his parents. "I want to go home."

Jo watched as the Morris' got inside their vehicle and drove away.

Jo and Ford were walking back toward Ford's car when the reporters turned their attention on them and began haranguing Jo for a comment or statement.

"That's enough," Ford told them. "Thank you for your time."

The two piled into Ford's Crown Vic. The hubbub of reporters outside was muted as Ford slowly made his way out of the parking lot.

"What's your opinion on beer?" he then asked.

"I've never been a huge fan," Jo said. "But right now, it sounds like the best thing in the world."

***

Ten miles away, the man was seated in a bar. He stared at the glass of bourbon in front of him. He had his head in his hands as he took his time finishing his drink.

The bartender, a burly man with a towel over his shoulder, sighed and said, "You want another?"

The man shook his head.

The bartender checked his watch. "You've been working on that drink for an hour, buddy. If you're not gonna buy any more, I gotta ask you to clear out so other customers can sit there."

The man nodded. He was running out of cash. He could barely afford the drink he'd already bought. Downing the last of the bourbon, he proceeded to tip the bartender before slipping off his stool. He turned to head toward the doors but stopped when his eye caught the television above the liquor shelves.

The man squinted. The television was showing footage outside of the King County prison, where a group of reporters were surrounding what looked like a family reunion. The man's eyes suddenly went wide as he realized he was looking at the same woman he had nearly approached at a hot dog stand just days before.

"Special Agent Johanna Pullinger," the voice of the news anchor said as the FBI agent shook hands with a weary-eyed young man on the screen, "along with Seattle P.D. detective Bryan Ford, were instrumental in securing the release of Timothy Morris. The man who had been charged with the murders of Rene Stansfield and his family…"

The man tuned out the news anchor as he stared at the face of the FBI woman on the screen. He only had a face when he approached her before. But now, thanks to the six o'clock news, he had a name.

Hands in his pockets, he moved swiftly toward the doors.

He pulled up his hoodie as he set about making his next move.

FORTY-SEVEN

Ford placed a bottle of beer in front of Jo. He slipped down in the seat across from her as Jo's eyes remained glued to the television mounted in the corner of the dive bar. The television was showing the footage of Jo and Ford speaking with Tim and his parents.

"So," Ford said, "what now?"

Jo sipped her beer and put it down. "That's the question of the hour," she replied. "Now that Morris is cleared, we need to figure out which lead to follow up on."

"We're on the same page that whoever killed the Stansfields also murdered Kellerman. I've already placed calls with every gun shop in town to try and get a lead on where the murder weapon came from. I feel like it's a wild stab in the dark, though."

Jo nodded. "The gun is old, based on what we know. Point being, it could've come from anywhere."

"Well," Ford said, "let's cite what we know."

"What we know," Jo said, "is that Rene and Richard had a strained relationship because of those drug trials and that Richard was having an affair with Justine."

Ford nodded. "And one of those two things ended up snowballing to the point that it forced someone to kill Rene and his family as a result."

"Indeed." Jo leaned back in her seat. "So, what do you suggest in terms of a game plan?"

Ford said, "We question everyone who was close with Rene and Justine. Someone has to know something about the affair Justine was having with Richard. Rich people have social circles. Gossip floats around. In terms of Rene and Richard's relationship, we need to contact more people inside Stansfield-Kellerman that are willing to talk about the drug trial."

"I'll take the lead on the drug trial angle," Jo said.

"And I'll take the lead," Ford said, "on the Richard and Justine affair."

"Any ideas where you'll start?"

Ford nodded. "Karen Caldwell. Justine's closest friend. If anyone might have information about the affair, Vegas odds sway in favor of her possessing that knowledge." He gestured to Jo. "What about the drug trial angle? What're you going to do?"

The lines in Jo's brow wrinkled. "I have a feeling," she said, "that Mark Tully might know more than what he's leading us to believe."

"I'm thinking that he's going to keep quiet, based on our last conversation with him."

"I believe that, too. But maybe if I tail him, maybe if I can corner him somehow, he'll give up something of relevance."

"Well," Ford said as he held up his beer in a toast, "sounds like a plan to me."

Jo clinked her beer against Ford's. The two sat in silence for a moment and sipped their drinks as "Come to Mama" by Ann Peebles played through the bar's speakers.

Ford said, "I like this song," and tapped his finger on the table to the beat.

Jo said, "I pegged you for an oldies guy."

"Oh, yeah? Why's that?"

Jo gestured to Ford's hair. "The gray near your temples."

Ford laughed. "You're calling me an old-timer?"

Jo shook her head. "I was going to say, 'distinguished'."

"That's just a fancy way of saying 'old'." Ford looked over his shoulder. "What do you say to one more beer before we jump back into this thing?"

"I'd like that very much," Jo said.

FORTY-EIGHT

Ford appraised Karen Caldwell's house as he slipped out of the car. The residence was a three-story mansion resting near the ocean, gated off and requiring someone to buzz Ford into the circular driveway upon arriving. He peeled off his sunglasses. The bass from the music playing inside the house was spilling outside.

Ford approached the front door, badge on his hip. He knocked twice. The door opened. A younger-looking man in workout gear answered with a smile on his face.

"Yeah?" the young man said. "Can I help you?"

Ford looked over the young man's shoulder. "Is Mrs. Caldwell home?"

The young man laughed. "It's *Ms.* Caldwell. And yeah, we just finished a session."

"Who are you?"

"Her trainer." He looked Ford over from toes to head. "You got a solid build. You need some personal lessons? I charge two hundred an hour."

Ford wasn't in the mood. "Please inform Ms. Caldwell I'm here."

The young man shouted out for Karen. Moments later, Karen Caldwell appeared in pink-colored workout gear. She was tall, blonde-haired, and she had a complexion that showcased what looked like a dozen plastic surgeries. And a smile that revealed whitened teeth.

She dabbed the sweat off her brow and walked into the foyer.

"Thank you, Devon," Karen said as she patted the young man on the back. "I think that's enough for the day."

The trainer kissed Karen on the cheek and told her he would see her in two days. He told Ford to "give training some thought" before grabbing his bag and heading out the door.

"Please come inside," Karen said. "And please close the door if you don't mind."

Ford went in and closed the door behind him.

"Can I get you anything?" Karen asked. "A vitamin water?" She then giggled. "Something stronger?"

Ford pointed to the stereo in the living room. "If you could turn the music down, that'd be great."

Karen obliged as she thumbed the power switch and began rolling up the workout mats on the floor. "I had a feeling you'd stop by," she said. "The police, I mean."

"Is that so?"

Karen nodded. "It was quite a stir when those charges were dropped from the kid who killed Rene and Justine."

"You sound like you believe he still did it."

Karen shrugged. "Doesn't matter what I think. I mind my own business." She giggled again. "I'm just a divorcee living my best life."

Thoughts of the trainer floated through Ford's mind. "I can see that. You're rather transparent."

Karen shrugged again. "I don't see the point in presenting myself in any other fashion."

"Then, in the interest of transparency," Ford said as he took a step forward, "I'd like to pick your brain about the affair Justine Stansfield was having with Richard Kellerman."

Karen's smile melted into a frown. "I see."

"You know something."

"You don't beat around the bush."

"Time is of the essence, Ms. Caldwell," Ford said. "Whoever killed Richard Kellerman and the Stansfields is still out there. It's possible whatever affair Richard was having with Justine may have something to do with it."

Karen said, "And you think that *I'm* the one who's going make sense of it all?"

Ford nodded. "You were close with Justine. The calls and texts I dumped from her phone confirm this. I've read them all. So, I believe you know something, and I need you to tell me what that is."

Karen sat down on the couch. She breathed, composing herself. "Justine and Richard's, I don't know, *fling* was an off-and-on thing."

"How long did it go on?"

"A few years, maybe. The timeline is messy."

"Did Rene know about it?"

"I'm not sure," Karen said. "Well, I think maybe he was starting to become suspicious. Justine told me a week before she died that Rene was asking a lot of questions about Richard."

"What kind of questions?"

"If there was anything going on between the two."

"And what did she lead him to believe?" Ford asked.

"She deflected," Karen said. "Justine was an expert at making Rene believe what she wanted him to believe." She laughed. "Like mother, like daughter, I guess."

Ford furrowed his brow. "What do you mean?"

Karen sat back. "Justine and Lindsey had Rene wrapped around their little fingers. They were his world. He did everything for them."

"Stick to the affair," Ford said. "Did Rene know, or did he not?"

Karen sighed. "I think he did. The last time I saw them, all of them, was a couple of days after Justine told me Rene was asking about Richard. Something was off. You could feel the tension between them."

"Was the tension between Rene and Justine out of the ordinary?"

"Like I said, he adored Justine and Lindsey. He did everything to give them a life of comfort. And that meant he had to work long hours. Justine would tell me in the early days of their marriage that he even slept on the couch in his office. He was so focused on making the company a success." Karen paused a moment. "To answer your question, all marriages have tension, and Rene and Justine's marriage was no different. But this time, it felt different—like something had fractured between them, you know."

Ford made a mental note. "The night of the murders, you spoke with Justine several times over the phone. What did you speak about?"

"Nothing specific. We were making plans to get our hair done the next day. At one point, the texts stopped. I thought maybe she had gone to bed. I didn't think anything of it." A tear rolled down Karen's cheek. "We all know what happened after that."

"Karen," Ford said as he stepped closer, "I'll ask you flat out: do you believe that Justine's affair with Richard may have had something to do with her death?"

Slowly looking up, Karen said, "I do."

"Tell me why," he said. "And please, don't spare any of the nitty-gritty details."

FORTY-NINE

Jo knocked on Mark Tully's door. It took two more knocks for him to answer. When he did, he huffed and quickly said, "I have nothing more to say to you people."

Jo showed Tully her palm. "Mr. Tully," she said. "Just a couple of questions, and I'll be out of your hair."

Tully shook his head and crossed his arms defensively. "I already said too much the other day. I was drunk. I should have never let you guys in my home."

"It'll be very quick."

"I'm done talking. Unless you cuff me, read me my rights, and take me in, that's all I have to say on the matter." He shut the door.

Jo sighed. Shook her head. She headed back down to her car, pulled out her phone, and plugged in Ford's number.

"Yeah?" Ford answered.

She got in the car. "Tully just slammed the door on me like I was an air conditioner salesman."

"You're surprised?"

"Not in the slightest. Nonetheless, I'm at a stalemate here."

Ford said, "What're you gonna do now?"

Jo eyeballed Tully's apartment complex through the windshield. "I'm going to sit tight and see if he goes anywhere. Maybe I'll get lucky, and he'll head out to a bar to load up on liquor. Maybe he'll be more inclined to talk then."

"Gotta play the hand you're dealt with."

"Indeed," Jo said. "How are things going with Karen Caldwell?"

Ford said, "I'm still here. But I'll be leaving in a minute. I need to call my lieutenant and give her an update, but we should meet up soon. How long are you going to stay on Tully?"

Checking her watch, Jo saw that it was a quarter to six. "Give me a couple of hours. I'll call you when I'm on my way back to the field office."

"Good luck."

"You, too." Jo hung up the phone. It was a stab in the dark that Tully would be more approachable as the night wore on. All she could do was wait and try. Turning on the car radio, she listened to an oldies station and kept her eyes peeled on Tully's complex.

***

An hour and a half had passed, and the sun had gone down when Mark Tully stepped out of his apartment building. Switching off the radio, Jo sat back and held a hand to her face to hide it as Tully took a look over both shoulders. He looked nervous. Worn out. Antsy. He fished out his keys and walked toward a battered Ford Pinto parked near the sidewalk. Tully got in the car, started the engine, did a U-turn, and headed down the street.

Jo, starting her car, followed after him. She made sure to maintain her distance, following Tully as he drove out of midtown. He got on the I-5 and drove for twelve minutes before taking the exit. The exit spilled out into a seedier part of town known as Rainier Beach. Tully turned onto South Ryan Street and then onto 51st before linking up with Renton Avenue. Renton turned into 55th Avenue, and as Jo tailed from a hundred yards away, she found that most of the town was run-down, boarded-up, and covered in graffiti.

The Pinto idled near a stop sign. It didn't move for ten whole seconds.

A short distance away, Jo pulled the car to a stop and killed the headlamps as she watched a figure dressed in a skirt approach the passenger's side of Tully's car.

"What are you up to, Mark?" Jo whispered.

The figure spoke to Tully a few steps away from the door. When the figure moved closer to the light, Jo was better able to make her out. She was scantily dressed. Jo smirked, knowing full well what was taking place. She watched the woman get into Tully's car before Tully made a right turn at the stop sign.

Jo throttled the engine. She closed the gap on Tully's vehicle. As soon as she was ten yards out, she thumbed the switch for the emergency lights mounted on her dash, flew past Tully's car, and came to a stop in front of it.

Jo swiftly got out of the car. She drew her gun. She approached the driver's side and told Tully to roll the window.

"Hands up!" Jo said. "Slowly!"

Tully complied as Jo pointed her weapon inside the vehicle. Seated next to Tully was a girl who looked years younger than him. Her eyes were wide, and she looked like she was about to faint. The color on Tully's face had drained. His shirt was halfway unbuttoned.

"Good evening, Mr. Tully," Jo said. "You feel like talking now?"

Tully rested his head against the steering wheel as Jo pulled out her cuffs and opened the driver's side door.

FIFTY

Jo entered the interrogation room. Tully looked up. His hands were shackled. He glared at her.

"Hey, Mark," Jo said with a smile.

"Lawyer," he replied.

"That's not going to fly."

"*Lawyer*," Tully said as though it were a curse word.

Jo pulled out a chair. She sat down in front of him. She folded her hands in her lap and stared right into his eyes. "How many times have you done this?"

Tully said, "Done what?"

"Pick up women to solicit sex."

"*Lawyer*," Tully said again.

Jo shook her head. "I've got all the time in the world," she said. "You don't, but I do. I'm on the clock. I'm resolved to stay here all night if need be."

Tully sighed. "Get bent," he said.

"That's quite rude of you."

"I want my lawyer. I'm not telling you a damn thing."

"Your lawyer is on the way," Jo said.

Tully crossed his arms. "Then I plan on sitting here and saying nothing until he does."

Jo checked her watch. "You're going to be waiting a while because he's driving across the city to be here. But if you don't want to talk, I will. You can just listen."

Tully said nothing.

"You know," Jo said, "it says a lot about a man who has to patrol the streets to find satisfaction. That goes for everything else: drugs, companionship, et cetera. It means he's desperate. At his wit's end. Stressed out."

Tully again said nothing.

"It speaks volumes, too," Jo said, "that a man would also be foolish enough to pick up a sex worker without vetting her age."

Tully furrowed his brow. "What do you mean?"

"Oh, *no*," Jo said. "You don't know…"

Tully leaned forward in his chair. "Know *what*?"

Jo stood. "You know, you're right. I think you need a lawyer. The charge of solicitation is bad enough. The *other* part of it is a whole other debacle." She moved to leave.

"Wait!" Tully said. "What the heck are you saying?"

Jo shook her head and pointed over his shoulder. "That woman," she said, "that *girl* you picked up is fifteen." She sighed. "Again, that's going to cause a whirlwind of headaches once they file formal charges. You might get slapped with endangering a minor, and you'll have to register as a sex offender—"

"Hold on!" Tully said, holding up his hands. "I didn't know that girl was underage. She said she was eighteen!"

"Well, she's not."

"Please!" Tully's eyes went wide. "I didn't know. I swear!"

Jo molded her palm on the door handle. "The judge will care less about that."

"I'll talk!" Tully shouted out. "I didn't know she was a minor. I would have never let her inside my car if I knew that was the case. Please. Just sit. Forget about my lawyer. I'll tell you whatever you want to know."

Jo walked back to the table. She sat down, crossed her arms, and said, "Tell me about Comoxin. Tell me what happened during the drug trials."

Tully closed his eyes. "The trial was a disaster."

"A disaster? How?"

"Comoxin caused life-threatening side effects in six out of ten patients in the trial."

Jo said, "So, what did you do then?"

Tully said, "I told them to shut it down and redirect what money was left to compensate the people that were affected. Certain people didn't take that well, one person in particular."

Leaning forward, Jo said, "Who?"

Tully looked Jo squarely in the eye. "Rene Stansfield. He tried to cover it up."

FIFTY-ONE

Tully, seated in an interrogation room at the field office, held his head in his hands. Jo, watching from the other side of the glass with Ford, looked at Tully as though she had caught a trophy fish.

"Not bad," Ford said with a smile. "I guess the stars aligned for you tonight."

Jo said, "I'd like to think so."

"So," Ford asked as he sat on the desk in front of the window, "what did he say?"

"He told me everything," Jo said.

"How'd you pull that off?"

"I told him that the girl he picked up was underage."

Ford huffed. "That's not good for him."

Jo said, "It's also not true."

Ford laughed. "Really?"

"Nope. But it got him talking."

"His lawyer might have a field day with that."

"He might," Jo said. "But I still found out what I needed to. As soon as I mentioned the mandatory sentence and fines for soliciting a sex worker, he was speaking so fast that I had to make him slow down. I asked him about the drug trials, his part in it, everything."

Ford said, "What did he tell you?"

Jo paced the room. "When Tully discovered that Comoxin caused myocarditis in sixty percent of the patients in the trial, he urged them to pull the plug."

"Good God," Ford said. "Comoxicin was causing heart inflammation?"

"In most of the patients, yes," Jo said, "Tully told Rene and Richard they needed to scrap everything and go back to the drawing board."

Ford said, "Based on what we know, that didn't go well."

"No, it did not," Jo said. "They were worried about the blowback after all the PR they put into marketing the drug. Tully told them they were getting ahead of themselves when they started running their mouth prematurely about the drug, but they thought they knew better." Her eyelids flickered. "*Stansfield* specifically."

Ford furrowed his brow. "Tully's saying that *Rene* was the one who pushed back when he told him to terminate the project?"

Jo nodded. "Without question. Tully came to both him and Richard when the trials went south. Richard was inclined to listen. Rene wasn't."

Ford said, "Why do you think that is?"

Jo said, "Apparently, for Rene, it was about saving pennies on the dollar. He's cut corners on the smallest things. Something like Comoxin souring, a flagship drug that was about to become their game-changer, was not something he took lying down."

"So," Ford said, "Tully blew the whistle, Rene freaks out, he essentially blacklists Tully into financial ruin, and the relationship Rene and Richard had ended up dissolving because of it."

Jo nodded. "Tully also gave us a list of the people involved in the drug trials. All of them wanted to file lawsuits against the company."

"Didn't they have to sign NDAs to join the trial?"

"They did."

Ford said, "Then it would be like kicking water uphill. It'd be near impossible to get in front of a judge because no lawyer would take on a case with a signed NDA on file."

"Exactly," Jo said. "And that's why we haven't heard anything related to Comixon in the media."

"Except for the lawsuit from Tully."

"Yeah, except for his, and even that one led to him losing everything. His job. His savings. His reputation."

Ford shook his head. "If you're the little guy, you can't fight and win against Goliath."

"Not in our legal system, anyway."

There was a moment of silence.

"What about Karen Caldwell?" Jo then asked. "Did anything pan out with her?"

"It did," Ford replied. "Apparently, Justine and Richard's affair goes back farther than just a few years. And it was on and off throughout Rene and Justine's marriage."

"And Rene never knew about it?" Jo said.

"He was suspicious only towards the end of his life, and I think I know why *now*."

"Okay."

Ford said, "Rene and Richard were best friends since college, yes?"

"Sure."

"They were also partners in a successful venture—one that made them both very rich. But it was only when the Comoxin trials failed—which caused a divide between the two—that Rene became wary of Richard. I figured, once the friendship fell away, Rene began to pay more attention to his partner's behavior towards his wife."

"Do you think that Richard knew Rene was suspicious?" Jo asked.

"I see where you're going with this," he said with a smile. "It would make sense if Justine and Richard were both dead and Rene was not. Then we could use the motive of a scorned spouse against Rene. But now that they are *all* dead, it leaves us with no motive or suspects."

Jo thought a moment and then said, "Did Karen shed any light on anything that happened during the night of the murders?"

"Apparently, Lindsey and Rene were supposed to go to a movie that night, but Lindsey got into an argument with her father, and it got canceled. Karen said that Justine texted her about it."

"Did you look at the text messages?"

"I did. But it doesn't say what they fought about."

Jo turned to the one-way mirror. Tully had his arms wrapped around himself as he stared at the floor.

She sighed. "Bringing him in was a waste of time."

"It might not," Ford replied.

She turned to him. "What do you mean?"

"Maybe the names of the patients he gave you could help us break this case open," Ford replied.

FIFTY-TWO

Tim Morris picked at his meal as his mother sat beside him at the dinner table. "Tim, sweetheart," she said. "You need to eat. You're so skinny."

Morris shrugged and slowly pushed his plate away. She was right, he knew. He was underweight. He looked more like a boy now than he did before he was arrested. "I'm not hungry, Mom." He sighed. "I can't stop thinking."

Jonathan Morris, standing in the living room, parted the window curtain with his finger. "Damn news vans," he grumbled. "They're still out there."

Deborah waved her husband off. "Don't give them a reason to poke their nose in here," she said. "They'll go away eventually."

Morris shook his head. "They've been out there all day. They won't leave me alone."

His father approached and patted him on the back. "Someone from CNN called," he said. "They want to do an interview with you."

"I don't want to talk to them," Morris grumbled. "I just want everyone to leave me alone."

Deborah wrapped her arms around her son. "It'll go away soon, Tim. I promise. The important thing is that you're home. You're safe now. It's over."

With a grunt, Tim stood and pushed out his chair. "It's *not* over," he said. "Whoever killed Lindsey is still out there." Eyes wide, he patted his chest. "And it's my fault. I could have stopped them. I should have stopped them."

"Tim," Deborah cooed, "there was nothing you could do. This is not your fault. Don't think for a second that it is."

"I loved her!" Morris said, a tear rolling down his cheek. "I should have treated her better. I shouldn't have let my emotions get the better of me." He walked over to the couch, plopped down, and began to sob.

His parents walked to him, sat down, and held their son tight. "I'm so sorry, Tim," Deborah said.

"Don't blame yourself, son," Jonathan added. "I know that's tough to hear right now, but it's true. We're going to get through this. All of us."

After the family spent several minutes on the couch hugging and crying, Morris made his way to his room. He sat on his bed. All he could think about was Lindsey. He batted his eyes. He stood up. He walked over to his desk, retrieved his phone, and began scrolling through the photos of him and Lindsey.

"This is all my fault," he whispered as he placed the phone down.

He walked to the window. He peeked through the blinds and saw the backyard was dark and quiet. He glanced around and saw the neighbors' backyards on both sides were quiet as well. The neighbors probably figured it was better to stay inside, lest they wanted to see themselves on the six o'clock news. Or worse, being hounded by news reporters to make a comment about their neighbors and their son, who had just escaped a triple homicide charge.

He shuddered at the thought of being locked up for life.

He sighed.

He was so frustrated with being cooped up. He wanted to leave. He wanted to go somewhere—anywhere where the news vans weren't. He wanted to see Lindsey. He wanted to say goodbye one last time.

He locked his bedroom door and waited for his parents to switch on the television. He then grabbed his jacket and slowly opened his bedroom window. He looked down.

He had done this so many times—the first when he was only twelve—that he didn't hesitate for a moment. He grabbed the trellis next to his window and slowly climbed down.

At the bottom, he looked around. The neighbor on the left had a dog, but it was likely inside with its owners.

He knew the backyard had sensor lights that switched on if they detected motion. But with his parents glued to the TV, he wasn't worried they'd come out to check. Also, they'd seen raccoons in the backyard who were always triggering the lights. Even if his parents did see the backyard lights come on, they'd think it were rodents.

Still, he knew he had to be careful.

He took a deep breath and then raced across the yard.

By the time he'd reached the end, the lights had already gone on and off. He looked back and saw there was no movement in the house.

He then heaved himself over the fence.

There was a narrow path that led from the back of the house, which led to a road further away. He knew the moment he reached the road, he wouldn't have to worry about reporters or anyone else catching him, for that matter.

Without wasting another second, he hurried away.

FIFTY-THREE

The man waited in his battered Honda Civic around the corner from Tim Morris's house. He didn't know who the kid was before the news started broadcasting his name on an endless loop, but now that he knew, he felt pressed to try and inch his way toward Morris.

The man was certain Morris had no idea who he was. On the night of the murders, he had snuck out of the house without anyone seeing him—but had he known it was Morris who was in the house, it would've been like killing two birds with one stone.

Tapping his finger on the steering wheel, the man sensed a tightness settling over his chest. Anxiety was getting the better of him, he knew. But he felt as though the sickness that was plaguing his body might kill him at any moment.

The man drew a breath. Tried to compose himself. He debated getting out of town but knew that he wouldn't get far. Not in his condition. He needed a plan. He needed to divert the investigation onto someone else before the police and the FBI showed up on his doorstep.

I have to do something, he thought. *I need to get out of this. They're going to find me. I'm going to spend the remaining months of my life in a cell.*

In the distance, he could see the media gathered in front of the Morris residence. He didn't dare get close. But he desperately wanted to get his hands on Morris. Find out what he knew. And whether it could lead back to him.

His hands shook. He gritted his teeth. The pain came in waves, and it seared his insides, causing him to break into a sweat.

He shut his eyes and waited for it to subside.

I shouldn't be here, he thought. *I'm exposed.*

The thought that one of the reporters might see him sitting in his car and come over with a camera made him shudder.

He decided to leave. Come back when there was less heat. Maybe he'd get lucky and find Morris alone at home. Then he would ask his questions. But not right now.

His trembling hand moved to turn on the ignition.

He caught something out of the corner of his eye.

A figure had jumped over a fence and was walking toward him.

His Civic was parked adjacent to a narrow path behind all the houses on the street.

He shifted in his seat. A moment later, the figure came into the light.

It was Tim Morris!

Morris looked left toward the news vans parked outside his house.

Morris quickly turned right and began walking in the opposite direction.

He was certain Morris hadn't seen him.

He reached over and pulled out a worn and battered Heckler and Koch firearm from the glove compartment. He disengaged the safety and rested the pistol comfortably on his lap.

He turned the key and started the ignition.

He pulled the Civic away from the curb and began to follow Morris.

FIFTY-FOUR

Jo and Ford were hovering over McKinley's shoulder. McKinley, seated in front of a laptop, rubbed his eyes and looked like he had been up for close to twenty-four hours.

"When's the last time you slept?" Jo asked.

McKinley replied, "What time is it?"

"Late," Ford said.

"I'll get around to it," McKinley said, pointing to his laptop. "Anyway, I pulled a list of patients in the Comixon drug trial. There were ten in total."

Jo watched as the screen populated with names, faces, and addresses.

"I'll have to do a little more digging," McKinley said, "so everything I have in front of me right now is just a brief rundown. Like I said, there were ten patients in total. I used the information that Tully gave you, cross-referenced it with the DMV and a few other departments, and this is what I came up with."

Jo read the list. She discovered that four of the patients died before the trial came to a conclusion. Two were in different hospitals—their cancer had spread to the point that they needed constant monitoring. Two were in remission, and she couldn't tell if it was due to Comixon, but they had moved to other parts of the country. The last two, a man named Daniel Walsh and a woman named Sarah Mueller, were still Seattle residents.

"Tell me about Sarah Mueller," Jo asked.

McKinley leaned closer to the screen. "She's a kindergarten teacher. She's married with two young children. And according to this, she had no side-effects to the Comixon drug."

Ford said, "What about this guy Walsh? Find anything interesting on him?"

McKinley shrugged. "Nothing came up when I searched. It was a little odd. All I could get was a driver's license, expired, and a few instances of him filing with state unemployment."

Jo examined the photo on the driver's license. Daniel Walsh had dark circles under his eyes. He was gaunt and pale, and he had a haunted look about him. His cobalt-blue eyes sent a shiver up her spine.

Ford nudged her. "What's up?"

Jo shook her head. "I'm not sure. Something feels off about him."

"Is that a sixth sense of yours talking?" Ford asked.

She turned to him, confused. "Sixth sense?"

He shrugged. "I mean, you know, you've got a killer's heart, don't you?"

She looked down at her chest.

"Does it give you special powers to sense out bad guys or something?"

"It helps to keep the blood flowing throughout my body," Jo replied curtly. "Nothing else."

Ford put up his hands defensively. "Didn't mean to offend you."

By now, Jo was used to the comments about her transplant, but that didn't mean she wasn't annoyed by it.

She had fallen in love with someone who she thought loved her back. He turned out to be the son of the Bridgeton Ripper—a serial killer who had terrorized the city for decades. The betrayal had broken her already frail heart. As a consolation, though, she now had *his* heart beating inside her chest.

"Anything else on Walsh?" she asked McKinley.

"I'll keep digging," McKinley replied. "I'll let you know what I find as soon as I stumble across it."

Ford and Jo moved away from the desk. Ford said, "What do you want to do about Mark Tully? We left him in the interview room to stew."

"Cut him loose," Jo said. "But we need to keep tabs on him."

"You think someone might knock on his door?"

"Possibly. He's a person of interest. He's at the center of this whole drug trial thing."

"But," Ford said, "both Rene Stansfield and Richard Kellerman are dead. From what we know, Rene was the one who wanted to cover up the failure of the trial."

Jo said, "Point being?"

"That there's nothing else to cover up. The person who was intent on covering it up is dead."

Jo held up a finger. "The company is still in operation. Just because Richard and Rene are gone doesn't mean that people with vested interests in the company won't attempt to reach out to silence others. Also, the person responsible for all of this is still out there. He may come back to tie up loose ends."

"That'd be a risky move on his or her part," Ford said.

"It would be, yes," Jo said. "But it's still worth checking out."

FIFTY-FIVE

Crickets chirped, and the wind blew as Morris climbed over the gates leading into the cemetery. It was dark, the only illumination from the lights built into the pathway that snaked through the cemetery grounds. Headstones of different shapes and sizes stuck out of the ground. The eerie setting made the hairs on the back of his neck stand up.

He stuffed his hands into his pockets. He looked over his shoulder. He was certain that the news vans didn't pick up on the fact that he had slipped out of his house. If they had, they'd be on him by now.

Traipsing through the cemetery, he approached a trio of graves. The grass in front of the headstones had not yet grown in. Fresh earth was in the process of smoothing over, so he knew he was at the right spot.

His heart racing, he stopped at the foot of the headstones, where his eyes fell on the name engraved on the headstone to the far left:

Lindsey Rebecca Stansfield
December 29th, 2006 -April 3rd, 2022
Our Beloved Daughter

He dropped to one knee. He looked away from the grave. A single tear slid down his cheek. He thought about the day he met Lindsey. She had slid him a piece of paper in their World History class with her cell number jotted down on the page; a little heart was drawn beneath it.

For several minutes, he said nothing. He just stared at her grave. A part of him wanted to reach down through the dirt and touch her, feel her skin against his. It was a morbid thought, he knew. She was dead, after all, but that was how much he missed her.

"I'm so sorry, Lindsey," he said. "This is all my fault."

Tears began to freely roll down his cheeks. He didn't bother wiping them. His heart ached for her, and it felt good to let it out.

He didn't know how long he'd been crying, but he finally wiped his face with the back of his sleeve.

His eyes fell on Justine's headstone. Then on Rene's. His jaw muscles tensed as he thought back to how poorly they had treated *him*. They thought he was a bad influence on their daughter. They'd wanted them to break up the moment they saw him. But none of it mattered now. They were gone. Lindsey was gone. And now he had to figure out how he was going to move on.

A twig snapped. He turned his head. He stood up and took a scan of his surroundings and thought maybe a critter was passing through.

"Hello?" he said, just in case.

No reply.

He looked around. He saw nothing. He heard nothing more. Certain that it was his mind playing tricks on him, he turned his attention back to the headstone.

Another twig snapped.

His heart fell into his stomach. He turned back around and hoped that he would spot a cat or other large rodent meandering its way through the grounds. But it was no four-legged critter approaching him from behind: it was a man with a gun in his hand.

The gun was directly aimed at him.

He threw up his hands. "Please, don't—"

"Shut up!" the figure shrouded in darkness grumbled. "You saw my face, kid. You *saw* me."

Morris was trembling. "I don't know you, man! Please, don't do this."

"I said shut up!" The figure took a step closer and coughed. "This ends tonight. *You* end tonight. I need to get away from this. *All* of this."

Something clicked in Morris's brain. He lowered his hands. He looked at the figure blanketed in black, drew a breath, and said, "It was you, wasn't it? You... You killed Lindsey. You killed her whole family."

The figure reared back the hammer on his weapon, squeezed his finger around the trigger, and pulled.

FIFTY-SIX

Jo checked her watch. It was a little past one in the morning. *I need to power down soon*, she thought. *I'm going to pass out at any second.*

Ford placed a cup of coffee on her desk. "A little liquid boost," he said.

Jo wanted to smile. But she was too taxed. It took everything she had just to grumble, "Thanks."

Ford asked, "How are you holding up?"

Jo replied, "Hanging in there by a thread." She gestured to McKinley over at another desk. "Kid is working overtime to pull up more info on the list of clients that Tully gave us."

"He's still here, by the way."

"Who? Tully?"

Ford laughed. "Yeah, I think he's worried about the fact that he told us more than he should've."

"I thought his lawyer was here to take him home?"

"He already came and left."

"And Tully's still in the interview room?" she said, surprised.

"He won't leave."

"Why not?"

"He's scared that whatever happened to Kellerman might happen to him."

"I don't blame him. The killer is still out there."

"That's why we need your boy, McKinley, to track down Walsh for us. When I called the number on the address we got off Walsh's driver's license, it was someone else who was living there. Apparently, Walsh had moved out a long time ago, and he never bothered to update his driver's license."

"Seems strange, doesn't it?" Jo said.

"What does?"

"Walsh disappeared right around the time the drug trial was shut down." She saw Ford rubbing his ring finger. "When did you get divorced?" she then asked.

Ford's brow furrowed. "Who said I was divorced?"

Jo gestured to his ring finger. "I can see the tan line. Doesn't take a seasoned detective to figure it out."

Ford held up his ring finger. "My wife is, well, estranged."

Jo leaned forward. "What do you mean by 'estranged'?"

"We haven't seen each other in a while," Ford said. "We're trying to work things out. She's living in Vancouver right now."

Jo said, "Can I ask why?"

Ford took a moment before replying, "A guy I put away a long time ago came to our house after he got out of jail. Things got messy. My wife and daughter saw the whole thing. It's just taking her some time to cope. I guess the cliché of the broken-hearted detective is true in my case."

"I didn't know you had a daughter," Jo said.

Ford smiled. "Her name is Hazel. She's a big fan of the Beach Boys."

Jo returned the smile. "Takes after her old man, I bet."

"A little bit," Ford said, still smiling. "It's been a while since I've seen her, though. I just hope that it's sooner rather than later."

The more he spoke about his family, the more Jo realized there was more to him than met the eye. "I'm sorry, Bryan," she said.

Ford laughed. "That's the first time you called me by my first name."

"Is that all right?"

"Only if I can call you 'Jo'."

Nodding, she said, "It's a deal." She averted her gaze. "And if it's any consolation, I'm not perfect, either. I, uh… I have nightmares. They happen almost every night."

Ford said, "What are they about?"

Jo shrugged. "Stuff from the past. I guess what I'm trying to say is that I understand how the job can haunt you."

"Well, aren't we a pair, Agent Pullinger."

Laughing, Jo said, "It appears we are, Detective Ford."

Ford's cell phone rang. He answered.

Whatever he heard caused his eyes to go wide.

"We have to go," Ford said, hanging up, "We have to go *now*."

Jo stood up from her desk. "What happened?"

"Tim Morris," Ford said as he moved toward the elevators. "Someone just shot him."

FIFTY-SEVEN

After shooting Tim Morris, the man fled under an overpass. His mind was spinning. His stomach was turning in knots as he laid eyes on a shanty town comprised of tents, cardboard huts, and a few tattered couches lined up in rows. The homeless population was booming in virtually every city nowadays. He knew it was his best chance at hiding out.

Police sirens wailed in the distance. The man ducked next to a tent and stayed low until it faded away. *This is bad*, he told himself. *They're going to find me.*

"*Hey*," a voice grumbled from inside the tent.

He turned to run when a man with a dark complexion poked out his head.

"Hang on," the vagrant said. "You don't gotta run, fella. It's all right. You're not disturbing me."

He stopped in his tracks. He looked at the vagrant smiling at him and gesturing for him to come closer.

"Take it easy," the vagrant said. "I'm not going to hurt you. No one here is dangerous. Well"—he pointed to a green tent at the end of the row spaced far away from the others—"Henry over there has got some problems—mental health problems, so steer clear of him." He laughed. "My name's Georgie. What's yours?"

The man said nothing.

"Come," Georgie said as he motioned for him to join him. "You look tired, son. Take a seat. You look hungry. When's the last time you ate?"

He did the math and realized it had been more than twenty-four hours.

"Get in here," Georgie said warmly. "I got a TV dinner I couldn't finish. You can have the rest. Come on, now. I'm not going to take no for an answer."

He knew there was nowhere to go, nowhere to hide—not yet, at least. The police would be swarming the cemetery by now. And soon, they would start canvassing the nearby areas—looking for someone matching his description. Plus, he should eat something, he knew. The adrenaline would begin to wear off, and he needed the energy. So, he went inside the tent and sat down. There were piles of books in the small space, making it feel even smaller.

"Here you go," Georgie said as he handed over a plastic tray. "Take a bite. It's not the best, but it's not nothing."

He used his hands to scoop the rice and lentils and devoured them. It was a bit sour—but it was still something.

"You look disturbed, son," Georgie said. "Everything all right?"

He shrugged. "I'm in trouble." He coughed and held his hand to his chest.

"You sick?"

He nodded. "You won't catch it. It's not a cold or anything."

"You should get to a hospital."

He shook his head. "I can't."

Georgie sighed. "You in trouble?"

He nodded again. "A lot."

"That's okay," Georgie said. "All of us are here because of bad luck, bad choices, whatever. No one is going to be looking at you differently, I assure you."

The man hung his head. "I have done bad things in my life. That's for sure. And I just *did* a bad thing now."

"Well"—Georgie held up his hands—"I won't judge you, son. I'm not in a position to do so." He clapped his hand on the man's bony shoulder. "Cut yourself some slack. Things will be all right."

"No," he said. "They won't."

Georgie sat back. "Stay awhile." He gestured to his books. "I've got plenty of entertainment. You can share the tent with me for the night."

"I can't stay long," he said. "They're looking for me."

"The police?"

"Yeah…"

Georgie nodded. "Again, whatever you did, I won't hold it against you. It's between you and God. Heck, even if you hurt someone, I won't speak on the matter. Again, I've done my fair share of bad things." He smiled. "It'll be okay, fella. I promise."

It was the first time in a long time that the man had been offered any shred of comfort. It nearly made him break down and cry.

"Thank you, sir," he said. "I appreciate this. I really do."

"Whatever you've done," Georgie said, "learn to forgive yourself. There's always a second chance waiting for you."

Not for me, he thought.

Georgie asked, "What's your name? It would be nice to know who I'm sharing my home with. But if you don't want to tell me, you don't have to."

The man cleared his throat. "My name's Walsh," he said. "Daniel Walsh."

FIFTY-EIGHT

The Crown Vic screeched to a halt in the ambulance bay of the UW Medical Center. Jo was out of the car before it came to a full stop, with Ford right behind her. The two of them rushed through the doors of the ER wing and flashed their identifications to the nurse at the front desk.

"Tim Morris," Jo said. "Where is he?"

The nurse clacked away at her keyboard. "He's in surgery," she said. "Second floor."

Jo and Ford ran as fast as their feet could carry them. They weaved their way through a sea of doctors and patients, and visitors, before taking the stairs to the second floor and asking where the trauma wing was. After a moment of searching, they spotted Tim's parents. They were seated on a bench. Next to them were a pair of swinging doors that led to the trauma center. They stood up the moment they saw Jo and Ford.

Jonathan Morris wiped the tears from his eyes. "Detective Ford," he said.

"Mr. Morris," Ford said. "Are you two okay?"

Deborah Morris nodded. "We're okay."

Ford gestured to Jo. "This is Agent Pullinger. She's from the FBI."

Jonathan shook Jo's hand.

"Is Tim all right?" Jo asked. "Where is he?"

"We just spoke to the doctor," Deborah said. "He was…" Tears welled in her eyes. "He was shot in the chest."

Oh, no, Jo's mind prattled. *Please, let him be okay.*

"He was lucky," Jonathan said with a long sigh. "The bullet punctured his lung, but the surgeon said he's going to pull through."

Jo breathed easy. "I'm so sorry, Mr. and Mrs. Morris. I know the two of you have been through a lot."

"Thank you," Deborah said. "We're just glad he'll be okay."

Jo was relieved that Tim Morris would be all right. She knew that he would need rest and time to fully recover—but right now, she wanted to find out who was responsible for pulling the trigger. She needed to hear it from Morris.

An hour later, she was granted her request.

FIFTY-NINE

Tim Morris's eyes peeled open as Jo and Ford walked into the room, followed by his parents. Monitors beeped. His arms were tethered to machines. The area where he was shot was covered by a mound of bandages. His skin was grey. A breathing tube was in his mouth.

Deborah smiled, approached the bed, and rested her hand on top of her son's. "Tim," she said softly, "the police and FBI are here. They want to ask you a few questions."

Morris blinked.

Jonathan shrugged. "He's got a tube in his mouth."

"That's okay," Jo said. "We'll try to make this as easy as possible. We won't stay long."

The parents stood aside as Jo approached the bed. She grabbed a chair and sat down. She watched as Morris's eyes slowly met hers.

"Tim," Jo said, "I'm just going to ask you a few 'yes' or 'no' questions. Blink once for 'yes.' Blink twice for 'no.' Can you do that for me?"

Slowly, Morris blinked once.

Jo smiled. "That's good, Tim. Listen, I know it's tough right now. I imagine you feel pretty run down, so I'll just ask a few things, and then we'll let you get some rest. Is that all right?"

Morris blinked once.

"Okay," Jo said. "Now, you slipped out of your parents' house tonight, right?"

Morris blinked once.

"You went to the cemetery to visit Lindsey's grave, is this true?"

Morris blinked once.

"Did you see anyone follow you there?"

Morris blinked twice.

"Okay. Now, this is the most important question. Did you see the man who shot you?"

It took Morris a moment, but then he blinked once.

"Was he tall?" Jo asked.

Morris blinked twice.

"Short?"

Morris blinked twice.

"Average height?"

Morris blinked once.

This will take too long, Jo thought. *Whoever shot him is on the run. I need to think quickly.*

Something occurred to her. She reached into her pocket, took out her cell phone, and pulled up the drug trial patients' records. Jo scrolled until she found the picture of the man with the haunted look in his eyes: Daniel Walsh. She expanded it and held it up.

"Tim," Jo said, "did the man who shot you look anything like this man?"

Morris's eyes went wide. His hand trembled. He pointed a finger, pointed to the photo, and blinked his eyes once.

"This is the man?" Jo said, wanting to confirm. "You're sure this is the man who shot you?"

Tears rolled down Morris's cheeks as he slowly nodded.

SIXTY

"I knew it," Jo said as she raced down the hallway outside of Morris's room. "When I saw this guy"—she held up Walsh's photo—"I just knew there was something off."

Ford, pulling out his own phone, punched in the number for his lieutenant. "Walsh's probably long gone by now."

Jo furrowed her brow. "Why would he go after Tim Morris?"

"Maybe he was tying off loose ends."

Jo understood. "He waited until Morris was out of prison before he went after him."

"Exactly," Ford said. "He must have hoped Morris would take the fall for the Stansfields' murder. But once he was let go, he knew the attention would divert back to finding the real killer: *him*."

"Exactly."

They piled in the car, Jo pulling up McKinley's number and hitting "Send." The kid answered after just one ring. "McKinley."

Jo said, "It's Pullinger. Did you pull up anything else on those patients' files?"

"A few things, yeah."

"I need everything you have on Daniel Walsh. We just got a positive ID from Tim Morris that he's the man who shot him."

McKinley told Jo to hang tight. Jo, looking over at Ford, listened to him relay the same information to his lieutenant.

"Pullinger?" McKinley said.

"Go ahead," Jo told him.

"Everything I've got on Walsh is pretty slim. One thing to note is that he's got a military record. I pulled that from a Department of Defense database. Looks like he served six years in the Marine Corps."

The info that a suspect had military training didn't sit well with her. They were always more dangerous than civilians. "What happened with Walsh in the Marine Corps?" she asked.

McKinley said, "Honorable discharge. According to his VA file it mentions the discharge was illness-related. The term 'burn pit' came up a few times."

Jo huffed. Burn pits were basically toxic waste dumps the size of football fields. The army would burn everything in them: bodies, trash, human waste, weapons, and anything else in-between. "It's well known," she said, "that a slew of people who served ended up experiencing life-threatening illnesses as a result."

"Well," McKinley said, "it looks like our guy Walsh ended up developing Stage Three Lymphoma as a result."

"It makes sense," she said.

"What does?"

"Why he'd take part in the cancer drug trial. He's sick, and he may be dying."

"Oh. That's rough."

"What else did you find?" she asked.

McKinley said, "It looks like the VA gave him the shaft when it came to covering his medical expenses. I'm still trying to piece together what happened to him after that. The paper trail sort of expires after June of last year. I've got no cell phone, no permanent address, but I do have a bank account number. Walsh opened up a savings account at a local branch. It's going to take time to look into it. I'll have to make a couple of calls."

"Get on it. Forward everything to Grantham. Get him in the loop ASAP and get back to me as soon as you can."

"Will do."

Jo hung up the phone and listened in to Ford's conversation.

"That's right," Ford said to his lieutenant. "The suspect's name is Daniel Walsh. Five-foot-six. Auburn hair. A hundred and fifty-six pounds."

"He's a Marine Corps veteran," Jo told him. "Put that out there."

Ford's jaw muscles tightened as he relayed that info. "He's dangerous. Possibly armed. Put out an APB and dispatch all available units around the Morris home. We'll need to work with the FBI and coordinate our efforts."

Jo tapped her finger on the armrest as Ford spoke for a few more minutes. He ended the call and turned to her.

"What are the chances," he said, "that Walsh is still in the city?"

"He *should* be running," Jo said. "Taking a shot at Morris wasn't smart."

"But *is* he running?"

Jo shook her head. "No. He's still here. I can't explain it." She looked at Ford. "But I can feel it."

SIXTY-ONE

The field office was bustling with activity when Jo and Ford walked in. The atmosphere was like the engine room on an old ship: chaotic but organized. They caught McKinley down the hall. He waved to them to follow after him.

"I've got something," McKinley said. "I called the manager at the bank where Walsh opened an account. He almost freaked out when I told him I was with the FBI. He cooperated immediately and gave me everything he could on Walsh's account."

Jo said, "What did you find?"

McKinley sat down at his desk. "Walsh received only one deposit in his account. It happened about three weeks after he opened it." He pointed to his monitor. "Look at the date."

Jo squinted and saw April 2nd, 2022, on the page. "That's one day before the Stansfields were murdered."

McKinley nodded. "Exactly. Now, look at the amount."

Jo leaned in and saw that the amount of five-hundred thousand dollars had been deposited in Walsh's account. "It has to be him," she said. "Walsh was paid to kill the Stansfields."

Ford said, "Can you trace who made the deposit?"

McKinley said, "It's going to take some time. I need to call up Agent Harrison. He works in white-collar crime. He knows how to trace this stuff better than anyone."

Jo told McKinley to make it happen. Moments later, Lieutenant Griffin emerged from the elevator. Jo and Ford greeted her. A minute later, they were all gathered in Grantham's office.

Grantham, standing in front of his desk, addressed the group. "How many units do you have patrolling the streets?" he asked Griffin.

Griffin said, "I've got two units covering the six blocks surrounding the area where Tim Morris was shot. I'm sending out more to blanket the rest of the areas further away. Long story short, half of the Seattle P.D. is tearing apart the city looking for this guy."

Jo looked at Grantham. "We need to get Customs and Border Protection involved too. He can't fly. Trains are too risky. He might try and hop his way over the border to Mexico by car. It's a long shot, but it's still a possibility."

"I'll make the necessary calls," Grantham said. He then crossed his arms. "Tell me, what is the probability that the guy we're looking for is the same man who killed the Stansfields and Richard Kellerman?"

"All but certain," Jo said. "If you're asking for the statistical probability, I'd settle on a solid ninety-five percent."

Ford said, "The doctors who treated Tim Morris at the hospital have sent the slug they retrieved from his lung to your techs over here. I'm told they are looking at it as we speak."

Grantham nodded. "Good." He then looked at Jo. "Why do you think he'd expose himself by going after Tim Morris? It was a risky move."

Jo shrugged. "Only Walsh knows why. It's clear, though, from his bank account that someone paid him to kill the Stansfields."

"Do you have any theories as to who that might be?"

Thoughts of the affair between Justine and Richard popped into Jo's mind. "If I had to take a guess, I'd say it was Richard Kellerman. Based on the text messages between Justine and Richard, we can tell that he was trying to get back with her, but Justine wasn't on board with this. She turned down his propositions several times. Apparently, Rene found out about the affair not long before he was killed. We believe Richard hired Walsh to kill Rene and his entire family."

"Including Justine?" Griffin said with a raised eyebrow.

"He must have known she would never leave Rene for him. He also must've feared that with their relationship strained, Rene might try to oust him from the company. So, it was better to get rid of them all. Sort of like, hitting two birds with one stone. With Rene out of the picture, he could take full control of the company, and with Justine gone, he would never have to worry about the affair becoming fodder for the news."

"And what about the daughter, Lindsey?" Griffin asked.

"I'm afraid she was collateral damage."

There was a moment of silence before Griffin said, "I can see validity in your theory, but didn't the same person who killed the Stansfields also kill Richard Kellerman?"

Jo said, "We believe so too."

Griffin frowned. "If Richard Kellerman paid Walsh, then why would he kill *him*?"

"Maybe Kellerman had second thoughts. Maybe the guilt got the better of him. And he wanted to turn himself in. We don't know this with certainty, of course. But it would make sense for Walsh to go after the person who paid him in order to tie up loose ends."

Grantham asked, "And why would Kellerman choose Walsh?"

"Walsh," Jo said, "took part in a drug trial he thought might cure his Lymphoma. After the trials failed, Kellerman must have approached Walsh with a proposition: kill Justine and Rene for a hefty sum. With Walsh's background in the military, and with his condition deteriorating due to the cancer, I'm sure Walsh thought it was a good idea to take the money."

Griffin's cell phone rang. She answered it. She prepared to move toward the door as she hung up the phone. "We've got a problem," she said.

Jo asked, "What is it?"

"A man named Morris Hackman was shot."

"Who shot him?" Ford asked.

"Daniel Walsh."

SIXTY-TWO

Walsh felt as if the walls were closing in on him. He couldn't run. There was nowhere to hide. Not in his deteriorating condition, anyway.

Maybe that was the reason he went back to the same motel that cost twenty dollars a night. He thought maybe the police would find him there, that they would kick in the door and bring an end to the chaos.

He turned on the television. The broadcast was covering the manhunt. The police and the FBI were scouring the streets looking for him. It was a miracle the clerk at the front desk didn't know he was a fugitive. If he did, Walsh would've sensed it. The clerk was old, near-sighted, and he was more preoccupied with the book he was reading than what was happening around him.

It would've helped if the clerk had a TV running in the background. Walsh saw no TV anywhere in the space, which told him the clerk had no idea he was on the run.

But that didn't mean he would be free forever.

The only question that remained was if he would take it lying down or standing up.

Walsh continued watching the news. He debated his choices: death or handcuffs. If he turned himself in, he would go to prison. He would probably die there. But at least he would be able to bare his soul and feel the burden of the situation lifted off his shoulders.

I can try and shoot my way out, he then thought. *I can go down in a blaze of glory.* He had done the same thing when he was deployed to the Middle East.

Several times he had been under fire and managed to find a way out. *So*, he told himself, *how is this any different?* He was trained to fight. The Marines had instilled the will in him to survive.

He coughed and saw a peppering of blood in his hand. He knew that survival was something he could only do for so long. Sooner or later, his body wouldn't comply, even if his mind was prepared to fight.

He suddenly had the urge for a candy bar. He wasn't sure why. Maybe something sweet would give him a bit of comfort while he figured out his options.

He walked out to the vending machines at the end of the hall. He collected the quarters and dimes in his pockets, popped them into the machine, and watched a chocolate bar fall to the tray. He took the bar out and prepared to open the wrapper when he saw the little boy from before—Joseph—poking his head out the door of the room beside his.

"It's you," Joseph said.

Walsh's nerves spiked. *Should I run? Did this kid see the news?*

"You're the sick man," Joseph said. "You were here before."

Walsh took a look around. He saw no one else.

"Where are your parents?" Walsh asked.

Joseph shrugged. "My mom works late," he said. "I don't know where my dad is."

"You shouldn't be alone."

Joseph pointed. "*You're* alone."

"I have to be."

"Why?"

Walsh shrugged. "I just… am."

Joseph squinted. "Don't you have a family?"

"No."

"Don't you have any kids? It'd be nice to play with someone." Joseph gestured into his room. "All day, I just watch TV."

Walsh's eyes narrowed. Children were so innocent. Whatever memories he had as a child were hard to recollect. "Anything good on?" he asked.

Joseph nodded. "A war movie."

"You're too young to watch that stuff."

Joseph shrugged. "My mom doesn't care." He looked sheepish. "I'm actually grounded. I'm not *supposed* to be watching TV."

Walsh asked, "Why not?"

"I did something bad."

"What did you do?"

Joseph bit his lip and shifted his weight. "I said a bad word. I shouldn't have. It wasn't nice to say it."

A smile crept across Walsh's face. "That's not so bad," he said. "I had to put a quarter in a jar when I said a bad word."

"Do you have a mom?"

Walsh shook his head. "No."

"*Everyone* has a mom."

"You're quite curious, aren't you?"

Joseph nodded and smiled. "I want to be a policeman one day. I saw a show with policemen. They ask a lot of questions. I'm practicing." He squinted. "Are *you* a policeman?"

Walsh shook his head.

"What do you do?" Joseph asked.

"I… was… a Marine."

Joseph lit up. "Cool!"

Walsh's heart sank into his stomach. More than anything, he wished he were a kid like Joseph. He'd be able to start his life over again.

Joseph stepped out of the room. "Why are you so sad? Your eyes are all watery."

"Because," Walsh said, "I did a bad thing, too."

"Did you get grounded for it?"

Walsh shrugged. "Not yet."

"You should just say you're sorry. That makes everything better." Joseph smiled. "Trust me."

The kid's words rattled inside his head. He got down on one knee. He held out the chocolate bar. "Here," he said. "You earned it."

Joseph's eyes went wide with excitement. "Really?"

Walsh held up one finger. "On one condition. You have to do what your mom says." He nudged the kid playfully. "And stop cursing."

Nodding, Joseph took the chocolate bar. "Thanks, mister."

Walsh patted the kid on the head. He went back to his room. As he shut the door behind him, he began to think that maybe it was time he turned himself in and ended this nightmare once and for all.

SIXTY-THREE

Police cruisers with lights flashing and sirens blaring passed by Ford's Crown Vic. Jo watched them through the passenger-side window. A full-on manhunt was playing out. She was certain Walsh would be caught. The only question was how it would go down when it happened.

Ford, behind the wheel, rubbed his eyes. "Stay awake," he told himself.

Jo said, "Where's this guy Hackman lives?"

"Virginia Mason. It's just a couple miles from here." Ford patted the dashboard. "Thank God for sirens, right?"

Jo glanced in the side-view mirror. People on the street were watching the police units barrel down the street. The glow from the emergency lights on the Crown Vic's dashboard lit up her face. "We'll end this tonight, one way or another," she said, more to herself than to Ford. "That's what troubles me," Ford said. "Walsh is desperate. Why else would he shoot another person on the same night?"

The notion of Walsh killing more people made Jo feel queasy. She tried not to focus on it. She needed to keep her head in the game. Her cell phone rang. She looked down, and Sam's name flashed on the caller ID.

"Hey," Jo answered.

"Good morning," Sam said with a laugh. "It's almost two a.m. Where are you?"

"Sorry, I meant to call you," she said. "It's going to be a long night, Sam."

"Are you okay? You sound stressed."

A little bit, Jo thought. "We're making a break in the case," she said. "I can't say much."

"You're okay, though?" Sam asked. "I don't need to worry?"

The less you know, the better.

"I'm fine," Jo said. "Don't wait up. Give Chrissy a kiss for me, okay?"

"Will do," Sam said before Jo terminated the call.

Ford asked, "Who was that?"

"My brother."

"I didn't know you had a brother."

"I've got a niece, too."

Ford said, "I have a nephew. My brother's kid. He's sixteen."

Relishing a brief moment of reprieve, Jo asked, "Do you get along with him?"

Ford shook his head. "My brother isn't the smartest guy in the world. I guess he passed that on to his kid." He glanced at Jo and smirked. "So, no, not really."

The comment made Jo laugh. She appreciated it. Laughter on the job was like meals: you had to take them where you could get them.

SIXTY-FOUR

Jo and Ford walked into their second hospital of the night. They asked the nurse at the station where Morris Hackman was. They were instructed to go to the emergency wing. Five minutes of looking brought them to a room where they found Hackman seated on the edge of a table. His arm was held in a sling. A fresh bandage had been placed over his shoulder. A Marine Corp tattoo—"USMC"—was permanently inked into his arm.

"Mr. Hackman?" Jo said as she showed her credentials. "I'm Agent Pullinger of the FBI." She pointed to Ford. "This is Detective Ford with the Seattle P.D."

Hackman didn't appear fazed. He just looked slightly perturbed. "Morning," he said.

"Are you all right?"

Hackman looked at his sling and laughed. "I've been through worse. Bullet fractured my clavicle, though."

"I'm sorry to hear that."

Hackman shrugged. "Walsh could have killed me. I think he let me off easy. The guy was always a good shot."

"So, just to confirm," Ford said, "you are saying it was Daniel Walsh who shot you?"

"Without question." He glanced at the floor. "Matter of fact, I think I might be in some hot water with you guys."

Jo said, "Why is that?"

Hackman took a moment to answer. "I had given Walsh the gun he used on me. He said he needed it for protection. When he came to see me tonight, I realized that wasn't the case no more."

Jo, crossing her arms, said, "Go on."

Hackman held up a finger. "Hold on a second. I'm all for transparency. I want Walsh brought in just like you guys. But I don't want to tell you things that'll end up having me thrown in prison just because I was in the wrong place at the wrong time."

"We can help you," Jo said. "We don't want *you*. We want Walsh. But we can't waste time. Walsh is now the prime suspect in four murders, and after tonight, two attempted murders as well."

Hackman sighed. "Yeah. Yeah, it's a real mess. I get it."

Ford said, "How do you know Morris?"

"We were in the Corps together. Three years. The guy was a great Marine." Hackman shook his head. "After that stuff with the burn pits, though, it really did him in."

Jo said, "Walsh had Stage Three Lymphoma."

Hackman said, "It's Stage Four now. The guy doesn't look like he used to. He used to be jacked. Built solid. Once he got cancer, it ate away at him. He tried to go to the VA for help. They didn't do a damn thing." He clenched a fist. "They never do."

Ford said, "Tell us about your time with him—recently, that is."

"I've seen him in spurts since he moved to Seattle. He came out here for a change of scenery. He used to live in Vegas. He looked me up. We had a beer from time to time. He wasn't working. He was getting sicker. Every time I saw the guy, I thought it was going to be the last time."

Jo asked, "Do you know where he was living?"

Hackman shook his head. "No, he just said he was couch surfing. Didn't say with who, though."

Ford asked, "Did he mention anything about being a part of a cancer treatment trial?"

"No," Hackman replied. "That's news to me."

"What about the gun you gave him?" Jo said.

"Walsh came to me about three weeks ago. He said he needed a gun. I didn't think anything of it. Vets carry guns. It's not that big of a deal. I knew Walsh had no money, so I gave him an old Heckler and Koch pistol I owned. Really worn down. I figured he just needed something for protection. He was living on the streets."

Jo said, "What happened after that?"

Hackman drew a breath. "Tonight, he came to my house. He looked really bent out of shape. I sat him down. Gave him some water." He closed his eyes. "And then he told me what he had done."

Jo and Ford waited for the rest.

"Walsh told me he shot a kid. I asked him why. He told me that he was scared. I asked him about what." Hackman pounded his fist on the bed beneath him. "That's when he told me."

"Told you what?" Jo asked.

Hackman replied, "That he got paid by someone to kill a rich guy a few weeks ago. He had never planned on killing the guy's whole family, but it happened. Walsh also told me that he finished off the job by killing another guy." Jo figured it was the Stansfields and Kellerman Walsh was referring to. "After he confessed, I gave him a minute to calm down. I told him he needed to turn himself in. I told him to give me back the gun I gave him. That's when we started arguing. He tried to run. I tried to stop him." Hackman held up his sling. "That's when he shot me."

Ford said, "Did Walsh say who paid him to kill that family?"

Hackman shook his head. "I asked, but he didn't tell me. He got all defensive when I tried to press him."

Jo asked, "He didn't say anything else?"

"No," Hackman replied. "Things went bad. He pulled his gun. I tried to wrestle it away. He shot me. I tried to catch him, but I passed out. By the time I woke up, the ambulance had rolled in. The neighbors called it in." He laughed. "I need a vacation after this."

Jo asked Hackman a few more questions. Ford did the same. After they were finished, they took Hackman's info and told him to stay by the phone before making their way back to the car.

"It's just a matter of time until a unit rolls up on Walsh," Ford said.

Jo said, "I don't know why, but I get a bad feeling he might off himself."

"Why do you think that?"

"He's sick, and he's cornered. He might do something drastic if we don't get to him soon."

"Let's hope that doesn't happen." Ford checked his watch. "What do we do now?"

Jo thought about it. Something in her mind told her she needed to go back to the start of the ordeal: the Stansfield residence.

SIXTY-FIVE

The Stansfield residence looked haunted at this time of the night. Jo rolled up in her vehicle and parked in the empty driveway. Unlike the last time she'd been there, there was no officer stationed at the house. All available resources were being deployed to find Walsh. Even Ford had gone back to the station to help with the manhunt.

She approached the front door. The exterior was dark and eerily quiet. She felt as though the spirits of the Stansfields were lingering about, keeping a close eye on her until their deaths were avenged.

She ducked underneath the yellow police tape and produced a lock pick kit. Breaking and entering was not taught at the academy. It was something she'd picked up on her own. She had taken the precaution of calling Secure & Safe to ask them to deactivate the alarm because she needed access to the property.

After fiddling with the locks for a couple of minutes, she was able to open the front door. A wave of cool air hit her face, sending a shiver up her spine as she walked into the foyer.

"Oh, Jo," she whispered to herself. "Why are you here?"

She moved up the stairs to the second floor. She walked into Lindsey's bedroom. The blood on the floor had turned black. After a moment, she made her way into the study. The stale scent of death still lingered in the air. Rene's bloodstains, like Lindsey's, had turned to black. She left the room, walked down the hall, and entered the master bedroom. She eyed the stain on the floor where Justine's body had been found.

Jo stood looking around, trying to figure out what she had missed, if anything, from the last time she was here. Everything looked as it had during her initial viewing. Nothing looked like it had been moved. And why would it? The crime scene had been sealed off from the public.

"Come on, Jo," she said to herself. "What are you looking for?"

When no answer came, she turned to leave.

Her eyes fell on the closet.

She thumbed the light switch and appraised the space inside the massive walk-in closet. Boxes upon boxes of shoes were organized in neat rows. Dinner dresses, pantsuits, casual clothing, and fur coats lined the racks. Looking around, Jo spotted boxes of jewelry on the shelves. The boxes were expensive. Glazed. Trimmed with gold. One box on the upper shelf, however, caught her eye.

She pulled the box down; it was cheaply made, and floral designs were crudely etched into it. It was the kind of thing one bought from a merchant in a foreign country on a whim. She got down on her knees, placed the box on the floor, and opened it.

Inside, she found a seashell. Next to it was a room key for a place called Bahia Principe Resort in Mexico. Underneath were several photos. Jo pulled them out. The first one was of Justine and Rene, younger, smiling and waving at the camera from inside the lobby of the resort. The second photo was of a pristine beach with blue waters and white sands. Beneath that was another photo of Rene, Richard, and Justine toasting with a trio of Pina Coladas. Finally, Jo looked at the last photo: it was of just Richard and Justine.

Something about the photo caught Jo's attention. Justine and Richard appeared to be on the beach. A campfire roared in the background. Justine's eyes were closed, her nose pressed against Richard's neck. It was an intimate moment, one that Justine felt the need to hide at the bottom of the pile.

She flipped the photo over. There was a date handwritten in blue ink: 6/2/2006.

The gears started working overtime in Jo's brain. She did the math, and she came to a sudden and unexpected realization.

SIXTY-SIX

After leaving the motel, Walsh had taken refuge in an abandoned warehouse some distance away. He knew Joseph wouldn't rat him out. The boy considered Walsh, his friend. After all, Walsh had given him a chocolate bar. But it was the other guests of the motel he was concerned about. The owner of the motel might not watch the news, but that didn't mean the guests didn't either. And it wouldn't take them long to call the police on him.

He peeked out of the tattered blinds covering the warehouse's broken windows. He needed to stay on the move. He could hear the sirens in the distance. It felt like the heat had been turned up around the entire city. For a moment, Walsh wondered how much of it was his sickness and how much was the tension from the situation.

A police cruiser closed in on the warehouse. Walsh took a step back from the window. He pulled out the weapon he'd procured from Hackman and cocked the hammer.

"Don't make me do it," Walsh whispered. "Stay away."

The sirens of the cruiser were blaring loudly now. They were just moments away from arriving at the warehouse doors. *They'll kick them in*, he thought to himself. *They're going to kill me.* He held the gun to his head. *I can't go to jail.*

The cruiser moved by the warehouse and kept driving. Eventually, the sirens faded away.

Walsh peeled the gun away from his temple. His body was shaking uncontrollably. He closed his eyes and shook his head, hoping that he was just living out a bad dream. But he knew he wasn't. He had killed four people. Tried to kill two more, one of which he used to call a friend.

He moved to a wall, pressed his back against it, and sat down. He coughed. His lungs felt raw. His head felt light. His heart weighed heavy. He examined the gun in his hands. It would get fired again, Walsh knew with certainty. It was just a question of would it be fired at the cops or used on himself.

A tear rolled down his cheek. *How did things go so bad?* he wondered. He wasn't always this desperate. At one point, he was a happy man. A competent Marine. A dutiful father and husband. The sickness took that away from him. Stansfield-Kellerman promised him a cure. What they ended up doing was throwing white gasoline on a fire.

Walsh's thoughts went back to Joseph, and a smile crossed his face. He then remembered what the boy had told him: "Just say you're sorry."

Those words rattled around his head for several minutes, getting louder as they did.

He then stood up. *I need to do the right thing*, he told himself. *I need to turn myself in. It's the only way this thing will end.*

SIXTY-SEVEN

Grantham furrowed his brow. "You want *what*?" he asked Jo.

Jo, standing in the doorway to Grantham's office, repeated her prior request: "I need whoever's on deck to pull the DNA samples taken from the Stansfields and Richard Kellerman. All of them."

"To do what with them, exactly?"

"I need them to run Lindsey Stansfield's DNA against Richard Kellerman's. I have a theory. I need to see if it pans out."

The SAC pinched the bridge of his nose. "You understand that we have a city-wide manhunt currently playing out, don't you?"

"I do."

"I have every available agent working in tandem with the Seattle P.D. to find this guy."

"I know."

"Then what is the relevance of running DNA profiles at this point in time?" Grantham asked.

"Because," Jo replied, "I need to be sure of something. I think I may have stumbled across the motive for these killings. Walsh is on the run. There's a good chance that he might get killed or take his own life. The latter is possible because his health is deteriorating rapidly, and he might look for a way out. If that happens, the answers to our questions die with him. This needs to be done now, sir. Also, I don't think that the people we have in the lab are going to be needed on the streets."

Grantham shook his head. "A DNA match is going to have to run through the Washington office. The resources we have on hand can't provide you with what you need. It'll take at least two or three days."

Jo pulled out her phone. "We can get the Seattle P.D. to do it."

The SAC held up his hand. "Okay," he said. "Let's say I believe you when you say that you have a hunch here. But clue me in as to what that might be."

Jo drew a breath. "I believe that Richard Kellerman may be Lindsey Stansfield's biological father. If this is the case, then that proves that Kellerman decided to have Rene killed in a bid to move closer to her and Justine. And that's why he'd paid Walsh to take out Rene. But something must have gone wrong the night of the murders, and Walsh ended up killing everyone, including Justine and Lindsey. That explained why Kellerman was so torn up at the funeral. His tears weren't for Rene but for Justine and Lindsey. Furthermore, if my hunch is correct, then it explains why Kellerman was murdered as well. Guilt must have gotten the better of him, and before he could confess to the police, Walsh finished him off."

Grantham mulled it over. He then nodded. "Okay. Get Seattle P.D. on the horn." He pointed a finger. "But I want you back out on the streets as soon as possible. Every stone we're turning up hasn't revealed Walsh. He's out there, and I want to find him before we have another dead body on our hands."

"Yes, sir," she said, leaving the office and dialing Ford's number. He answered after two rings.

"Go ahead," he said.

"I need you to do me a favor," Jo said.

"Your timing is impeccable."

"I know. But this needs to be done right away. I need to double-check something."

"How can I help."

"I need you to have your people in the lab run a DNA profile. I need them to check Lindsey Stansfield's DNA against Richard Kellerman's. I have reason to believe that he may be her biological father."

"Oh, man," Ford huffed. "That makes a lot of sense."

"My thoughts exactly."

"Give me a couple of hours. I can't move any faster than that."

"Understood," she said. "We'll need to link up soon. We need to hit the streets and see if we can get a line on Walsh."

"I'll call you in twenty."

Jo hung up the phone. She moved to her desk, calling over McKinley and instructing him to forward all information he had on Daniel Walsh to her email. She would sift through it all and see if there was anything that they might have missed that could lead them to him.

"Pullinger!" Grantham called out from his office.

Jo stood up. "Sir?"

Grantham, thumb pointed over his shoulder, said, "He's on the phone."

"Who?"

"Daniel Walsh. He just called the main line asking for you."

SIXTY-EIGHT

Jo wasn't sure if she'd heard it right until Grantham repeated that Daniel Walsh was on the line for her. Her first thought was that it was a sick joke. It was not uncommon to receive calls from the public claiming to be one person or another. And with Walsh being the most wanted person in the city, some deranged caller figured he'd get his fifteen seconds of fame.

Regardless, she had to check it out.

The other agents watched her as she entered Grantham's office. Their heads peeked out of cubicles like groundhogs checking the weather. Support staff stood still as statues, their eyes locked on Jo.

Walking over to the phone on Grantham's desk, Jo picked up the receiver and pressed the button to answer the call.

"This is Agent Pullinger," Jo said.

Dead silence hung on the other end of the line.

"Hello?" Jo said. "Are you there?"

Breathing came through the earpiece— strained and labored. "This is Daniel Walsh," a trembling voice said. "This is the FBI, right?"

It's him, Jo thought. *It's definitely him.* "Yes, Mr. Walsh," she said in a calm tone. "You wanted to speak to me?"

Walsh coughed. "Yes, I do. I'm not sure who else to call."

Jo noted the raspy nature of Walsh's breathing. *He's sick*, she thought. *Very sick.*

"That's quite all right, Mr. Walsh," Jo said. "Can I call you Mr. Walsh?"

"Call me Daniel," he said.

"Okay, Daniel," Jo replied. "Are you okay?"

"No. No, I'm not. I have the entire city looking for me."

"I trust you understand why."

His voice strained, Walsh replied, "Don't patronize me."

"It wasn't my intention. We just want to talk to you. You've caused quite a stir. Things are a bit hectic right now. We just want to make sure that you're safe."

Walsh laughed. "You're good, Agent Pullinger. How many hours did you log for this kind of training?"

Jo said, "More than a few. It turns out you've had some training yourself in the Marine Corps. Based on what I've seen, you had a spectacular record."

"Until they let me die," Walsh said with a depressed tone. "Those bastards are the reason this happened. That's how I see it. If they had just helped me out, none of this would have happened."

Empathize with him, Jo told herself. *This is what you were trained for.* "I heard about those burn pits," she said. "What happened to you and other military members was despicable. None of you deserved that."

"No, we did not."

"You just wanted help."

"That's right."

"So," Jo said, "that's what brings us to the point that we are at now, Daniel. What's happened has happened. There's no changing that. But we need to figure this out without any more people getting hurt."

Walsh said, "That's why I called." He sighed. "I think my options are starting to run out."

Jo's eyes flickered to Grantham, who watched her with a dutiful and curious gaze. "So," she said to Walsh, "what do you want to do, Daniel? What's the best solution to this problem from your point of view?"

Walsh was silent for a moment. He then said, "What happens if I turn myself in?"

"Like I said, we talk about what happened—"

"No," Walsh cut in. "I meant, what happens to me after you charge me for these murders? Don't lie to me. I know you guys have me pegged for what's happened. I got sloppy." He coughed. "This is my fault. I did this to myself."

Jo said, "I'm not sure what's going to happen. But coming in on your own accord will definitely make it easier."

Walsh uttered a curse. Jo thought she heard the phone being slammed down. She was worried he might have hung up. But seconds later, Walsh spoke again: "I can't go to jail. I won't live long enough to carry out my sentence. I'll die before I even get to trial."

"You don't know that, Daniel. We can help you."

"*How*?" Walsh grumbled. "Did you find the cure for cancer?"

Jo said nothing.

"That's what I thought," Walsh replied. "Either way, I'm screwed."

Jo said, "That's not true. We can help you, Daniel. Just come in. Let's talk. I promise that no one will harm you. You have my word."

Seconds passed that felt like minutes. Jo looked at Grantham. Then she looked at the other agents in the bullpen staring right at her. After a moment, Walsh continued talking: "I'll come in," he said defeatedly. "I'll talk to you, but only to you."

Jo said, "That can be arranged. How do you want to do this?"

"Someplace public. Someplace I know I won't get hurt."

"You pick the place. I'll be there."

"Pike Place Market," Walsh said. "Thirty minutes. Come alone." With that, Walsh terminated the call. Moments later, McKinley entered the room.

"We traced the call," McKinley said. "It came from a pay phone near Pike Place Market."

Jo said, "He's already there. We have him." She held her head high. "Let's finish this. Let's bring this guy in."

SIXTY-NINE

Ford, inside the armory at the field office, watched as Jo gathered two magazines for her weapon and a Kevlar vest. "This is dicey," he said. "I don't think you should do this."

She checked her weapon and said, "We don't have a choice."

"I'm voting against this," Ford said. "*Officially.*"

"Noted," Jo replied.

"I managed to pull Walsh's record," Ford said. "He served for a good length of time in the military."

Jo said, "I'm aware."

"Are you also aware that he was diagnosed with PTSD? When he was discharged, his psych evaluation said he had PTSD coupled with possible schizophrenic paranoia. He doesn't know which way is up. As terrible as it sounds, it means he's not thinking straight and is also very dangerous."

"I'll keep that in mind."

"Jo," Ford said, taking a step forward, "there are other ways—"

"Bryan," Jo cut in, "this ends tonight."

"Walsh is on edge," Ford said. "We can't predict what he will do."

"We can't *not* do anything."

"If we leave him be, he might, well, expire on his own."

Jo's eyelids flickered. "And you're fine with that being how it ends? We'll lose out on any answers we're looking for."

Ford shoved his hands in his pockets. "I think it's safe for me to say at this point that I care what happens to you. I don't want to see you get hurt."

Jo smiled. "You asking me out on a date?"

Ford shook his head. "No, no way. I'm very much in love with my wife." He shrugged. "Besides, you're not my type."

"An independent thinker?"

"No," Ford said. "You're too surly."

Jo said, "I have to do this, Ford. It's the only way."

Ford nodded. "Just promise me that you'll come back in one piece."

"I'll try."

Ford stuck out his hand. "Good luck, Jo."

Jo took up the offer and shook. "Thanks, Bryan," she said before donning her Kevlar vest.

SEVENTY

Jo tightened the Velcro straps on her Kevlar vest. She checked her watch and saw that it was creeping in on five in the morning. She was seated in her vehicle with a clear view of the Pike Place Market.

A crackle came over the radio resting on the dashboard.

"Pullinger," Grantham said. "You there?"

Jo grabbed the radio. "I'm here, sir."

"You ready?"

Jo nodded. "I'm ready."

"Good," Grantham said. "We have four agents waiting in the wings in case something goes wrong. They'll be watching you the entire time, so you don't need a wire."

Jo said, "Have they spotted anyone?"

"No, not yet. The market is empty. We cleared out the fish merchants who were just arriving for the day. There's no sign of Walsh."

"Okay." Jo took a deep breath. Her nerves were spiking. Adrenaline was starting to kick in.

Grantham said, "Someone's on the line for you. Hold on a minute."

Jo waited and then heard Ford's voice come over the airwaves: "Good morning, Jo."

"Detective Ford," she replied.

"I'm a block away from you," Ford said. "I'm waiting with the Hostage Rescue Team. We'll be on you in no time if you need us."

The notion that Ford was close by offered Jo a bit of comfort. "I appreciate that," she said. "I just want to get this thing done."

"Slow and easy," Ford said. "Walsh wants to come in. He's looking for salvation. Just close this thing out so we can all go home."

"I'm on it," Jo said.

"Good luck," Ford told her before terminating the call.

She closed her eyes. She breathed in, held it, and breathed out. She pulled her sidearm. This wasn't the first time she had found herself in this kind of situation. She just didn't want it to be the last.

She thumbed the slide on her gun and checked the rounds. She then secured the weapon in her holster, stepped out of the car, and slowly made her way toward the market.

SEVENTY-ONE

Pike Place Market was an ideal, postcard-worthy setting. The ocean waters rested just beyond the market. The smell of fish coupled with coffee grounds was in the air. It wasn't a pungent aroma. It was actually somewhat appealing.

Jo walked down a sloping walkway that led to the front of the market. Neon traced the buildings in vibrant colors that lit up the early morning skies. The sun, rising up from the east, blanketed the terrain with a dull tangerine hue. For a moment, Jo was worried that this would be the last sunrise she would ever lay her eyes on.

She came to a stop just outside the entrance to the market. She waited. Though no one was around, she could feel the eyes of the people watching her. She took a scan of her surroundings and checked her watch one more time.

"Where are you, Walsh?" she whispered. "Show yourself."

Two minutes passed. Then three. Then four. Jo took another look at her watch and saw that Walsh was past the agreed-upon time.

"Come on, damn it," she said. "Where are you?"

The cell phone in Jo's pocket buzzed. She pulled it out and saw Grantham's name on the caller ID.

"Yeah?" she answered.

"It's Walsh," Grantham said. "I have him on the other end of the line."

"Put him on."

Seconds passed before Walsh's voice came over the line. "It's me," he said.

"Where are you?" Jo asked.

"You know that I was in the military."

"I do."

"Then you know," Walsh said with a cough, "that I'm not stupid."

Oh, no, Jo thought. *He's on to us.* "Walsh—" she began.

"Shut up," Walsh cut in. "I told you I wanted to come in. I told you I wanted this to be easy. Instead, you surround yourself with guys packing assault weapons. You didn't think I'd see that?"

"Daniel."

"No," Walsh said. "This is not how I wanted this to go. I was prepared to turn myself in. It's clear you wanted to ambush me."

Jo shook her head. "No, I swear to you—"

"*You* did this, Agent Pullinger. Not me. We're done talking. I'll see you all on the other side."

Walsh terminated the call.

Jo fought the urge to hurl the phone as far as possible. She then turned, waved her hand, and hollered, "He's gone!"

Seconds later, two black SUVs with blue emergency lights flashing pulled up to the market. Black-clad men with assault weapons piled out. Grantham, wearing a Kevlar vest, was in tow.

"What happened?" he asked.

Jo shook her head. "We spooked him," she said. "He saw the HRT team."

Grantham gritted his teeth. "Damn it."

Jo said, "Canvas the area. He might still be around."

Grantham began barking orders as Jo pulled down on the Kevlar that was digging into her neck. She stopped at one of the SUVs and rested up against it. A moment later, Ford appeared.

"Jo," he said.

Jo offered him a wry smile. "Ford," she replied.

He jutted his chin toward the market. "I had a feeling this was too good to be true."

Jo hung her head. "We almost had him. He wanted to come in. I should have come by myself."

"It is what it is. Walsh can't go far. It's only a matter of time. We lost this one. But we'll win the next one."

Jo said nothing. Time was running out for Walsh. The last thing she wanted to see was him dead—*and* taking someone along with him.

Ford checked his watch. "You need to get some rest. We both do."

Jo nodded. "You're right."

"We'll pick this up soon. We've got plenty to work on in the meantime."

"Agreed."

Ford clapped his hand on her shoulder. "We'll figure this out. We'll get him."

Jo smiled before heading back to her car. She pulled out her phone and texted Sam that she was on her way home.

She didn't realize that in the distance, Daniel Walsh, seated in the Honda Civic he had stolen only hours before, was watching her every move.

SEVENTY-TWO

Walsh gritted his teeth as he watched the FBI team descend on Pike Place Market. His blood was boiling. What he had asked for was simple. But the FBI couldn't even extend him that courtesy.

"*Damn you*," Walsh whispered, tightening the Mariner's ball cap around his head. "All you had to do was come alone."

Jo Pullinger spoke with a detective. Walsh could tell based on the way the guy was dressed. The two spoke for a moment. Walsh noted the disappointment in Pullinger's posture even from a distance.

"This is on *you*," Walsh grumbled. He coughed, covering his hand with his mouth. He pulled his hand away. He saw a few droplets of blood in his palm.

He felt like his heart was melting, and not in a pleasant way. He knew he was dying. It was only a matter of time. Maybe days. Maybe hours. Maybe minutes. He was angry, angry at the Marines, the VA, the man who hired him to commit murder, and the FBI, who wanted to take him down for doing nothing more than wanting to survive.

He clenched his jaw. *Joseph was wrong,* he thought. *I shouldn't have taken advice from a damn kid. What the hell was I thinking?*

He now knew with certainty that surrendering wasn't an option.

He looked at the gun in his hand. He still had a full clip.

If it's war they want, he recalled an old sergeant in the Corps saying, *it's war they'll get.*

He stuffed the weapon in his waistband.

Walsh watched as Pullinger approached her car. She stripped off her Kevlar vest. She said something to a tall and brooding man. Walsh figured he was the agent in charge. She then got behind the wheel. She started the ignition. She pulled away from the scene and headed away from the action.

She's probably going home, Walsh thought to himself.

Walsh started the Civic and followed after.

SEVENTY-THREE

Jo's eyes snapped open. She saw Chrissy jumping on her bed. "Wake up, Auntie Jo!" her little niece squealed. "It's a new day!"

Every muscle in her body felt sore. Her head was pounding from getting home early in the morning after the debacle at Pike Place Market. "Good heavens," she said as she smiled pleasantly. "What time is it?"

Chrissy pointed to the clock on Jo's nightstand. "It's noon!"

"Shouldn't you be at school?"

Rolling her eyes, Chrissy said, "It's *Saturday*, Auntie Jo. Come on! Mommy is making sandwiches for lunch!"

It took every bit of energy for Jo to sit up in bed. Chrissy pulled on her arm, urging her to get up and follow her into the kitchen. Jo indulged her little niece and walked out into the dining room to find Kim placing a plate full of sandwiches on the table.

"Good afternoon," Kim said with a smile. "Come on, eat something. You look famished."

Jo took a glance outside the window. The sun was full and beating down hard. She would have to eat fast. Walsh was still out there. But, she knew looking for him on an empty stomach wouldn't serve her in the slightest.

It took her less than ten minutes to finish her meal, but it gave her the opportunity to speak to Kim about their weekend plans, which was a welcome relief from the stress of searching for Walsh.

The front door opened. Sam walked inside. He was dressed in running pants and a T-shirt. He checked the smartwatch on his wrist in order to log his run time.

"Well, well," Sam said as he looked at Jo. "If it isn't the female Elliot Ness."

Jo rolled her eyes. "Haven't heard that one before."

Kim nudged Chrissy. "Come on, baby girl. Let's go to the backyard and play on the swings while Auntie Jo and Daddy catch up."

Chrissy followed after her mother as they disappeared through the sliding glass doors. Sam sat down at the table.

"Haven't seen you in a couple of days," Sam said. "You look tired."

Jo got up from the dining table, walked over to the sink, and filled her glass with water. "I'm beat."

"You okay?"

Jo nodded. "Just wrapping up a case."

Sam glanced over his shoulder and lowered his volume. "Does it have anything to do with that guy that the police are looking for?"

Jo said, "You've been watching the news."

Sam nodded.

"Yeah," Jo said. "We almost had him last night—I mean, this morning if you consider the time. He's on the run again."

"Should *we* be concerned?"

Jo shook her head. "There's nothing to worry about." The muscles in her chest suddenly tightened. It had been a few days since she was tormented by her heart condition. And somehow, it had decided to rear its ugly head now.

"You don't look too good," Sam said. "Maybe you should take a day off."

"Doesn't work that way," Jo said. "I can take a break *after* we catch this guy."

"You sound like Dad."

Jo said, "I guess it's hereditary."

"Really, though," Sam said. "Is everything okay? The news said this guy is dangerous."

Jo said, "We'll get him." She pinched her thumb and index finger together. "We're this close."

A look of concern washed over Sam's face. "Just be careful," he said.

"I will," Jo replied, emptying her glass of water. "I have to get back to work."

"Come back early tonight if you can. I'm barbecuing."

"I'll try."

Kim came back in. "Sorry to intrude on your conversation," she said. "It's sunny but chilly outside. I need to get a light sweater for Chrissy."

"Don't worry," Jo said. "I was getting ready to head out."

"Oh, before I forget," Sam said, turning to Kim. "Some guy was parked in front of the house last night. I saw it on the doorbell camera. I think it was Jerry Miller from down the street. He said he was stopping by at some point to return my cordless drill. Did he leave it?"

Kim shook her head. "No, I don't think so."

Jo moved to her room to get dressed. The mention of a car parked in front of the house tickled her brain.

She then shook the thought away.

SEVENTY-FOUR

Ford was already waiting for Jo in the field office by the time she arrived. She had two cups of coffee in her hands, one for her and the other for Ford.

"You've been here so much," Jo said, "I'm starting to think you work here now."

Ford shrugged, took the coffee, and held it up in thanks. "You think I could make a move to your job?"

"I don't know," Jo said playfully. "Do you play by the rules?"

"Sometimes."

"Are you good with filing tons of paperwork?"

Ford shrugged. "I'm used to it."

Jo gestured to Ford's tie-less dress shirt. "You would have to abide by the muted tone and tie uniform, though. Is that a dealbreaker?"

Ford nodded. "Absolutely. I can't stand ties, so I don't think this is going to work out."

The two laughed and then approached McKinley's desk. The kid had circles under his eyes. He smiled wearily as he looked up from his monitor.

"Detective Ford," McKinley said. "Agent Pullinger."

"Good afternoon," Jo said.

"It's afternoon already?"

"Yes, it is."

McKinley pursed his lips. "Man, I need to get some rest."

Jo said, "You look a little worse for wear."

"I'll call it quits soon." McKinley pointed to his monitor. "The bank is working on figuring out who sent Walsh the bank transfer. I just spoke to the bank again. They said they'll call when they have something for me."

"Pullinger," Grantham called from his office. "Can I see you for a moment, please?"

Ford followed Jo into Grantham's office. Ford lingered near the door, ready to leave at a moment's notice.

Grantham motioned for him to come inside too. "It's okay, Detective," he said. "You're practically a regular around here now."

Ford nodded and slipped into a chair.

"So," Grantham said as he sat down at his desk. "I trust you're properly rested after last night's little outing?"

Jo said, "As much as I can be. Any word on Walsh?"

Grantham shook his head. "No, not yet. I suppose that's a good thing. He's either hiding or on the run. I'm inclined to think after what happened last night that it's the latter."

"Let's hope not."

Grantham looked at Ford. "What about Seattle P.D.? Did you guys unearth anything?"

"No," Ford said. "Units are still scouring the city, although Lieutenant Griffin had to pull some units off so they could get back to their regular patrols. But we're still searching."

"Very good." Grantham sat back in his chair. "Well, until we catch wind of Walsh or receive any updates, we're at a standstill." He gestured to both Jo and Ford. "The two of you seemed to have paired off nicely. I assume that you'll be doing that for the remainder of the investigation."

Jo said, "If that's all right by you, sir. Detective Ford here has been invaluable. As a matter of fact"—she shifted her weight—"I would like to go on record and state that Detective Ford should be considered for an official commendation when this is all over."

Ford couldn't help but smile.

"Noted," Grantham said. "I was pressed by the Governor for an update. I explained to him that Daniel Walsh is our prime suspect. All evidence points to him having been hired by someone within Stansfield-Kellerman to commit these murders. He was a bit dismayed when I couldn't elaborate on who it could be, even though I know your working theory is that it was Kellerman."

Ford said, "I would hold off on making any official statements until we know for certain."

Jo's brow furrowed. "We do know it was Kellerman, don't we?"

Ford said, "I've been thinking about the case all night. Justine was shot more times than Rene or Lindsey. It looked more deliberate. As if she was the target. The shots were well-placed, but considering the fact that Walsh is a military vet, this makes sense. But the shots fired at Rene and Lindsey were a bit, well, sloppy. Done on the fly. It appears that it was something Walsh wasn't *planning* on doing but *had* to do to cover his tracks."

Grantham said, "What's your point?"

"My point," Ford said, "is that something doesn't add up. If Kellerman hired Walsh to kill Rene, then Rene's injuries should have been more precise. He was the target, after all, and Walsh wouldn't have been careless in the mission and, somehow, let Rene survive the ambush."

"Maybe," Jo said. "Because of his sickness, Walsh couldn't perform his task as well as he'd planned."

Ford mulled it over.

Grantham said, "Until this can be proven as fact, it's all conjecture, and it must not be released to the press."

Jo said, "Which is why we need to hang onto the hope that Walsh is still alive. We need his testimony. Only he knows the true story."

Ford's cell phone rang. He answered. He asked the person on the other end if they "were sure" before hanging up.

Jo said, "You got something?"

Ford nodded. "Very much so. The DNA between Richard Kellerman and Lindsey Stansfield is a match. Kellerman is Lindsey's father. The lab guys are absolutely sure."

The room was silent. Even though one mystery had been solved—that Lindsey was indeed Kellerman's biological daughter—it still didn't explain why she and Justine were also murdered on that fateful night.

SEVENTY-FIVE

Jo and Ford were seated at a diner near the field office. She thanked the server as a BLT was placed in front of her. The server then placed a plate of corn beef hash in front of Ford and left.

"So," Ford said, "how does it feel?"

Jo, stabbing her food with a fork, replied, "How does what feel?"

"Being the smartest person in the room."

Jo huffed. "I'm hardly the smartest."

"You've been right at almost every turn," Ford said. "If it wasn't for you sticking your nose in, Morris would still be in jail."

Jo said, "The truth would have eventually come out. Morris was innocent. It was just a matter of time."

Ford shook his head. "Plenty of innocent people have been put away for crimes they didn't commit. It's not a new story. I'm just glad that Morris was put in the clear."

Gazing out the window, Jo became lost in thought as she counted the facts on hand: *Walsh is hired to kill Rene by Kellerman. Justine and Lindsey are caught in the crossfire. Walsh goes on the run and panics. Now we're chasing him down.*

"Your food's getting cold," Fords said, snapping Jo out of her reverie.

"Sorry," she said.

"Don't apologize to me. It's your meal."

Jo shook her head. "It's happening again."

Ford asked, "What's happening again?"

Pointing to her temple, she said, "Something's nagging in the depths of my brain. I can't quite put my finger on it."

Ford put his fork down. "What is it?"

Jo sighed. "Have you ever been on a few dates with someone?"

Ford replied, "I have a *kid*, remember?"

"No, I know. What I meant to say was, have you ever been on a few dates with someone where everything, at least on paper, was lining up perfectly? You have all the same interests. You're pretty much on the same page with your life, your goals, et cetera."

Ford said, "Sure."

"Well," Jo said, "have you ever had that happen and thought: *This person is a good match—but there's something missing?*"

Ford nodded. "I have, actually. That happened with a woman I dated in college. I liked her. But the chemistry wasn't there. I tried to make it work but couldn't for one reason or another."

"That's exactly what I mean," Jo said. "Chemistry. That thing that tells you you're on the right path."

Ford asked, "Are you saying you're having a rough dating life or something?"

Jo's eyes narrowed. "No."

"If you are, we can get you signed up on a few dating apps—"

"*Ford.*"

He laughed. "I'm just messing with you."

"I know," she said. "I guess what I'm trying to say is that the example I just gave you is how I'm feeling right now with this case. We have all of the facts. Something is just not lining up, though."

Ford said, "The DNA proved what you were suspicious of. Kellerman is Lindsey's father. Also, Walsh himself said he was hired to do the killings. So, we have the motive and the means for the murder. Kellerman wanted to be closer to his daughter, and he used Walsh to do it."

Jo was silent a moment. "You're right," she said. "It does make perfect sense when you lay it out like that."

Ford smiled. "Exactly."

But as Jo dug into her meal, she couldn't push away the nagging feeling that something wasn't adding up.

SEVENTY-SIX

Walsh was in the parking lot of a recreational center three blocks away from Jo Pullinger's house. He was watching a pair of kids kick around a soccer ball twenty yards away. His mind drifted to the time he served in the Middle East. Two Iraqi kids were doing the exact same thing. They were barefoot as they kicked the ball to each other. He was in his Humvee, observing a checkpoint. Making sure no one went in and out of the marketplace without them knowing. Even so, he couldn't help but stare at the kids. They were maybe seven or eight. Their laughter could be heard in all corners of the marketplace, and it made him smile as well. One of the kids spotted him looking their way and waved him over. A part of him wanted to go over and join them. The joy on their faces was infectious. But as it was just him and another Marine, he couldn't leave his post. He waved back at the kids and shook his head. What he didn't realize was that an insurgent had gone into the marketplace at that very moment with a vest full of C-4. The blast not only killed the two kids—injuring countless others—but it nearly killed him and his comrade.

Even after all those years, the two boys' smiling faces were forever etched in his brain.

He blinked himself out of the memory. He was tired of the pain. Tired of the nightmares. Tired of the trauma that had gotten the better of him.

He looked into the rearview mirror. He was taken aback by what he saw. He was gaunt. Pale. A specter of a man. But it wasn't his fault. The military made him sick. They turned their back on him. Stansfield-Kellerman lied to him. The FBI did the same.

His thoughts turned to Jo Pullinger. What was about to happen in a few hours wasn't her fault. She was simply the Bureau's messenger. But someone had to pay. An example had to be made. People would have to die so that he could send a message to the world.

He looked at the paper resting on the passenger seat. It was his manifesto, his last words. He would leave it behind when all was said and done:

To the world,
This is what happens when you turn your back on the warriors. This is the price you pay for casting us by the wayside. Let what happened here serve as an example.

He glanced at the clock on the radio. The time read 4:06 p.m. He retrieved the Heckler and Koch firearm from the glove compartment and checked the rounds for the umpteenth time. It was a habit he'd picked up while in the Marine Corp: make sure his weapon was functioning before going into battle.

SEVENTY-SEVEN

Jo watched the sun slowly descend into the west through the window near her desk. It was a postcard image—colorful and vibrant—but she didn't feel the warmth she would have otherwise felt. Her mind was distracted and anxious.

There was still no word on Walsh. The units the FBI and Seattle P.D. had pooled together were turning up nothing. She was starting to think that Walsh was either dead or on his way to the next town.

"Pullinger," Grantham said.

Jo looked up and saw the SAC looking down at her. "Yes, sir?"

"Go home. There's nothing more you can do right now."

Jo gestured to her desk. "If it's all right, sir, I'd like to stick around in case something comes up on Walsh."

"You'll be the first to get the call if it does," Grantham said.

"But—"

"Go home, Agent Pullinger," Grantham said. "You've done your part. Walsh isn't going to come to us with his hat in hand. That time has passed. He'll surface again. I have no doubt about that. But the legwork you put in is done. All we can do is wait."

"Then I don't see why I just can't wait here, sir," Jo said.

"Because you're nodding off," Grantham said. "Consider this an order from your superior."

Jo glanced at her clock. Sam was probably getting the barbeque going.

285

Grantham is right, she thought. *I'm just killing time here.*

She got up and grabbed her jacket from the back of her chair. "You'll call me the moment *anything* happens."

Grantham nodded. "You have my word."

"Thank you, sir." She moved toward the door.

"Agent Pullinger," Grantham called out.

Jo waited.

"Nice work."

Jo offered Grantham a smile and walked past McKinley's desk. The young agent had the phone to his ear, rubbing his eyes and looking worse than she did.

"McKinley," Jo said.

McKinley told the person he was speaking with to hold the line. "Yes," he said to Jo. "Do you need something?" He pointed to the phone. "I can keep them on hold—"

Jo shook her head and stuck her hand out. "I just wanted to thank you for all your hard work, Agent McKinley." She glanced at Grantham as he walked back to his office. "I can assure you it hasn't gone unnoticed."

Smiling, McKinley shook her hand. "Thank you for giving me a chance."

"I'll see you tomorrow."

"Likewise."

She took the elevator down and made her way to her car in the underground parking lot. She pulled out her cell phone. The signal was strong, so she decided to call Sam. She wanted to let him know that, for once, she would be on time for dinner. She could almost see the smile on his face when she told him. Chrissy would be beyond ecstatic. It would also be nice to finally help Kim around the kitchen, seeing that she was expecting and all. And that she had let her stay over at their house.

Maybe I should grab something on my way over, she thought.

Wine was out of the question. Kim was pregnant, and neither she nor Sam would drink in front of her. Maybe a sweet dish. Kim's favorite was key lime pie. Even Chrissy would enjoy that.

Having decided what to take with her, she reached her car and dialed Sam's number.

SEVENTY-EIGHT

Sam Pullinger loaded the Jetta with the final items on his grocery list. He'd just picked up raw steaks for himself, chicken legs for Kim, and corn for Chrissy. He would also put a couple of beef patties on the barbecue for later. The patties would come in handy when they made burgers the next day.

He took one last look at the trunk, wanting to make sure he had everything. Ketchup. Mustard. Buns. A case of beer. Coals. And the main attraction: the meat.

Once satisfied, he got behind the wheel and pulled out of the parking lot.

He was fiddling with the radio dial when his cell phone rang. He fished it out of his pocket and smiled when he saw Jo's name on the caller ID.

He put her call on speaker and said, "Hey there, stranger."

"Evening," Jo said.

"Didn't think you'd be calling this early."

"I know. I'm coming home sooner than I thought."

"Really?" Sam said. "That's great news. I'm just done picking up everything for the barbecue. I know how much you love my steaks."

"I can almost taste them," she said.

He smiled. "I'll put one on the grill just for you."

"You do that."

"Is everything wrapped up with your case?" he asked.

"In a sense," Jo replied, "There's not much more we can do at the moment. Either way, I think I'm done with the late hours for the time being."

"Well, Chrissy and Kim will be ecstatic that you're coming home for dinner."

"Good. I plan on getting some facetime in with my niece."

"I won't tell her you're coming early. We can let it be a surprise."

"Sounds good," Jo said. "I'll see you soon."

"See you soon."

He ended the call. He tapped his finger on the steering wheel. He was elated that the entire family would get to spend the evening together. He could see them in the backyard, talking and laughing and just enjoying each other's company.

It's gonna be a good night tonight, he thought.

Almost six blocks away from the house, he fiddled with the radio and landed on a station. "Sister Christian" was playing. He turned the volume up and smiled as the piano intro kicked in.

Lights flashed in his rearview mirror. He looked up. A car was twenty yards behind him. He figured his eyes were playing tricks on him. He adjusted his glasses. Focused on the road.

The lights flashed again.

"What the heck?" he said as the drums and guitar riffs kicked in over the radio.

The lights flashed again.

He looked in the rearview mirror again. *Do I have a flat?* he thought. He checked his dashboard and saw no lights were on. The tires were fine.

The lights flashed again in the back.

Maybe it's my gas cap, he thought.

The lights flashed once more.

He held up his hand. "Okay, okay," he said as he turned on his signal and pulled over to the right.

The car behind him came to a stop. He watched the mirror as a figure got out of the car, obscured by the lights in front of him. Sam pursed his lips. He figured it was Jerry Miller. Jerry had done this once before. He'd parked in Sam's driveway and honked his horn until Sam came out. Turned out that Jerry was drunk and couldn't find his way home, even though it was a couple of houses away.

"Oh, Jerry," Sam said as the figure approached the driver's side. "What have you gotten yourself into now?"

The figure rapped its knuckles on the glass. Sam rolled down the window, making "Sister Christian" flow out into the evening air.

"Is that you, Jerry?" Sam asked as he turned his head and smiled.

Something metal touched his skin. He looked up and saw the barrel of a gun pressed against his head. He tensed up. A man with pasty skin and circles under his eyes crouched down and came to his eye level.

"Slide over," the man said. "Do it slowly."

Sam's heart raced. His mind tried to process what was happening as the man cocked the gun's hammer.

SEVENTY-NINE

Jo squinted as she pulled into the driveway. Sam's Jetta should have been there by now. It wasn't.

"What the heck?" Jo said, killing the engine. She got out of the car, looking around and hoping that maybe Sam was about to pull up. She waited thirty seconds and figured that maybe Kim had asked him to make another stop.

She grabbed the key lime pie from the passenger seat. She fished out her house keys, made her way to the front, and opened the door.

"Auntie Jo!" Chrissy shouted.

Jo placed the pie down, got on one knee, and embraced her little niece. "Hey, troublemaker."

Chrissy scrunched her face. "I'm not a troublemaker!"

"Oh, yes, you are!"

Jo tickled Chrissy to the point that Chrissy was rolling on the floor. Moments later, Kim entered the room and laughed.

"I thought you were Sam," Kim said.

Jo looked around. "Yeah, I thought he'd be home by now."

"He should be." Kim checked her watch. "Maybe he stopped off for something. We're doing a barbecue tonight. Maybe he was grabbing a six-pack. The man can't seem to have steaks without a beer."

"Yeah," Jo said as she stood up. "Maybe that's it."

"Mommy," Chrissy said as she squinted at Kim. "What's beer?"

Kim said, "It's an adult beverage, honey."

291

"Can I have one?"

Kim's eyes went wide. "Absolutely *not*."

Chrissy stomped her foot. "How come?"

Sighing, Kim said, "It's spicy. You wouldn't like it."

"Yuck!" Chrissy said as she stuck out her tongue. "I *hate* spicy!"

Kim, winking at Jo, whispered, "Works every time."

Jo laughed. She then remembered the pie. "I brought something sweet."

"I hope it's key lime pie?" Kim said.

"It is, indeed."

Kim smiled and took the pie from her. "How was your day?"

"Not bad. I'm just happy to be home."

Chrissy hugged Jo's leg. "Are you home *all* night, Auntie Jo?"

Jo kissed her niece on the head. "I'm home *all* night, little lady."

The three proceeded to set the table in the backyard. After some time had passed, and everything was set, Jo checked her watch.

"It's getting late," she said. "I wonder what the heck Sam is doing."

Kim reached over and grabbed her phone from the table. "I'll ring him up. He probably just got sidetracked."

Kim dialed and held the phone up to her ear. After what felt like a full minute, Kim shook her head and hung up.

"He's not answering," Kim said, concerned.

"Let me try," Jo said, pulling out her phone. She dialed. It rang six times.

Strange, Jo thought. *Where is he?*

"I'm sure everything's fine," Kim said.

Jo wasn't convinced by her tone.

"Yeah," Jo replied flatly. "I'm sure it is."

Jo walked over to the front door. She stepped outside. Crickets chirped. Other than that, the neighborhood was silent. She walked down the driveway and stopped in the spot where Sam's Jetta would've been parked. She looked to the left and then to the right.

No one was coming. Everything was eerily still.

She looked up at the sky. It was black, save for the sprinkling of stars.

A chill licked at the back of her neck. She hugged herself.

She suddenly had a sinking feeling that something was not right.

EIGHTY

Sam, blindfolded, shuddered as he heard the sounds of duct tape being stripped apart. He was seated on cold concrete. He couldn't see where he was, but he could tell by the lack of oxygen in the room that he was somewhere confined and unforgiving.

A moment later, the blindfold was pulled off his eyes. He shut them. He could smell the rancid breath of his kidnapper just a few inches from his face.

"Look at me," the man grumbled.

Sam shook his head.

The man slapped him across the cheek. "Look at me!"

Sam slowly peeled open his eyes. A haunted face stared back. The man violently coughed, covered his mouth, and drew in a raspy breath.

Sam looked around. He saw that he was inside a storage unit. His Jetta was parked a few paces away, crammed into the space that was smaller than Chrissy's bedroom.

"W-what," Sam stammered. "W-what are you d-doing with me?"

The man held a finger to his lips. "You must understand, what's about to happen to you is nothing personal," the man said.

Sam said nothing.

"You might live," the man said, "or you might die. The choice is up to your sister."

Oh, no! Sam thought. *Jo, what's happening?*

The man took the duct tape and secured Sam's arms with several wraps. He placed the duct tape down. He then moved toward the Jetta. He took a pipe that he had placed in the back seat and gripped it tightly in his hands.

"Please, don't hurt me," Sam said.

The man closed his eyes and stood there in silence as if he was meditating. He then shook his head.

"Please," Sam said, "I can—"

"No more talking," the man grumbled. "Stand up. Now."

Sam followed the man's orders.

"Go to the trunk and get inside," the man said as he popped the trunk open and stood by it, the pipe still clutched in his hand.

Sam crawled into the trunk. The man ordered him to close his eyes.

Sam was certain that he was about to die.

EIGHTY-ONE

Jo went back inside the house, the cell phone to her ear and McKinley speaking to her on the other end of the line.

"Hey, Jo," McKinley said. "What's going on?"

"Lewis," Jo said, "I need you to do me a favor."

"Sure, go ahead."

"I'm going to forward you a cell number. I need you to run a trace on it."

McKinley said, "I need to run to a different department really quick.

Jo replied, "I'll wait."

Chrissy tugged at her pants. She was looking up at Jo with a curious set of eyes. She was holding her teddy bear in her arms. Kim stood behind her with a look of concern on her face.

"Auntie Jo," Chrissy said softly, "is Daddy okay?"

Jo forced herself to smile. "Daddy's okay, honey. Auntie Jo is just…"

Think! Make something up!

"Auntie Jo is just doing a little work." She turned her focus on Kim. "Maybe Chrissy should go in her room for a moment."

Kim ushered Chrissy off to her bedroom. Moments later, she returned.

"Jo," Kim said with a trembling voice, "what's going on?"

"It's okay," Jo said. "It's probably nothing."

"Is Sam hurt? Did something happen to him?"

Jo's sixth sense screamed that something was wrong. The sister part of her wanted to panic. But the professional part of her knew that no good would come from upsetting Kim or Chrissy.

"I'm sure everything is fine," Jo replied. "I'm just being cautious, that's all."

McKinley came back on the line. "Jo?" he said.

"I'm here."

"They're running a trace on the number you just forwarded to me. Give me some time—"

Jo's phone began to buzz with another number. She looked at the display and saw Sam's name. "McKinley," she said, "I'll call you right back." She switched over the line. "Sam! Are you okay?"

No one replied.

"Sam?" Jo said. "Are you there? Is everything all right?"

Still, no one spoke.

"Sam?"

"Is this Special Agent Jo Pullinger?" the voice of Daniel Walsh said.

EIGHTY-TWO

Jo closed her eyes. *This can't be happening,* she thought. *Please, tell me this isn't happening!*

"Hello?" Walsh said. "Are you still there?" He coughed. "I know this is hard to take in, but I need your full attention."

Jo glanced at Kim. She held up a finger and told her that she would be right back. She stepped outside and closed the door behind her. She switched the phone over to her other ear.

"Where are you?" Jo said. "What have you done to my brother?"

Walsh said, "I haven't done a thing to him. Not yet, at least."

"If you harm one hair on his head—"

"*Stop,*" Walsh cut in. "If you value your brother's life, you'll do exactly as I say."

Jo's heart was racing. She worried that the strain would finally do her in. Taking a moment to catch her breath, she walked down the driveway and saw Kim poking her head through the curtains in the living room.

"Is he safe?" Jo asked.

"He is," Walsh replied. "For now."

"I want proof."

"Well, you're not going to get it."

"How do I know that he's not hurt?"

"He isn't. You'll have to take my word for it."

"You have to give me something," Jo said. "If you want something in return."

Walsh coughed. He sighed. "Hold on one second," he said.

The front door opened. Kim rushed out. "Jo," she said. "What's going on? Tell me right now."

"Kim," Jo said, "I need you to be patient."

Walsh came over the line: "Are you there?"

"I'm here," Jo said.

"Here he is…" The sounds of the phone being shuffled came over the line, followed by Sam's voice: "Jo?" he said wearily.

"Oh, my God," Jo said. "Sam, are you okay?"

"I'm locked in—"

"That's enough," Walsh cut in. "You have your proof. Your brother is alive. If you want to end this, you're going to do exactly as I say."

Jo said, "What do you want, Walsh?"

"We're running out of time," Walsh said. "So, I'll keep this brief. I want that kid I shot at the cemetery. You're going to bring him to me, and then I'll tell you where your brother is."

"This is insane. What's your endgame?"

"The same as yours: I want all of this to be over with."

"And you plan on killing Morris? Is that it?"

"Maybe," Walsh said.

"Why?"

There was silence on the line.

"Tell me why you want Morris," Jo pushed.

"He was on the list."

Jo was confused. "List? What list?"

"He was also a target."

"What?" Jo was horrified. "You were planning on killing *him* too?"

"That's not important," Walsh spat. "Just bring him to me if you want to see your brother."

Jo shook her head. "This isn't the way to do it, Walsh. You can't kill your way out of this—"

"*Shut up*!" Walsh snapped before coughing. "I'm tired. I'm tired of all of this. This is all your fault. The cops. The feds. *You* guys did this. You boxed me in. You pushed me to the edge."

"Listen to me," Jo said. "Just let my brother go, and I'll come and bring you in myself. No backup. Just me."

"Enough talking," Walsh said. "I'm going to hang up. You're going to stay by the phone. I'll call you back shortly. When I do, I'll give you a location." He coughed again. "You'll meet me there with the kid at a time of my choosing. If you don't, you'll be attending another funeral before the weekend draws to a close."

The line went dead.

Jo felt like her heart had dropped into her stomach. She quickly dialed McKinley, and he answered after one ring.

"Did you trace the number?" Jo asked.

"He's within the twenty-mile radius from where you are right now."

"That could be anywhere," she fumed.

"It was the best we could do under the circumstances."

She knew he was right. The only way to directly locate a caller was to triangulate their position off of cell phone towers. Even then, there was no guarantee they'd be found if they were on the move.

McKinley said, "We'll keep working on it. We have his number."

"Okay," Jo said. She hung up and ran back into the house. She grabbed her jacket and started scrolling for Ford's number on her phone.

Kim, looking as though she might pass out, said to Jo, "Talk to me. Tell me what's going on."

Jo stopped in her tracks. She looked at Kim. She held her hands up in the air. "Kim, something has happened."

"Where's Sam?"

Jo swallowed the lump in her throat. "Someone took him," she said.

Kim brought her hand to her mouth. Tears streamed down her cheeks. She walked over to the couch, sat down, and held her head in her hands.

Jo knelt down in front of her. "Listen to me," she said. "I'm going to find him. Everything is going to be okay. I need you to trust me."

Kim shook her head. "Please, Jo, you have to bring him home! We need him!"

"I will," Jo said. "But I need you to stay here with Chrissy. I need you to remain calm. We can't lose our composure. We have to stay strong."

Kim nodded and wiped the tears from her face.

EIGHTY-THREE

With the lights flashing and siren blaring, Ford's Crown Vic screeched to a halt in front of the Pullinger residence. A Seattle P.D. cruiser accompanied him. A uniformed patrolman jumped out of the car and hustled up to the front door with Ford in the lead.

Jo opened the door. "Bryan," she said. "Thanks for coming so fast."

"Has he called?" Ford said.

Jo held up her phone. "Not yet. My people weren't able to get a trace on my brother's phone yet. We need to head out."

Ford pointed to the patrolman. "This is Gibbons. He's going to stay with your family until we figure all of this out."

"Come on inside," Jo said, heading into the living room. Ford followed after her. He spotted Kim Pullinger on the couch with Jo's niece in her lap. They looked shell-shocked, turning their eyes up at Ford and Gibbons wearily.

Jo moved to the couch and got down on one knee.

"Kim," Jo said, "this patrolman here is going to stay with you until we have Sam. Everything is going to be fine."

Kim nodded and hugged Chrissy tightly.

Jo and Ford hurried out of the house and piled into Ford's Crown Vic. The car peeled away from the curb and did a U-turn. The other cars on the street cleared out of the way once they saw the lights and sirens. The needle on the speed gauge settled at 85 miles per hour.

Ford said, "We need to head to the station. I already called my lieutenant. They're dispatching every available unit to try and find your brother."

Jo nodded. "I called my SAC. He's doing the same." She glanced out the window. "Sam couldn't have gone far."

"We'll canvas the surrounding area. Did your people triangulate *any* kind of position when Walsh called?"

Jo said, "The cell tower that got pinged showed that Walsh and my brother are somewhere within twenty miles."

"Twenty miles," Ford said. "We're close to the marina and a few warehouses. Maybe he has him there."

"I checked on my phone, and there is also a slew of old apartment complexes." Jo shook her head. "He could be anywhere."

"At least he's close by," Ford said, trying to sound reassuring.

Jo was silent.

Ford then said, "What about your brother? When you talked to him on the phone, did he give you a clue as to where he could be?"

"Kind of," Jo said. "He said he was locked up, but that could mean anything."

Ford nodded as if in thought.

The Crown Vic barreled down the road, even passing through red lights.

"How did Walsh sound?" Ford asked. "What did he tell you?"

Jo's mind was running in circles, but she replied, "He asked me to bring in Morris. Obviously, that's not going to happen."

Ford said, "What does he want with Morris?"

"He said something about him being on a list."

"What kind of list?"

"I'm thinking a hit list?"

Ford's face tightened. "Do you think Kellerman had hired Walsh to kill Morris as well?"

"That's what it sounded like."

"But that doesn't make sense," Ford said. "What does Morris have to do with Kellerman?"

"I don't know!" Jo said, throwing her hands up in frustration. "I have no idea how any of this links up. All I want is my brother!"

"*Easy*," Ford said. "It's going to be all right. We'll figure this out."

Jo looked at him. "I'm sorry," she said, calming down. "I can't let anything happen to Sam. We need to find him, Bryan. We need to bring him in safe—him and Walsh."

"We will," Ford said. "We'll find him, Jo. We'll bring your brother back alive."

Saying nothing more, she looked out the window. "I'm coming, Sam," she whispered. "*I'm coming.*"

EIGHTY-FOUR

Sam could hear Walsh coughing from inside the trunk. He tugged at the duct tape, binding his hands together. He was worried that the trunk would open at any moment, a gun would be held to his head, the trigger would be pulled, and he would never have the opportunity to say goodbye to his wife and daughter.

The trunk opened. Sam shuddered. Walsh coughed, looked down at him, and flexed the grip he had on his pistol.

"Please," Sam said. "Don't kill me."

"I'm not gonna kill you."

"Then please let me go," Sam begged.

Walsh's lip trembled. "I can't," he said defeatedly. "I've come too far now."

"You can do the right thing. You don't have to do this."

Walsh closed his eyes. He winced. He coughed. He shook his head. "What was I thinking?" he said. "What the hell did I get myself into?"

Sam said, "There's still time to turn back. Please, sir. Don't do this. Just cut me loose, and I'll walk away."

Walsh stared at Sam for a long moment. He hung his head. He nodded. He then took out a switchblade from his pocket, snicked it open, and went to cut the duct tape binding Sam's hands.

Thank God! Sam thought. *Just breathe. It's over. He's going to let me go!*

"I can't do this," Walsh said. "I can't do this anymore." He made a small incision in the restraints—and then he stopped. He stood back. He clicked the blade closed and stuffed it back into his pocket. "No. What's done is done. You need to be made an example of."

"Please!" Sam said, his last hope of being free snatched away from him. "You don't have to—"

"*Enough*," Walsh said. "Stay here. Don't say another word." He moved around the trunk to the front of the car. He returned with a hose and a roll of duct tape. He proceeded to stuff the hose into the exhaust, sealed it with several strips of duct tape, tossed the hose on the floor, and slammed the lid shut.

Sam trembled. He felt as though his bowels would give way at any moment. He felt the car sway to the side as if someone had gotten behind the wheel. It was followed by the engine coming to life. He waited.

Seconds later, he could smell the fumes from the exhaust trickling its way through the hose, filling the air inside the storage unit.

EIGHTY-FIVE

Seemingly every member of both the Seattle P.D. and local FBI field office had been gathered inside a conference room in what was dubbed "the crisis room." Jo, standing next to Ford, watched as Grantham addressed everyone.

"Sweep every street," Grantham said. "Time is of the essence." He pointed to the map on the wall behind him with a red circle covering a twenty-mile radius. "Our suspect, Daniel Walsh, is somewhere in this area. Most likely, he's staying put. He has a hostage with him, and we need to move as quickly as we can to find him before it's too late."

Grantham fielded questions. The plan of defense was reiterated. Grantham then clapped his hands together like a football coach, and everyone in the room broke their collective huddle.

"Pullinger," Grantham said.

Jo walked over. Her heart was still pounding, her thoughts dwelling on her brother. "Yes, sir?"

Grantham crossed his arms. "I'm worried about a conflict of interest here."

Jo had a sense that the SAC would say something like that. "Walsh wants me, sir. He's going to call me and only me."

"Walsh is bent. He doesn't know what he wants. He's a rat trapped in a box with a blowtorch heating the lid."

"I understand," Jo said. "But I can't walk away from this. Not unless you order me to. This is my brother we're talking about. If you were in my position, I'd be inclined to think that you would do the same thing."

Grantham nodded. "Understood. And you're not wrong." He pointed. "But I want you to tread carefully. Don't let your passions get in the way of this. The smallest mistake might end up costing your brother his life."

Jo could only nod.

Moments later, her cell phone rang. The caller ID said, "Unknown." Grantham snapped his fingers and told McKinley to begin tracing the call. Jo waited for McKinley to get settled. Grantham then nodded for her to proceed.

Jo said, "It's me."

"I know," Walsh replied. "Do you have the kid with you?"

"I do."

Walsh paused. "You're not lying to me, are you?"

Jo said, "No. But we're wasting time here."

"Yes, we are. Your brother is in a—let's say, perilous position."

Compose yourself, Jo told herself. *Stay calm. Stay cool.* "I did what you asked," she said. "Now tell me where to go."

"Cowen Park Bridge," Walsh said. "It's not far from where you are now, assuming you're at your field office."

"I am."

"Good. Then head over there now. If I see cops, if I see any of your people, I will not be happy."

Jo heard the sound of some kind of door being rolled down. She took a note of it. She was almost certain she had heard that sound before.

"Agent Pullinger," Walsh said.

"Yes," Jo said.

"I should add, your brother will not be with me when we meet. He's someplace safe for now. But, if you play games with me, you will never find him. Got it?"

"No games," she said.

"Good. Then I'll see you soon."

Walsh terminated the call. She looked over at McKinley. McKinley shook his head and informed her that the call ended too quickly to trace it.

Grantham said, "All right, we know where we're going."

"Sir," Jo said, "I need to go alone."

"Pullinger—"

"Walsh will sniff us out if I arrive with the cavalry. He already did that at Pike Place Market. It's too risky."

"Well," Grantham said, "I'm not letting you go in there alone."

Ford chimed in: "Jo is right. As a matter of fact, we need to pull a few of the units off the streets. Walsh is wound tighter than a spring coil. We can't give him any reason to harm Sam."

Grantham thought about it and then nodded. "All right. I'll make the call. The two of you head over to the bridge. But I'm going to send a chopper up to keep an eye on you. I'll make sure it maintains its distance, but I can't have you two out there all alone."

Jo shook her head. "I think Ford should take the lead on finding my brother."

309

"We don't have any solid leads," Grantham said.

"We do," Jo replied. "I heard something over the phone when I spoke with Walsh. It sounded like a door closing. It had the same kind of sound a rolling sectional door makes, like from a garage, maybe a storage unit."

Ford walked over to the map. "McKinley," he said, "I need you to pull up everything you can in the twenty-mile radius in regards to storage units or warehouses."

"I'm on it," he said.

It was decided that while Ford would scour the streets looking for Sam, she would head off to meet Walsh.

EIGHTY-SIX

The toxins seeped their way into the trunk, causing Sam to hack and wheeze. He could hear the idling of the car engine, the throaty vibrations beneath him as he lay on his side.

The storage unit is going to fill up in no time, he thought. *I can't stay here. I need to get out!*

He coughed and batted his eyes. The sting from the carbon monoxide was forcing him to close his eyes. He turned over on his right side. The rear seats were near his heels. Sam recalled the salesman at the car lot demonstrating how they folded down when he'd purchased the Jetta.

The fumes from the exhaust were becoming overwhelming. Sam did the math quickly in his head: the size of the storage unit and the time it would take for the exhaust to spew out of the tailpipe and fill it entirely. The result made him sick to his stomach. He had no time to spare.

He tucked his knees in. He kicked at the back seats with the minimal force he could apply. He kicked again. And again. And again. Still, nothing budged. He shut his eyes as a thought ran through his mind, telling him he would be smothered in the trunk of his family's car.

No! he thought defiantly. *I'm not going to die in here!*

He tucked his knees in again. He kicked. He pulled in his knees once more. He kicked the seats again. Finally, on the third kick, he saw the back of the seats budge and caught a quick glimpse of the interior of the car. Coughing and straining from the exertion, he saw a glimmer of hope on the other side of his terrible predicament.

He continued kicking with all the strength he could muster.

EIGHTY-SEVEN

Jo weaved her way through traffic and merged onto the highway. Ford spoke to her through the speakerphone as she headed toward the Cowen Park Bridge. It was a twelve-minute drive, less than ten, with the lights and sirens on and the other cars on the freeway clearing out of the way.

"Okay," Ford said over the speaker. "I've got a shortlist here of possible locations where your brother could be, assuming your theory about the storage unit is true. There are three storage facilities resting inside the twenty-mile radius."

Jo said, "How far apart are they?"

Ford sighed. "They're spaced out. It's going to take me thirty minutes in total to check each one."

Jo balled up her fist and punched the steering wheel. "That's a lot of time that'll get chewed up." *Easy,* she reminded herself. *A level head is what's going to win this situation.* "But it is what it is," she continued, calming down. "Just move quickly."

"I will."

"Bryan?"

"Yeah?" he said.

"Find my brother," Jo said. "I'm depending on you."

"I'll bring him back alive."

"Thank you."

"Thank me when this is over. And Jo?"

"Yeah?"

"Be smart," Ford said. "You know as well as I do that Walsh doesn't plan on being taken alive."

"I know. But maybe I can talk to him. He can't depend on anyone but himself. I'm not surprised that he asked to meet at the bridge. Part of me is worried that he's going to jump—that this is all for show."

Ford said, "I thought the same thing, too."

Jo honked the horn at a driver driving too slowly in the middle lane. The driver pulled to the left. Jo moved around him and saw the exit coming up ahead.

"I'm five minutes out," she said. "As soon as I'm there, I'll call you back. I'll keep the call going so you can listen in on everything as it plays out. Call my SAC and let him know so he can listen in on the call too."

"Copy," Ford said. "Once it's done, once we get Walsh and bring in your brother, I need you to do something for me."

"What's that?"

"That diner we went to," Ford said, "the one from a couple of days ago. I really like their coffee. When we make it out of this in one piece, I want you to buy me a cup. Sound good?"

Jo smirked. "Buy *me* a cup of coffee, and you have yourself a deal."

"You got it," Ford said. "Stay sharp."

Jo replied, "You, too."

She terminated the call, took the exit, and turned down a road that led away from the city and into a dense and darkly lit forest that seemed to stretch on for miles.

EIGHTY-EIGHT

Ford's Crown Vic screeched to a halt outside the first storage facility. He jumped out of the car, flashlight in hand, as he spotted seven rows of small storage units cramped together, surrounded by a chain-link fence. He took a look around. He saw no one was around, so he hopped the fence and began running through the grounds.

"Sam Pullinger!" Ford called out. "Can you hear me?"

He continued to holler Sam's name, racing from one storage unit to the next. He pounded on the doors. He listened for any movements inside. He'd spent five full minutes searching when he came to a stop. He was panting and sweating from the exertion.

"Sam Pullinger!" he called one more time. "Are you there?"

There was no reply. Only the static buzz of the lights illuminated the surrounding area.

He gritted his teeth, hopped over the fence, and hurried back to his car. He jumped behind the wheel, threw it into gear, and did a U-turn out of the lot.

The clock was running out quickly—and he still had two more locations to cross off the list.

EIGHTY-NINE

The carbon monoxide had nearly filled the inside of the trunk. The pain in Sam's chest grew searing with each cough he made. Still, he continued kicking his feet against the back seats in a bid to knock them down. Sweat poured down his face. His head felt like it was filled with helium. His energy levels were quickly depleting with each thrust of his feet.

"Come on," Sam said, the effort to speak nearly draining him. "You're not going to die here."

He kicked the seats harder. He could already see the inside of the car, but the opening was not enough to move out of the trunk. He figured a few more kicks would knock the seats down all the way. He pulled his knees into his chest. He shut his eyes and thought of Kim, Chrissy, and Jo.

"I'm coming," he said. "I'm coming home."

With a quick thrust, he kicked in the back seats entirely. He turned over onto his side, shuffling his way into the interior of the car. He crawled to the front seats, reaching out his hands toward the ignition. He felt around for the key, ready to twist it and shut the vehicle off—and then he discovered that Walsh had stripped the key, wedging it into the ignition so that it couldn't turn.

No, Sam thought. *No! No! No!*

He fumbled with the ignition for several moments. But there was no way it was going to budge. He turned his attention to the locks. He pressed the button. The locks would not open.

Oh, God! Sam's mind raced. *He's locked me in!*

He crawled into the back seats. He coughed again. His field of vision was narrowing by the second. He rested on his back. He raised his feet again and started kicking at the windows—one, two, three, four times—but the glass held strong.

His eyes fluttered. He knew he would lose consciousness anytime. He raised his feet once again. He kicked, but it was a listless effort.

Utterly spent, he placed his head on the window.

He had no more to give. He'd fought as hard as he could. He was done.

NINETY

The car turned onto a dirt path, cutting through a forest that opened up onto a sprawling, gothic bridge. As soon as Jo arrived, she put the car in park and dialed Ford's number. He answered after one ring.

"I'm here," she said. "Did you find Sam?"

"Not yet," he told her. "I'm two minutes out from the second location."

Time's almost up, Jo thought to herself.

Ford asked, "Do you see Walsh?"

Jo, phone in one hand, slipped out of the car. A chilled nighttime breeze licked at her skin. She surveyed the bridge, surrounded on all sides by lush green trees. The bridge itself was an ominous sight, the kind of place teenagers went to smoke and drink.

"Jo," Ford said. "Anything?"

Jo was certain she could hear the faint chuffing of a helicopter somewhere off in the distance.

"Nothing," she said. She placed her palm on the grip of her service pistol as she slowly made her way to the center of the bridge.

"Jo," Ford said. "Your SAC is being conferenced in."

Jo waited. Her eyes were pinned to the other side of the bridge, searching for any signs of Walsh.

"*Pullinger*," Grantham said over the line. "The chopper keeping an eye on you is two miles out."

"Tell them to stay back," she said. "We don't want to spook Walsh. I'm putting my phone in my pocket. Just listen in. I'm going to walk out onto the bridge."

Jo stuffed her phone into the front pocket of her Kevlar vest. She felt exposed being out in the open all by herself.

"Walsh?" she called out. "I'm here."

There was no reply. Nothing but the sounds of a critter scurrying somewhere in the brush. Finally, after what felt like an eternity, Daniel Walsh stepped out from behind a tree with a gun clutched tightly in his right hand.

NINETY-ONE

Ford arrived at the second storage unit. This time, he decided to drive around the lot, beeping the siren and calling out Sam's name through the open window. The lot was smaller than the one before, with much less ground to cover. He drove up each row, hollering out Sam's name several times before killing the engine and listening in.

He heard something fall from a storage unit nestled in the third row.

Ford jumped out of the car. He drew his weapon. Ran to the third row. Called out Sam's name again and saw the light trickling out from underneath one of the doors. He ran up to the door. He threw it open and raised his gun. A man with long hair and a box in his hands stood frozen in his spot.

"Whoa!" the long-haired man said as he dropped the box onto the floor.

Ford trained his weapon on the man. "What are you doing here?"

The man held his hands high above his head. "I'm moving my stuff back into my ex-wife's place, man! Don't shoot!"

Ford took a look around the unit and saw box after box marked "David's Stuff" and "Michelle's Stuff." He cursed. He then holstered his weapon, ran back to the car, and set about driving the three miles toward the last location on his list.

NINETY-TWO

Walsh slowly approached Jo. He raised his gun. He hacked and wheezed and nearly doubled over from the exertion.

"Hands up," he said. "Hold them up high."

Jo complied.

"Walk out further," he demanded.

Jo did as he instructed.

Walsh kept the gun trained on her at all times. The closer she came to him, the more she could see how withered, pale, and emaciated he was. He looked more like a ghoul than a man. His eyes were manic and tinted with red.

"Where's your gun?" Walsh said.

Jo pointed to the weapon attached to her hip.

"Toss it over the bridge. Use two fingers. Do it slowly. If you make a wrong move, I won't hesitate to put a bullet between your eyes."

Jo's fingers slowly brushed against her service weapon. She pinched the grip with her fingers. She knew from her training that she should never surrender her weapon, but this was no ordinary situation.

She looked at Walsh. "Let's talk for a second—"

Walsh fired once. The bullet chewed up a piece of concrete near the tip of Jo's left foot. She shuddered slightly and thought for the briefest of moments that she had met her untimely end.

"Throw it now," he said. "I'm not going to tell you again."

Nodding, Jo removed her weapon with two fingers, held it up, and tossed it over the bridge. The gun fell a hundred feet before clattering onto the earth below. She was thankful she had stuffed a can of pepper spray behind her Kevlar vest, in case she needed a backup weapon.

"Good," he said. "Keep your hands high."

Jo asked, "Where's my brother?"

"He's safe."

"No more games, Walsh. I did everything you told me to do. Tell me where my brother is, right now."

Walsh coughed into his arm. His legs wobbled. He drew a raspy breath. "But you didn't do *everything* I told you."

She knew what he was about to say next.

"Where's the kid?"

"He's not with me. And you know better than anyone that as a member of law enforcement, I would not put an innocent person's life in danger."

Walsh didn't look surprised by the answer. It was as if he was expecting it. "You would risk your brother's life to save a stranger?" he said.

She paused. "I want my brother back, safe and sound. Just like I don't want anything to happen to you. And that's the truth. Whether you believe me or not."

He stared at her for a good thirty seconds. Then his shoulders slumped. "I never wanted it to come to this. None of it. I just wanted to get better, but they broke any hope that was left."

"Who did?"

"Stansfield-Kellerman," he spat. "They said they could make my cancer go away, and I believed them."

Jo shook her head. "You were joining a drug *trial*, Walsh. There was no guarantee it would be a success."

"That's not what they told me."

She waited for more.

"They said they had a miracle drug—one that could cure cancer. All I had to do was sign some papers, and I would get better."

Jo knew all pharmaceutical companies were looking for the elusive cure to cancer. One pill that could make it all go away. But the breakthrough was still a long way away. She wasn't sure if she'd see the cure in her lifetime.

"Why didn't you get chemo or radiation for your cancer?" she asked.

"I wanted to, but no hospital would take me without health insurance."

"What about Veterans Affairs? They would've helped you."

"You don't think I tried?" Walsh said. "They said that my cancer was so far along that no treatment would help."

Jo was horrified. "They left you to die?"

He looked away. He became lost in his thoughts. He then shook his head. "No, not exactly. During my time in the Marine Corps, I had seen so much bad. Done so much wrong. Stuff I am not proud of. When I started to get sick, I should've gone for help, but I wanted nothing to do with the VA. I hated everything they stood for. When I was discharged, they left me to find my way in the world. How can they do that? I had given the best years of my life to them. But by the end, I was a shell of my former self—the effects from the burn pits had started to slowly eat away at my body. It was only when my condition worsened that I went to the VA. By then, it was too late."

Jo sensed that Walsh was just angry at the world. At the military for putting him in a situation that caused him to get sick. At Stansfield-Kellerman for not making him get better.

"Is that why you killed the Stansfields? Because you were angry that their drug didn't work?"

He blinked. A tear rolled down his cheek. "It was just supposed to be *her*," he whimpered. "Not the others. It was an accident. The three of them weren't supposed to be there." He shook his head. "When I saw the others in the house, I panicked."

Jo's eyes narrowed. "Who was supposed to be in the house alone? Was it Lindsey?"

His face twisted. "No. Not the girl. I was surprised to see her there."'

"Then who was it? Justine?"

He fell quiet and then nodded. "Yes."

Jo's mind began racing. She had always thought Rene Stansfield was the target, but now that she knew it was Justine Stansfield, she was utterly confused. "Why would Richard Kellerman hire you to kill Justine Stansfield?"

Walsh's brow furrowed. "What are you talking about?"

Jo squinted. "Richard Kellerman hired you to kill Justine Stansfield. Was it because of their affair?"

"No," Walsh said. "*Rene Stansfield* hired me to kill his wife."

NINETY-THREE

"*Rene* hired you?" she said, shocked. "Rene Stansfield?"

Walsh nodded. "That prick paid me to do the job. He said if I did it, if I killed his wife while she was home, he'd give me a lot of money. He said I could use it to get better."

"But you killed them all," she said. "You killed the entire family."

"*I told you*," Walsh growled, "it was only supposed to be the wife. Rene wasn't supposed to be home, and neither was his daughter. But they were. I had no choice. All of them had seen my face."

"Explain, Walsh," Jo said.

He shook his head. "It doesn't matter."

"It does. You destroyed an entire family. It's because of your actions we are here now" She held out her hands. "You have to give me *something*."

Walsh closed his eyes. He drew a weary breath. "Rene was supposed to turn off the alarm. I was supposed to enter the house through the back— do the job and quietly leave. But when I got to the house, I saw the back door was locked. I thought maybe he forgot. I couldn't call him and ask. I'd left my phone in the car, which was parked about a mile away. I wasn't going to go back. So, I decided to walk around the property, and that's when I saw a window on the second floor was open slightly. I decided to go through there."

Jo remembered Morris telling them that Justine was always cold and so she'd turn up the heat high. Lindsey's room was straight below the furnace, and so her room was the hottest. She'd crack open the window to cool the room.

Something else occurred to Jo: the mystery calls that Rene had placed right before the murders. *He had tried to call it off*, she deduced. *He tried to cancel the plan because Lindsey had refused to go with him to the movies.*

Walsh continued, "I was going to make it look like an accident—like a break and enter gone wrong." He hung his head. "But the girl was in her room when I climbed in. She screamed. I had no choice. Then I heard Rene. I could hear him fumbling for something. I thought he was trying to double-cross me, so… I ran down the hallway and shot him."

Jo knew what happened next. "Once you killed Rene, you went over to Justine."

He sighed. "She was on the hit list. So, I had no choice."

"Was Tim Morris on the hit list too?" she asked. "Is that why you'd gone after him at the cemetery?"

He made no comment.

"Is that why you wanted me to bring him here tonight, so you could finish your job?"

He nodded. "As a good Marine, I follow my orders to the end."

"But why Morris? Why would Rene want him dead?"

"He didn't like him dating his daughter. He thought he was a bad influence."

"But they had already broken up," Jo said.

Walsh stared at her blankly.

327

Maybe Rene didn't know, Jo thought. *Maybe he had no idea Lindsey and Morris were no longer in a relationship.*

She then asked, "And Richard Kellerman? He was on the hit list too?"

"He was."

All the pieces had finally come into place. It was never Richard Kellerman who was behind the murders. It was always Rene Stansfield. He must have recently found out about the affair between Kellerman and Justine. After all, he was asking about it just mere weeks before the murders. With his friendship with Kellerman fractured over the Comoxin trials, he figured it was now a good time to finally get rid of him, and his unfaithful wife, all at once.

But Lindsey was never part of the plan. Rene had no idea she wasn't his biological child. If he did, he wouldn't have had a fight with her about going to the movies.

"You had no idea it was Morris in the house that night?" Jo asked.

Walsh's jaw clenched. "If I'd known, I would've finished my mission."

"But when he took the fall for the murders," she said, "you were in the clear. Isn't that, right?"

He looked away.

There was a moment of silence between them.

"Where's my brother?" Jo demanded.

He blinked. "What time is it?"

"What?"

"How long have we been talking?"

"Long enough."

He smiled. "Then I'm afraid your brother is dead."

A sharp pain shot through her heart. She almost felt like she would keel over and throw up. She placed a hand over her chest. Her eyes welled. "You said you'd tell me if I came to the bridge."

"I said I'd tell you if you came with Morris. You broke our agreement, Agent Pullinger. Your brother's death is on *you*."

Anger rose in her.

She moved toward him.

He aimed the gun at her head.

She stopped.

She then shut her eyes. The thought of Sam gone made her not care whether she lived or died. He was what kept her going.

I've failed you, Sam, she thought as tears streamed down her face. *I'm so sorry.*

"I can feel it," she heard Walsh say. "It's happening."

Jo opened her eyes. She was certain Walsh would pull the trigger. Instead, his expression slackened. He lowered the gun slowly and held it by his side.

She was confused.

A sliver of a smile crept onto his lips. "I can feel my life leaving me, Agent Pullinger," he said. "I'm… I'm dying."

Jo took a deep breath and stood up straight. She shook her head to control her emotions. She remembered Ford's words: *Be smart. Walsh doesn't plan on being taken alive.*

Even though Sam might be gone, she still had a job to do.

After all, she had a killer's heart beating inside her chest. She was alive only because of it. She might not have been able to save her brother's life, but she could very well try to save Walsh's.

Revenge wouldn't make the pain go away, she knew. Revenge only made it worse.

"You're not dying." She held out her hand. "Just give me the gun. We'll go to the station and talk this out, just you and me."

Walsh shook his head. He looked at the gun in his hand. "You know everything," he said. "You know what happened. There's nothing more to say." He closed his eyes. "Tell whoever might care that… that I'm sorry. I didn't mean for things to go this way. I… I just didn't know what else to do."

Jo sensed that something terrible was about to play out. "Walsh—"

He turned his back to her, walked over to the side of the bridge, and held the gun against his head.

He pulled the trigger.

NINETY-FOUR

Ford arrived at the last storage unit on his list just as he heard the sound of a gunshot cracking through the speaker on his phone.

"Jo!" Ford said as he snatched up the phone. "Are you okay?"

A few moments of silence held sway over the line.

"I'm fine," Jo said wearily.

"Where's Walsh?"

Another moment of silence.

"He's gone," Jo finally said.

Ford wanted to hear more—but he still needed to find Sam. He slipped out of his Crown Vic and ran through the rows of storage units, shouting Sam's name. He ran through the first row. The second. The third. The fourth. Finally, upon arriving at the fifth row, Ford made out the sounds of an idling engine.

"Sam?" Ford called out.

Something caught his eye—the last storage unit at the end of the row. He saw what looked like smoke trickling out of the bottom of the door. He ran toward it. He saw that a lock was secured over the latch. Ford stood back, raised his weapon, aimed it at the lock, and shot it apart. He tossed the pieces aside and threw open the door. He coughed as fumes billowed out of the unit. His eyes welled up instantly. He covered his mouth with the back of his sleeve and moved inside. He peeked inside the Jetta and spotted Sam Pullinger passed out in the back seat. He saw a hose was tethered to the car's exhaust pipe.

Ford coughed some more and batted away the smoke. He removed his jacket, held it up to his face as a shield, and punched at the glass with the butt of his gun. Two punches and the glass shattered. Ford reached inside the car and pulled Sam out. He dragged him out of the storage unit, laid him on the ground, and held two fingers up to his neck.

To his relief, he felt a pulse.

NINETY-FIVE

The spotlight from the helicopter washed over the bridge. Several FBI vehicles pulled up to the scene with lights flashing and sirens blaring. Jo, standing on the bridge, looked over and spotted the twisted heap of Walsh's body lying in the shallow water below.

Grantham, running toward her with a group of agents, held his radio to his lips and started barking out orders.

"Pullinger!" Grantham said. "Are you okay?"

Feeling more taxed than she ever had before, she continued to stare at Walsh's body. "It's over," she finally said.

"What happened?"

"He shot himself."

Grantham sighed. "*Damn.*"

Jo's phone rang. It was Ford. She quickly answered.

"Bryan," Jo said. "Tell me something good."

Ford said, "I found Sam. He's okay. I've got an RA unit inbound. He needs to get to a hospital, but he's going to be all right."

Jo closed her eyes and smiled.

"Your brother is all right," Ford said. "I got him."

Jo thanked Ford before hanging up the phone. She turned to Grantham and saw what felt like every law enforcement official in the county close in on the bridge.

Grantham, looking down at Walsh's body, said, "It's too bad we didn't get him alive."

Jo shook her head. "He wasn't going to come in. This was going to end with either him or me dead."

Grantham clapped his hand on Jo's shoulder. "Well, I'm glad it wasn't you." He turned to an agent beside him. "Let's move. We need to get down to the body."

The SAC set about cordoning off the area. Jo loosened the straps on her Kevlar vest, removed the can of pepper spray, and sat down on the bridge with her back resting on the wooden railing. She slowed her breathing. She then pulled out her phone and quickly dialed Kim's number.

"Jo," Kim said. "Talk to me."

"We've got him, Kim," Jo said. "We found Sam. Everything is going to be okay."

Kim broke down in tears. Jo could hear her telling Chrissy the good news. She told them both to stay by the phone. She would inform her where Sam was as soon as Ford got him to a hospital.

McKinley, part of the group of agents on the bridge, got down on one knee in front of Jo. He held out his hand. "Need a lift?" he asked.

Jo smiled, slapped her hand into McKinley's, and stood up with his help.

"Some night, huh?" McKinley said.

Jo nodded. "Yeah, some night."

"You did good, Agent Pullinger."

"You played a big role in that, Agent McKinley."

His face lit up at the comment.

As the FBI converged on the scene and the helicopter flew over the area, Jo took one last look at Walsh's body. Everything had come to a close. The journey to end the madness was finished. Though she was happy to bring things to a close, she still felt remorse over the fact that Walsh was dead. At the end of the day, she debated whether Walsh's actions were done out of selfishness or simply because Stansfield-Kellerman, Rene, and the military had used him to serve *their* agendas.

Turning away from Walsh's corpse, she decided it was the latter.

NINETY-SIX

The moment Ford relayed the name of the hospital that Sam was admitted to, she drove there like a maniac.

She ran down the halls and found Ford standing outside a room.

"He's fine," Ford said. "He's waiting for you inside."

"Thank you," she said.

She entered the sterile room and saw Sam lying on a bed. An IV was attached to his left arm, but he wasn't hooked up to any machines or monitors, which was a comfort to see.

He smiled when he saw her.

She rushed over and hugged him. "I'm so sorry," she said.

He swallowed and said in a raspy voice, "For what?"

"This is my fault. Walsh only went after you because of me."

He shook his head. "No. He went after you because *you* were doing your job."

Her eyes welled up. "I thought I'd lost you," she said.

He grinned. "You can't get rid of me that easily."

"Kim and Chrissy are on their way. They'll be here soon."

His smile widened.

"What did the doctors say?" she asked.

"Except for a scratched throat from all the coughing I did, I'll be fine."

She drew a breath. "I should've been the one looking for you, not Ford."

He swallowed again and said, "From what I've heard, you were needed elsewhere."

She was silent.

"Did you get him?" he then asked. "I mean, Walsh?"

"I did, but... he's dead."

He looked at her. "Did you...?"

"I wanted to—when I thought he'd hurt you— but no, he shot himself."

He reached over and placed his hand over hers. She gripped it tightly.

A moment passed before he said, "I was actually angry, you know. When he... Walsh jumped me."

"That's understandable. No one likes being kidnapped."

"No, I wasn't angry about that."

Her brow furrowed. "So, what were you angry about?"

"After he'd tied me up in the backseat and was driving me to the storage unit, Walsh had stopped by the side of the road."

"Why would he do that?" she asked.

"He didn't like the smell of the meat I'd bought for the barbecue, and he threw it all out."

Jo's mouth dropped. "And you were angry about *that*?"

He shrugged. "What a waste of good steaks, you know."

She rolled her eyes and then smiled. "I'm just glad you're okay," she said.

He smiled back.

NINETY-SEVEN

Jo rapped her knuckles on the front door of the Morris residence. Deborah Morris answered. She smiled upon seeing that it was the agent who had freed her son.

"Agent Pullinger," Deborah said. "What a pleasant surprise."

"Good afternoon, Mrs. Morris," Jo said. "Is it all right if I come inside for a moment?"

Deborah stood aside and gestured for Jo to enter. "Yes, of course."

Jo entered the home. Upon walking into the foyer, she felt a newfound sense of optimism lingering in the Morris household.

"I've been watching the news," Deborah said. "It was such a shock to hear about what happened with that man on the bridge."

"It was," Jo said. The two weeks of fallout and paperwork and bureaucracy from Walsh's demise were still fresh in her mind.

"Was it really him?" Deborah asked. "Did that man kill the Stansfields?"

Jo nodded. "He did."

"This is all so terrible."

"It certainly is," Jo said.

"That company has been in the news a lot, too," Deborah added. "Something about a drug trial going poorly."

"They're still sorting it out," Jo said. "But yes, Stansfield-Kellerman is in a lot of hot water after everything's that come to light."

Deborah shook her head. "I mean, it pains me to hear how things ended, but I'd be lying if I said that I wasn't glad this was over. It's taken a toll on our family. I'm not sure how much more we could have taken."

"That's actually why I'm here," Jo said. "I wanted to see how all of you were doing. Is your husband around?"

Deborah shook her head. "No, Jonathan went to the mall to fetch Tim a backpack. He's leaving tomorrow."

"Leaving for where?"

Deborah smiled. "He's joining the military. Tim thought long and hard on it. We're supporting his decision. It'll be good for him to get a start fresh, to get a little discipline in his life."

"Can I speak to him?"

Deborah led Jo to Morris' room. She knocked on the door. Morris told them to come in. Jo entered the bedroom to find a clean-shaven Morris with a crew-cut hairstyle, packing his clothes into neat piles on the bed. He was wounded but healing.

"Agent Pullinger," Morris said. "I didn't know you were coming by."

"I hope that's okay," Jo said.

Deborah, moving toward the door, said, "I'll leave you two alone for a moment," before ducking out of the room.

Morris continued to pack his clothes. Jo noticed that the kid looked a little more put-together than the last time she saw him. He still looked weary—but he was holding his head high.

Jo said, "How are you holding up?"

"I'm okay," Morris said. "Just taking things one day at a time."

"You sound better. You look better."

Morris took a deep breath. "Spending time in jail kind of shocks your system. It puts things into perspective." He grimaced, rubbing the bandaged area beneath his shirt. "Getting shot does, too."

Jo said, "I'm sorry this happened to you, Tim. I really am."

"I know," Morris said. "I'm just glad you guys cleared me of all of this. All I can really do now is, well, try to keep moving."

"I heard you were joining the military."

Morris nodded. "That's right. It was my idea. I figured maybe the military can provide me with something, I don't know, better."

"I'm glad to see you're doing okay and not letting your past dictate your future."

Morris ceased packing. He sighed.

He sat on the edge of the bed, wincing at a twinge of pain and rubbing his chest as he did. "I still think about what happened," he said. "I think about it all day, actually. I think about what would've happened if that guy wasn't there, if Lindsey hadn't been murdered, if I had shown up earlier than I did or maybe even pulled the trigger myself."

"But you didn't," Jo said. "This was all Daniel Walsh's fault. Well, it was Rene Stansfield's, too. Either way, it had nothing to do with you."

"Still," Morris said. "I was there. And what happened, happened. I'll never forget it. It will always stay with me." He gestured around the room. "But I can't sit here and dwell on it. I have to try and make something of myself. I know that's what Lindsey would've wanted."

Jo nodded. "She would be proud of you if she saw you now."

He stared at the floor for a moment. "I hope so," he said. He then looked up at her. "Thank you, Agent Pullinger, for what you did for me. And thank your friend, that detective, for me too. Without you guys, I don't think I'd be sitting here or even getting a second chance at life." "I'll let Detective Ford know," Jo replied. "You take care of yourself, Tim." With that, Jo left the room. She took one last glimpse over her shoulder and saw Morris packing his clothes in his suitcase.

She felt a renewed hope for him. He'd been through hell, and he'd come out on the other end a changed person.

He had a bright future ahead of him, and she had full confidence that he wouldn't waste this new opportunity that was given to him.

NINETY-EIGHT

Ford's heart raced as he walked up to the house he once shared with his wife and daughter. He knocked on the door and cleared his throat. His palms were sweaty, and he was nervous

A moment later, Kelly answered the door with a smile.

Ford beamed as he laid eyes on his wife. She was just as beautiful as the first day they'd met. Her golden hair was silky smooth, her eyes sparkled, and her cheeks dimpled as she smiled.

"Hey, Bryan."

"Hey, Kelly."

Kelly gestured for Ford to come inside. He stepped into the foyer. Kelly closed the door behind him.

Ford asked, "Where's Hazel?"

Kelly said, "She'll be back soon. She's next door playing with the neighbor's kid."

"That's great. I can't wait to see her."

Kelly moved into the kitchen. "Did you want water or anything?"

He was too excited to consume anything. "No, that's okay."

"Was it a long drive?"

"Just a little," Ford said, playing down that it took a little over three hours for him to get to the house from where he'd been staying.

Kelly said, "I'm glad you're here."

"Me, too," Ford said. "I didn't think the day would come."

"Well—" Kelly bit her lip. "I heard about what happened on the news. I didn't know you were working on such a big case."

Ford shrugged. "I didn't want to say anything. I thought it might upset you."

Kelly drew a deep breath. "When I heard your name on the news, it got me to thinking about everything that happened that night the man came to our house. I was… Well, I was scared."

Ford said, "You have every right to be. I understand why you needed your space."

Kelly took a step toward her husband. "I know your job has its risks. I just worry that it will affect Hazel and me. I thought if I put some distance between us, it would help. It has, in a way. I've been able to think a little more clearly about what I want."

Ford felt the moment of truth arriving. "What conclusion did you land on?"

Kelly took Ford by the hand. "I miss you, Bryan," she said softly. "*We* miss you. I'm tired of not having you around. I know what you do is dangerous, but I just can't stand the thought of you not being here."

Ford gently stroked his wife's cheek. "I don't want you to be scared," he said. "And I don't ever want anything to happen again like it did that night. I'll do whatever I have to so I can make it work."

"I've missed you, Bryan," Kelly said. "We both have. I want you to come back home." She smiled. "I'm *asking* you to come back home."

Ford, his eyes welling with tears, said, "Are you sure?"

Kelly nodded. "More than anything."

Ford embraced his wife. They said nothing for several moments. As soon as they broke their embrace, the front door opened.

Ford turned his head. A miniature version of his wife stood in the doorway. Hazel's eyes were wide. She was frozen in place as she looked at Ford as though it was Christmas morning.

"*Daddy*?" Hazel said curiously. "Is that really you?"

Ford, tears streaming down his face, got down on one knee. "Come here, you."

Hazel rushed into her father's arms. He picked her up and pulled his wife into the huddle.

Nothing was said as they held each other.

The only thing that mattered was that they were a family once again.

NINETY-NINE

Ford was seated at his desk at the Seattle P.D. when Lieutenant Griffin showed up.

"You got a minute?"

Ford furrowed his brow. "Yeah, sure. Why?"

Griffin forked a thumb over her shoulder. "You got a visitor."

Ford looked over. Standing in the doorway leading into the detective's bullpen was Jo.

Ford stood from his desk. He walked over, slipped his hands into his pockets, and jutted his chin as he said, "Agent Pullinger."

Jo replied, "Detective Ford."

"Let me guess," Ford said. "You've got another case you want me to take a look at."

Jo laughed. "No. Not yet, at least. I just wanted to stop by really quick. You left the hospital without me formally thanking you face to face."

Ford shrugged. "It's not necessary. I was doing my job."

"Regardless, thank you for saving my brother's life. If you hadn't been there... well, things might have turned out differently."

Ford asked, "How's he doing now?"

"He's making a good recovery. Just a bad lingering cough, but nothing serious."

"That's good to hear," he said.

There was a pause.

Ford asked, "How are you sleeping?"

Jo recalled the fact that she had been nightmare-free now for close to a week. "Better," she said. "A lot better. And how are things on your end?"

"Just got off the phone with my wife and daughter. Things are…" He smiled. "Well, they're looking up."

"That's good."

"I'd like to think so." Ford shrugged. "I guess with everything that happened, my wife decided we spent enough time apart."

"Listen," Jo said, "I just wanted to tell you that I couldn't have done this without you. Part of me wonders how this all would have turned out if we hadn't been saddled together on this."

Ford nodded. "I thought the same thing, too. Part of me thinks that Morris might still be in jail."

"I just saw him. He's actually joining the military."

"Wow."

"Yeah, and he wanted me to thank you."

Ford rubbed the back of his neck. "I'm not used to all the thank-yous."

"Get used to it. You've earned them," Jo said.

"Well, if you ever need a partner again, you know where to find me."

"I do." Jo stuck out her hand. "You take care of yourself, Detective Bryan Ford."

Ford shook it. "You, too, Special Agent Jo Pullinger."

EPILOGUE

After offering Ford her thanks for a job well done, she returned to the field office to drop off the Bureau-issued vehicle. She still hadn't purchased her own vehicle—she'd hit the ground running the moment she got to Seattle—but visiting a local dealership was on her to-do list.

She fetched a cup of coffee, called a cab, and waited outside the field office. Moments later, the cab arrived, and Jo got inside—and she was thrilled to see that it was Joe, the driver who had picked her up from the airport.

"Well, I'll be!" Joe said. "Look who it is. Miss FBI herself."

Jo smiled. "Good to see you, my friend."

"What are the chances I would be picking you up today? Ha!"

"I don't know, Joe," she said. "But I'm happy that you did." She gave him the location and sat back for the ride.

"So," Joe said, "how's life at the FBI?"

Jo shrugged. "It's a grind," she said.

"Any big cases recently?"

Jo thought about Walsh. About Morris. About Ford. About everything that had transpired in the past few weeks. "You could say that," she said.

"Care to talk about it? It's a bit of a drive to your destination."

Jo said, "Maybe some other time."

With a thumb's up, he said, "Fair enough." He pointed to the radio. "Anything you want to listen to?"

She asked, "Who was that artist you played for me the last time?"

Joe snapped his fingers. "I've got *just* the thing for you, ma'am." He pulled up his phone, punched in a song, and moments later, "I Believe In You" by Johnnie Taylor began to play.

"Not bad," she said. "Not bad at all."

Sometime later, the cab arrived outside the art museum in downtown. Waiting for her out front was Chrissy, Sam, and Kim. They waved to Jo as she got out of the car.

Jo, a cup of coffee in hand, approached her family.

"Auntie Jo?" Chrissy asked. "Do you have to work today?"

Jo shook her head. "Not today, little one."

The answer made Chrissy's eyes go wide. "*Really*? Are you staying with us all day?"

"Yes, ma'am. I'm not going anywhere."

Chrissy wrapped her arms around Jo's neck and squeezed tighter than she had before. After Chrissy let go, Sam wrapped his arm around Jo's shoulder.

"How'd it go?" Sam asked.

"Good," Jo replied. "I just stopped by to say thank you to Detective Ford."

"I'll never forget what he did. He's a good man."

"He absolutely is." Jo nudged her brother. "How about you? You holding up, okay?"

Sam had been struggling for a few days—nightmares, sweats, and a general sense of malaise. Nonetheless, he was happy to be alive and back home. "I'll be fine," he said. "Just promise me that I'll never be locked in a trunk again, and we're square."

Holding up her pinky, Jo said, "Deal," as Sam extended his pinky, wrapped it around hers, and squeezed.

"Auntie Jo," Chrissy said, "can I have some of your coffee?"

Jo shook her head. "It's spicy. You wouldn't like it."

"Yuck!" Chrissy said. "No, thank you!"

Jo looked at Kim. Kim winked.

"Works every time," Kim said.

They moved together toward the museum entrance. They paid for their tickets, walked inside, and spent the day strolling through the museum.

Not one minute went by during their visit that Jo didn't find herself smiling.

Visit the author's website:
www.finchambooks.com

Contact:
finchambooks@gmail.com

Join my Facebook page:
https://www.facebook.com/finchambooks/

JO PULLINGER SERIES

THOMAS FINCHAM holds a graduate degree in Economics. His travels throughout the world have given him an appreciation for other cultures and beliefs. He has lived in Africa, Asia, and North America. An avid reader of mysteries and thrillers, he decided to give writing a try. Several novels later, he can honestly say he has found his calling. He is married and lives in a hundred-year-old house. He is the author of the Lee Callaway Series, the Echo Rose Series, the Martin Rhodes Series, and the Hyder Ali Series.

Printed in Great Britain
by Amazon

47266994R00198